# BUBBA DONE IT

A DREAMWALKER MYSTERY

# BUBBA DONE IT

# MAGGIE TOUSSAINT

**FIVE STAR**
*A part of Gale, Cengage Learning*

GALE
CENGAGE Learning·

Farmington Hills, Mich • San Francisco • New York • Waterville, Maine
Meriden, Conn • Mason, Ohio • Chicago

**GALE**
CENGAGE Learning·

**LIBRARY OF CONGRESS CATALOGING-IN-PUBLICATION DATA**

Toussaint, Maggie.
    Bubba done it / by Maggie Toussaint. — First Edition.
    pages ; cm. — (A dreamwalker mystery ; 2)
    ISBN 978-1-4328-3067-0 (hardcover) — ISBN 1-4328-3067-8
(hardcover) — ISBN 978-1-4328-3058-8 (ebook) — ISBN 1-4328-
3058-9 (ebook)
    I. Title.
PS3620.O89B83 2015
813'.6—dc23                                                    2014047835

First Edition. First Printing: May 2015
Find us on Facebook– https://www.facebook.com/FiveStarCengage
Visit our website– http://www.gale.cengage.com/fivestar/
Contact Five Star™ Publishing at FiveStar@cengage.com

Printed in the United States of America
1 2 3 4 5 6 7 19 18 17 16 15

This one's for the Valona crew.

# ACKNOWLEDGMENTS

I am beyond grateful for all the friends and fans who have encouraged me along this journey. Critique partners Marilyn Trent, Keely Thrall, and Polly Iyer helped sharpen this manuscript. My brainstorming team of Ginny Baisden, Marianna Hagan, and Suzanne Forsyth helped come up with many of the twists and turns for my Bubba book. Without you ladies, this series wouldn't have nearly the texture it does. A special thanks to Craig Toussaint for relaying the account of the Bubba who forgot to turn in his golf score card some years ago during a tournament. When I heard the tale of how many men answered the call of the pro for Bubba to "get over here and turn in your card," I knew I had to write a story with the Bubbas in it.

# CHAPTER 1

"Help. Please. Help me," the thin male voice rasped over the police radio. "This is . . . Morgan . . . Morgan Gilroy . . . I've been . . . stabbed."

I strained to hear what the banker was saying, chilled by the realization that these might be his final words. Tension crackled in the air as the transmission ended. I glanced over at Sheriff Wayne Thompson.

His eyes were focused on the road, both hands locked on the steering wheel. "Thanks for the replay of the nine-one-one call, Dispatch. My consultant and I are en route to Sparrow's Point. Our ETA is three minutes."

Static crackled on the line. "Roger that, Sheriff. The ambulance is eight minutes out."

My fingers dug into the armrest as the Jeep barreled through a series of tight turns. The two-hundred-year-old oaks lining the twisting road flashed before my eyes. Long shadows and sunlight flickered across the windshield, adding a strobe-like sense of unreality to my already churning stomach. Sure, I was technically a psychic consultant, but I dealt with dead people and solid objects.

Not with knife-wielding assailants or bloody victims.

We squealed around another bend in the road, and I banged into the center console. "You trying to kill me?"

"Heck, no. I've got plans for us." The sheriff grinned and flipped the siren on.

My hands clamped over my ears to block the warbling noise. "There is no us."

His dark eyes widened appreciatively. "But there will be, Baxley."

"Get over yourself. I don't date married men. I don't date, period. Too busy raising Larissa."

"You'll weaken, babe, and I'll be there to catch you."

"Lordy. You need to get a grip. I have no intention of becoming one of your women. That's not in my future."

"You having one of your psychic moments?"

I snorted. "More like a reality moment."

He braked sharply for the turn onto Honeycreek Lane. "You want in on this homicide, you do as I say."

Air stalled in my lungs. "You think Morgan is dead?"

"If he ain't gone, he's knockin' on the door. Wait a minute—can't you tell? Can't you zap into the spirit world and look him up? That would sure save me a lot of investigating."

My dreamwalks are best done in protected surroundings. No way would I risk that level of vulnerability in a speeding vehicle. "It isn't that simple."

"Pity."

He jammed the gear selector into park. Blue lights splashed across the colonnaded front of the oldest, most historic house in Sinclair County, Georgia.

The sheriff pulled his gun and fixed me with a stare. "Keep your scrawny butt in here until I clear the house. Odds are the assailant is long gone, but I don't play the odds. I only bet on sure things."

With that he raced up the sweeping stairs of Sparrow's Point, leaving me alone. I hit the door locks and glanced around fearfully. Nobody with a knife running toward the vehicle.

I was safe for now.

My head throbbed from the siren blare during transit; strobing blue lights kept me off center as I waited. Islands of blooming heirloom azaleas dotted the yard. Under any other circumstances I would enjoy their beauty. Today the thick foliage and profusion of blossoms might be hiding a very bad person.

I hugged my arms to my middle and took a deep breath. And another. Nothing eased the edgy, needling feeling I had. It seemed as if I was trapped in that pre-sentient moment before something happened.

Was the sheriff right about it being simple to find a recently deceased spirit? I didn't usually get involved with cases until someone was long dead. I'd never tried to locate a newly deceased person.

Was a spirit trying to contact me? Was that why my nerves wouldn't settle?

Was Morgan's spirit here in the sheriff's Jeep? I couldn't tell. There were no voices whispering in my head. No new voices, that is.

If Morgan was dead and if he wanted to speak to me, I'd have to go to him, in a dreamwalk. Recently I'd taken over the job of county dreamwalker from my father, and I'd had some success helping people, but I had a lot to learn about my psychic abilities.

And there was the monetary benefit to consider. With every case I helped the sheriff solve, I received a sack of cash, under-the-table money that supplemented my meager income.

I could wait until the sheriff returned before I searched for Morgan among the dead. Or I could be the hero and solve this case almost before it began. That would certainly raise my worth in the sheriff's eyes. My competitive instinct flared. Yeah. This felt right. I'd beat the sheriff at his own game.

Time for a dreamwalk.

I double-checked that the doors were locked and settled into my seat. I superimposed Morgan's features on the inside of my eyelids, grounding myself physically at Sparrow's Point, but allowing my mind the freedom to seek the banker's spirit. With every deep breath, I drew further into myself, seeking the core of my power, the engine that would propel my spirit to an alternate plane.

A gateway opened up. My mind moved forward, passing through the psychic realm with a minimum of disorientation. Pride swelled within me. I was getting better at this. Murky twilight surrounded me. Transparent beings hurried past as if I were an inconvenient road block.

I turned slowly, wondering what I should do. With Morgan's image in my head, I expected to find him. Or at least to know which way to go.

I had nothing.

No direction.

No Morgan.

Had I wasted a trip?

"Morgan? You up here? Did you call me?" I asked.

Angry bees buzzed in the distance. By the time I recognized the sound, they were all around me, a thick knot of aggressive spirits.

"I called you," an older man said.

A young, tattooed woman shoved the white-haired man aside. "No. I called her. Listen up, traveler. My sister needs the bank robbery money."

Others shouted and pushed, pressing in on me, as if they were helpless against my magnetic pull. I glanced around, searching for an exit, but spirits stretched as far as I could see in every direction.

Panic clawed at me, and I pushed the spirits away. "Stop! Get off me. Let me be." My protest gained me a narrow cylinder of personal space.

Tattoo woman crossed her arms and glared. "You summoned us."

Even a novice like me knew not to stare into those glowing red eyes. "No. I didn't. I'm looking for Morgan Gilroy. Anyone know where he is?"

"Don't know the man," the older man said. "Never heard of him."

I ignored his gruff tone. "He'd be new to the spirit world."

"Then he wouldn't be here yet. Takes a while for spirits to find this place."

So much for me being the hero. I'd risked this dreamwalk to get a jump on solving the case. Looked like Wayne would have to stick to detective work after all.

"I have to go."

"Not so fast," tattoo woman said. "We know who you are. What you are."

"I don't mean any harm."

"You travel between worlds. You can't just come here whenever you want. There's a price to pay."

"There is?"

"And we mean to collect."

"Look, I don't know anything about that. I really have to leave right now." My hand went to my crystal necklace.

As one the spirits retreated.

Tattoo woman's voice followed me to the gateway. "I'm watching you."

Gradually my surroundings took on corporeal form. The solid seat beneath me. The mechanical whir of the Jeep's engine. The zebra-striped slices of sunlight across the lawn of Sparrow's Point.

Sparrow's Point.

I was at Morgan Gilroy's house. The banker had called for help, said he'd been stabbed. Urgency filled me, burning like

13

acid indigestion, and propelled me out of the Jeep.

I had to see Morgan.

It couldn't wait another minute.

I gained the porch, then the front door, which the sheriff had left open. My eyes strained to see in the dark corridor. The hallway spun. I gasped in a breath, and gravity reasserted itself.

So did reason.

Was the intruder still here?

I needed to find the sheriff fast.

I squinted into the gloomy corridor and took stock. Plastered walls. Wide planked wooden floors. An antique marble-topped buffet with a seashell display was to my left. A large conch shell caught my eye. I palmed it, liking the pointy edges and the smooth texture. If I stumbled upon a bad guy, I could whomp him with the seashell.

Every fine hair on my body stood on end. Energy arced from one raw ending to the next, urging me to fight or run far away. Dread mounted with each step.

I heard the sheriff's voice down the hall. He murmured something in a reassuring tone. I followed the sound, my eyes darting from the blue and gold carpet runner to the shadowed rooms I passed. My fingers tightened around the shell.

Almost there.

I gained the doorway to what appeared to be a library. My gaze swept the paneled bookshelves lining two plaster walls, the carved desk and empty chair across the room, and the dark stain on the Oriental carpet. Morgan lay face up in the center of the stain. A gasp slipped from my lips.

"I told you to stay outside." Wayne knelt beside the banker. "I haven't cleared the house."

I lifted my eyes to the sheriff's familiar rough-hewn features. Below his receding hairline were a handsome face and a trim, athletic body. If I kept looking at Wayne, I wouldn't see the knife planted in Morgan's chest or the bloody shirt. I edged toward a bookshelf, putting distance between me and the threshold. "I had to come."

"This is a crime scene. You can't be in here." His dark gaze narrowed. "What's that in your hand?"

"A conch shell."

He swore. "Put it down. Don't touch anything."

I clung to the shell and nodded toward the banker. "Is he dead?"

"Not quite."

No wonder I couldn't find him in the spirit world. He was still here.

The banker wasn't a close friend, but he had a teenaged daughter. She'd be devastated at losing him, just as my daughter had been when her father was officially declared dead.

What else did I know about Morgan? Twenty years ago he'd swooped into town, flashing cash and buying property. Last year he'd sniffed after my fixer-upper. I needed money something fierce, but I wouldn't part with my inheritance for pennies on the dollar. I'd told him where to shove his lowball offer.

Stop that, I told myself.

Be respectful.

You're in Morgan's home.

He's dying.

Morgan made a gurgling noise in his throat, rasping in a breath. This was the moment of death I hated most, the liminal moment when spirits slipped through the veil. I steeled myself for Morgan's passing, not wanting to watch, yet unable to tear my gaze away.

The breath wheezed out of him. Impossibly, his dulled eyes sought mine. I edged closer, my hand fisting over the pointy edges of the seashell. Slashes in his white shirt oozed thick crimson.

Blood.

I shuddered and breathed around the metallic smell.

Another inhalation from the dying man. Morgan's chin wobbled. A raspy whisper slipped out on his final exhale. "Bubba done it."

# CHAPTER 2

The sheriff closed Morgan's eyes. He stood and glared at me. "Darn it, Baxley, I told you to stay outside. You can't tell anyone what you just heard. That's privileged information."

Bile rose in my throat. Morgan Gilroy wasn't my friend, but I knew him. I swallowed thickly. I used to know him.

He was dead now.

Someone had killed him.

Someone named Bubba.

In Sinclair County, Georgia, we had a boatload of Bubbas.

"Don't move and don't touch anything," Wayne said. "I'm going to clear the house."

The sheriff and his gun left the room, leaving me with the dead guy. Cold seeped through my body, numbing my senses, shutting down my flight response.

Part of me wanted to do another dreamwalk, to catch Morgan while the event was fresh in his mind. The other part said no way. I needed to learn how to avoid those angry spirits I'd just encountered. Daddy would know what to do. I'd ask him later. I'd catch up with Morgan later, too.

I tried gazing at the distant marsh through the picture window, listening to the odd creaks and starts in the old house. But every time the wind kicked up, mossy branches danced, making me think someone was out there, watching.

Turning, I focused on the fancy books. Gold letters on the spines. Some looked like law tomes. Interspersed with the books were photos of Morgan's daughter, Connie Lee. Poor thing. Her life would be forever changed.

I heard the sheriff on the stairs. Unwittingly, my gaze went to the dead banker. While this chill was upon me, I could stomach the gruesome sight. The knife hilt in his chest was impossible to miss, as were the bloody slashes. My gaze traveled down to his hands. They lay at his sides, the pinkie finger on his right hand bent at an impossible angle. I shuddered at the pain he must have endured. I didn't like pain.

I didn't like death much either.

Who hated this man enough to stab him over and over again and leave him to die?

I saw now that Morgan had been holding on, waiting to tell us who had done this horrible thing to him. My hand tightened on the conch shell, the hard points pressing into my skin. I studied the shell. Shrimpers were forever catching conchs as they dragged their nets through the sea.

Shrimpers. I knew a Bubba who was a shrimper. Worse, he'd run afoul of the Gilroy clan nine months ago by spotting the overturned boat of Morgan's missing niece in the marsh. The Gilroys clamored for Bubba Wright's arrest, but there was no proof he'd killed the missing girl.

What about Bubba Paxton? During his wild years, he'd been the biggest crackhead in town. He'd caught religion in prison and recently opened a church. Even so, I wouldn't want to be in a dark alley with Bubba Paxton.

Another Bubba rolled into my mind. Big-mouth Bubba Jamison. His frequent letters to the editor of our paper sharply criticized the good-old-boys network, which had been Morgan's inner circle. Had his rants crossed the line to violence?

My brother-in-law was a Bubba. Worse, Bubba Powell had lost the love of his life to Morgan eighteen years ago. Had he finally exacted his revenge?

The sheriff returned, a boxy, metallic case in his hand. He set down the box and extracted a camera. "The house is clear."

I nodded, tight-lipped, still worried about my brother-in-law. After a dozen years of marriage to Bubba's younger brother Roland, I knew that Powell men didn't give affection lightly. The thought of Bubba Powell possibly involved in a crime of passion made my knees tremble. The room tilted.

Wayne snarled at me. "Suck it up, Baxley. I've got enough to worry about without having a puny female on my hands."

With his threat, my fear channeled into dark emotion. Anger churned in my cold gut. Old secrets slipped from a locked vault in my head. "Who are you calling puny? The woman who held your head when you tried to drink an entire case of beer in one night?"

He waved off my accusation. "Ancient history. I can hold my liquor now."

Like that was an outstanding accomplishment. It boggled my mind that a boy I used to help with his homework was the top law enforcement officer in our county.

Strangely, a sense of calm overtook me, a sense of being on the outside and observing this scene. I could still smell the blood and hear the approaching wail of the ambulance, but I'd gone to that trauma-free place in my head, same as when my husband disappeared.

My omniscient gaze returned to the dead man on the floor. No amount of testing, poking, prodding, or electric shocking would bring Morgan back to his family. That sharp hunting knife had severed Morgan's chances for survival.

The banker's murder would test Wayne's detective skills. Sinclair County was better known for car wreck fatalities, people dying from natural causes and, about nine months ago, a missing child.

But murder . . .

Murder was bad news.

It was also my reporter friend's fondest dream. What could I tell Charlotte without jeopardizing my consultant status?

Morgan lay on the floor of his study, his bloody cell phone inches from his right hand. The knife hilt looked like my late husband's nine-inch Bowie. Dirty-wine colored blood seeped from underneath him, saturating the Oriental carpet and the wide planked hardwood floor.

On his sleek desk were several open manila file folders, as if he'd been working at home when he'd been disturbed. There were no bloody fingerprints. No visible shoe prints. No sign that anyone had been there, except for the thick knife hilt protruding from the dead man's chest. That was no help. Those things were standard issue at the local hardware store. There were probably hundreds of them in our county.

I shuddered and looked away from the body.

Navy-blue leather wingback chairs and ottomans stood ready to receive visitors. Elegant tan drapes framed floor-to-ceiling picture windows that overlooked a hand-tiled swimming pool and the picturesque salt marsh beyond.

"Baxley, get out of here. The paramedics are coming," the sheriff said. "I've got to process this crime scene."

I leveled my gaze at him. "You are the rudest man I've ever met."

"Don't push me, babe. I've got a murder to work. Unless you're going to do your woo-woo stuff and rat out the killer."

"Not today and not here. This place is swirling with emotion. Whoever did this hated Morgan. Once we get Morgan to the morgue I can try to contact him. Or I can do a reading on the knife."

"Whoa there. Not so fast with the knife. I need to fingerprint it. But first I've got to take pictures of the scene."

"Who could have done such a thing?"

"I already know that. I've got a solid lead. I won't even need you on this case."

I blinked. " 'Bubba done it'? That's your lead?"

"Morgan named his killer. I'll round up the Bubbas and hold 'em until one confesses. It will be the easiest case I ever solved."

As a single parent, I relied on law enforcement officers to keep my family safe. Wayne's crude methods wouldn't be tolerated in a larger police system. Who made sure he did his job? Anxiety burrowed into my thoughts like an insidious worm, making me question the wisdom of moving my kid to a place with a shoddy police force.

Wayne barked out a request for the county coroner through his radio.

Paramedics arrived, and Wayne headed them off at the study door. "Sorry to have called you all out here. The victim didn't make it. I've summoned the coroner."

I clung to the conch shell to ward off the cloak of death. Help was on the way. My father was the new coroner.

Heavy footsteps mounted the back porch steps. The kitchen screen door squeaked open. "Morgan? Morgan? What's going on here?" a man asked.

"Christ. That's Ritchie Gilroy. Do something, Baxley." The sheriff reached for his camera. "Keep him out of here. He doesn't need to see his brother like this."

I had firsthand experience of what it was like to lose a loved one. Roland's funeral was two years ago and not a day went by that I didn't think of him. But I thought of him whole.

Wayne was right.

Ritchie didn't need to see his brother with a knife wedged in his chest.

# CHAPTER 3

Steeling myself for his questions, I stepped into the hall to intercept Ritchie Gilroy. "Come sit out by the pool with me."

He barreled past me. I hit the side of the wall to avoid him. It was either that or be mowed down.

"God! No! Morgan!" Ritchie fell on his knees beside his brother. He grabbed the knife hilt.

"Don't touch that!" the sheriff yelled, camera in hand.

Ritchie paled. He released the knife, sobbing openly. "Jesus. No. Not my brother."

"Get him out of here," the sheriff growled.

I shot Wayne a dirty look. So much emotion rolled off Ritchie that it snapped like electricity. I drew more inside of myself to protect my senses. "Let's go outside. Get some fresh air."

Ritchie swiped the moisture off his cheeks. "When will it end? Hasn't my family been through enough?"

I couldn't bring myself to touch him. The sensory overload would've been too much. I cleared my throat and pulled out my sternest parental voice. "I'm sorry, but you can't be in here. The sheriff needs to do his job. We have to leave the room."

Ritchie gazed at me in confusion. "Baxley? What are you doing here?"

"Come with me, okay?"

He stumbled to his feet, pushing off the front of the desk. "You catch this bastard, Sheriff. You make him pay for what he did."

"Follow me."

Ritchie huffed out another deep breath. "I heard the sirens from my yard. I'm sick about this. God. My brother is dead."

His cheeks were flushed. If I didn't know he'd sprinted from his place down the road, I'd have thought he breezed in from a tennis match. His pristine white shorts and white polo shirt screamed status, money, and power.

My jeans, tie-dyed T-shirt, waffle-tread boots, and two-tone hair didn't scream anything. After accepting the position of county dreamwalker, a center forelock of my dark brown hair had turned snowy white. Not that my appearance mattered right now. My power came from a different source, and I'd put it to work later, regardless of what Wayne said about needing me on the case.

Sympathy swelled within me as I accompanied Ritchie out the front door. He was at least four inches taller than my five-foot-six and outweighed me by about fifty pounds.

Ritchie glanced over at the concrete driveway. Morgan's big Lincoln snoozed next to the sheriff's Jeep.

"God." His voice warbled. "My entire family is slipping away from me. First June. Now Morgan."

"I'm sorry for your loss."

"I can't believe he's gone." He covered his eyes with his hands. "I saw him last night. Louise and I had Morgan over for dinner. He said he and Patty were going to try again."

I'd seen Patty a few days ago coming out of Cap'n Sandra's restaurant. She'd been with someone, but it wasn't Morgan. An image surfaced in my mind. My brother-in-law, Bubba Powell, had been with Patty. My stomach lurched. I sucked in a breath through my teeth.

"Oh, God. I have to tell Louise," Ritchie said.

The news had hit Ritchie hard, but he appeared to be moving past shock. His fragile wife would not be so resilient. "Where is she?"

"At the beauty shop." He fumbled in his shorts pocket for his cell phone.

I stepped away to give him privacy. I needed to get out of here. Though my extra senses were protected, negative energy lapped at my feet, draining me. With the dreamwalk I'd just taken, my reserves were already low. I envisioned a white light surrounding me to block the bad energy.

Distance was what I needed. Distance would help me gain perspective. Distance would allow me to figure out if my screw-up brother-in-law was safe from a murder charge. Distance would put me closer to the school bus and my precious daughter.

How would I get back to town?

It wasn't like I could take the ambulance or the sheriff's Jeep. No one was using Morgan's Lincoln, but I couldn't borrow the dead man's car. It might contain evidence. If I could bum a ride from Ritchie or Louise, that would be good. Failing that I'd have to call Charlotte or ask my mother to come and get me.

Mental note: always drive my own truck to future job sites.

"Baxley." Ritchie pocketed his phone. "Louise is meeting me at home. Would you come with me to tell her? I'm not up to the task."

Poor Louise. This news would hit her hard. "I'm sure you'll do just fine. I really need to get home and meet Larissa's school bus. Trouble is, I don't have a car."

"Borrow one of ours. Please, come with me. Louise went to pieces when June disappeared. I can't tell her about Morgan. I just can't."

His plea tugged at me. I'd been told since childhood that I had a healing way about me, a soothing quality. I'd shied away from actively using it with people, preferring instead to work with plants and animals. But here was a situation where I could do some good. Louise was a friend in need.

I glanced at my watch again. The school bus would arrive in less than an hour. It was at least a ten-minute walk to Ritchie's house along the paved road, less if we cut through the woods. If Louise fell apart, I couldn't count on getting out of there right away.

Time to make an alternate plan for my daughter. "I'll help, but let me make a call first."

Relief surged through his eyes. "Thanks."

I hit number three on my speed-dial list. Mama picked up on the fourth ring, which meant she was near the phone. She only answered on rings four, seven, or nine.

"I'm tied up out at Honeycreek Lane," I said. "Can you meet Larissa's bus and keep her until I can break free?"

A television blared in the background. I heard the faint symphony of wind chimes serenading my parents' tiny bungalow. "Sure thing. I've got a good groove going this afternoon. Larissa can help me paint the house."

Painting the house was a never-ending affair. My parents collected odds and ends of paint from everyone, adding natural pigments to create their own unique shades. I never knew what their house would look like, inside or out.

"Make sure she changes out of her school clothes first. And keep the music volume down to tolerable levels."

"Lighten up, dear. You've got plenty of Nesbitt blood flowing through those veins of yours. A little rock 'n' roll would mellow you right out."

"I mean it, Mama. I'm counting on you to act like a responsible adult."

"Don't you worry about a thing."

My biggest nightmare was that Larissa would embrace my

parents' counterculture lifestyle. She was ten going on twenty-one as it was. My daughter was all I had left of Roland. She was my heart.

"Thanks."

Ritchie and I struck out on the paved road and walked the distance at a brisk pace, each of us lost in our thoughts. Overhead the birds sang in the moss-draped oaks, the sun shone in the cloudless sky, and a light wind rustled through the palm fronds. Just another day in our coastal paradise. Except for the dead banker at Sparrow's Point.

We were almost there when Louise's car careened past us and skidded into the open garage. Ritchie caught my eye. "Do you think she already knows?"

# CHAPTER 4

Louise sure acted like she knew something. She could have given us a lift down the driveway or opened her window to greet us. Instead, she hurried inside the house as if the hounds of hell nipped at her high heels.

Ritchie and Louise's contemporary home wasn't as stunning as Morgan's house but it was upscale and well-maintained. Landscaped beds framed the two-story dwelling, the lush vegetation a dark contrast to the pale yellow stucco.

Second thoughts assailed me. I didn't understand Louise's rudeness, and that uncertainty stirred up butterflies in my stomach. Ritchie might not be empathic, but as Louise's husband, he certainly knew his wife better than I did. Had I made a mistake in assuming I could help? Moisture dampened my palms.

I would rather be anywhere else in the world but right here, witnessing another person's grief. My own sense of loss should have faded with time. Instead, my husband's death was an open wound that festered. Roland had been my best friend, my lover, my confidante until the Army declared him dead after a botched mission.

Like me, the Gilroys were no strangers to misfortune. Louise and Ritchie's ten-year-old daughter went missing nine months ago. Their June had hit it off with my Larissa, and June's disappearance hit us all pretty hard. Louise refused to accept that June was dead, but in my heart I feared that was the case.

27

June had been a happy kid, competent in a boat, full of Gilroy self-confidence. Her disappearance was an open case with no leads. Our community had rallied, trying to find her, but we'd failed miserably.

Precious bounded up to meet me when I entered the too-quiet house. The flat-coated Lab had the curliest hair on her ears and a lightness to her step that I envied. She was also one of my most challenging dog-walking clients.

At the bar, Louise clanked an empty highball glass on the granite counter. Booze sloshed into the glass as she refilled it.

Louise kept her rigid back to us. Her salt-and-pepper hair skimmed the top of her jacket collar. She wore a navy blue sheath, with matching jacket and pumps.

"Did they find June's body?" Louise asked.

Realization flashed through me. Ritchie's summoning her home must have triggered her worst nightmare. Poor Louise. I hadn't expected her to think this was about June. No wonder she'd raced for the bar to fortify her nerves.

Her husband cast me a beseeching glance. I crossed the ceramic tile floor to Louise. "Ritchie asked me to break the news to you, Louise. First, let me put your mind at ease. This has nothing to do with June."

Louise sighed audibly. Her head and shoulders drooped. "Thanks for that. I keep thinking she'll walk through that door any day now."

"I understand."

"Until they find her, I can't give up hope that she's alive."

The chances of June being alive were slim to none. Her boat had been found in the last outcropping of marsh on this side of the sound. My head knew this, but my heart wished a miracle had happened, that she'd been rescued and had been living on a freighter all this time. A silly fantasy, but I understood Louise clinging to the idea her daughter was alive. I couldn't bear to think of Larissa being anything less than whole and healthy.

"I don't understand what's wrong with that lousy sheriff," Louise said. Flags of red appeared in her pale cheeks. "He ought to have some leads in her case by now. He ought to have located June and brought her home where she belongs. It isn't right that a mother should endure so much agony."

Ritchie advanced toward his wife. "Lighten up, Louise. Everything that happens isn't about you. I lost a daughter, too. Now my brother is dead."

I scrunched my eyes shut, wishing I could rewind time and erase his words. There was nothing soft or comforting about them. His anger tainted the room.

Louise dropped her highball glass on the tile. Glass splintered the crystalline silence. She shrieked, causing my heart to miss several beats. So much for my being a helpful presence. So much for doing this as tactfully as possible. In one swift move, Ritchie had negated my reason for being here.

I forced in a breath of air. Louise stared at Ritchie, her pale face at odds with his now-florid complexion. With damage control on my mind, I guided her over to the sofa and wished Ritchie would take himself off to another room.

"What happened?" Louise whispered. Her hands were December-frost cold.

"Morgan's dead, Louise, just like Ritchie said. The sheriff is over at Sparrow's Point right now," I said. Now that the news had been broken, it seemed better to continue with the direct approach.

"Tell her the rest of it," Ritchie said from the doorway.

Louise's glassy eyes searched my face. In that moment, I felt a wave of empathy for Sheriff Wayne Thompson and other lawmen. I couldn't imagine having to routinely break the news of foul play to relatives.

Louise clutched the side of her navy jacket, rumpling the

crisp fabric. "What? You must tell me."

One look at her mascara-stained cheeks and I knew I wasn't up for this task. I should never have let Ritchie persuade me to come here. Whatever compassion I possessed, Louise wasn't picking up on it. I'd allowed Ritchie to play on my misguided desire to ease Louise's pain and walked wide-eyed into this maelstrom of emotion. Plants and animals were much more my style.

He'd used me. I wanted to get up and leave, right this second.

How tacky would it be to ask for their car keys right now?

Majorly tacky.

I had to see this through.

"Louise, it isn't good news," I said. "Morgan was killed. The sheriff is working on the case. He'll find Morgan's killer."

Louise sobbed loudly. I patted her shoulder and glanced over at her husband. This would be the perfect time for him to take Louise in his arms. He shook his head, his eyes brimming with moisture. He left the room.

Precious padded over and thrust her head in Louise's lap, and Louise clung to the dog. I squeezed her shoulder and wished there was more I could do. My heart went out to all of them. I'd stood in this chasm of grief myself, and the winds of loss still howled through my belly. At least this time the Gilroys had the comfort of a body to bury.

After awhile, Louise's sobs abated.

"This backwater place." Louise backhanded the moisture on her face. "Someone here has it in for Gilroys here. I'm gonna hire an army of private detectives. That stupid sheriff couldn't find his way off a sandbar at high tide. The only way we're going to nail the offender is with outside help. I should have hired someone nine months ago, but Ritchie trusted that do-nothing sheriff. Damn it. A mother knows when things aren't right. I should have trusted my instincts."

My instinct was to run screaming from this house, but it was a five-mile walk back into town where my truck was parked at the sheriff's house. If I could get Louise to calm down enough to borrow her car, I'd be home free. Until then I was her emotional hostage.

The level of anger in the room nearly blinded me. Waves of the stuff bounced off the walls, triggering my flight or fight instincts. I glanced out the sunny window where the twinkling high tide beckoned in the marsh, wishing I was outside and alone.

I'd walked into this with good intentions, knowing that loss invoked strong emotions. But instead of comforting Louise, my personal demons were resurfacing. I had to pull it together. I was supposed to be helping, not watching for the first opening to escape the taint of death.

I clasped my hands together, closing the circuit of my energy, strengthening my mental barriers. "You do what you need to do, Louise. If hiring a detective is what you want, I say go for it."

"That Bubba Wright is going down for this one. This murder and June's disappearance."

My breath hitched in my throat. It couldn't be coincidence that she'd mentioned a Bubba right away. "I don't understand."

"I always knew he had something to do with June's disappearance. I'm going to insist that bloodhounds search his boat, his dock, his crappy little seafood shop, and his trailer. No way is he getting away with this."

Her venom floored me. She might as well have smacked me in the head with a landscaping timber. "Louise, why do you think Bubba's involved?"

"He found the boat, didn't he? How many other shrimpers drove right past the boat and didn't see it? He saw it because he knew it was there. He's guilty. I want to catch him and make

31

sure he dies by lethal injection."

I tugged at the neck of my T-shirt. Conviction rang in her voice. Louise believed Bubba Wright was a stone-cold killer. "Finding something in someone's possession is a long way from proving they harmed someone."

"Yeah, but he's never looked me in the eye after June disappeared. Something else is going on with that man. He hates Gilroys. After he hurt my June, he went after Morgan. Who's next? Me? Ritchie? Or what about Morgan's daughter? Maybe I should hire bodyguards instead of private detectives. Either that or wake up with a bullet hole through my head."

It was on the tip of my tongue to tell her Morgan had been stabbed, but the sheriff had warned me to keep my mouth shut. Louise Gilroy was none too stable herself. I wouldn't put it past her to retaliate by shooting Bubba Wright. I needed to do some damage control here.

"Be reasonable, Louise. This is Sinclair County, not a huge metropolis with an ungovernable crime rate. Families have lived here in harmony for generations."

Louise sniffed. "Not those new people out at the north end. They want to change things."

Like what day the bridge club met. The ladies of the north end wanted to play bridge on a day that didn't interfere with their golf league. When the regulars refused to change from the first Tuesday of the month, the newbies launched their own bridge club. Some of the locals had defected to the new group, causing a shortage of players in the decades-old First Tuesday club.

"We're learning to live together, the new and the old. There's bound to be a few speed bumps along the way."

Louise reared back. "You calling my June a speed bump?"

"No. Goodness. Of course not." My gut twisted. Trust me to put my foot in my mouth. "I don't know what happened to

June. Her disappearance and Morgan's murder are unrelated events. We should stay out of it and let the sheriff do his job."

"I'm not staying out of anything. Bubba Wright is guilty. I'll make sure the whole world knows it."

# CHAPTER 5

Half an hour later Louise showed no sign of winding down. I could champion the peacefulness of Sinclair County and Bubba Wright's kind heart until swamp lilies sprouted on the moon, but Louise would never hear me.

I'd walked in Louise's shoes. When Roland disappeared, my life nearly stopped. But I'd had Larissa. Caring for her had pulled me back from the brink. Louise was still teetering on that sharp edge of dreadful hope. Waiting for answers had taken a terrible toll on her emotions. Bitterness, frustration, and anger boiled out of her mouth.

My work here was done.

"I have to go," I murmured and edged toward the door.

With her eyes on the shimmering water in the creek, Louise slugged back another whiskey and launched into track three of her recurring tirade. Her scathing tone followed me as I left the house. "That damned Bubba Wright. I bet he's in cahoots with the sheriff—"

I shut the door firmly, welcoming the sunny warmth of mid-afternoon and the ocean-fresh air of the incoming tide. In a pool of sunshine far away from the house, I turned my face skyward, closing my eyes, letting the pulse of nature cleanse my system.

I pulled the flaming arrows out of my wounded pride and pushed the negativity out of my thoughts. With Ritchie and Louise mired in grief, my transportation problem loomed large.

No way could I presume to borrow a vehicle from them.

Grimly, I surveyed my options. It was five miles back to town, definitely too far to walk. There were no taxis in Sinclair County. I'd already imposed on my mother to meet Larissa's bus, Daddy would be tied up at Sparrow's Point, so I called my friend Charlotte Ambrose at the newspaper. "You got a minute?"

"You got a million dollars?" Charlotte sighed seductively into the phone, her voice Marilyn Monroe–playful. "I'll do anything for a cool million."

I choked out a laugh. "A million dollars doesn't go as far as you think. I need a ride to town from Honeycreek Lane."

"Kip makes us punch a time clock. He owns me for another hour."

As much as I loved communing with nature, being stuck on Honeycreek Lane for sixty minutes didn't suit me. "There's something in it for you. Drive out here and be quick about it. There's a big story."

"I'm not leaving my air-conditioned office for a pet trick or a showy flower."

Impatience sharpened my tone. "Get your butt out here. And bring your reporter gear. Otherwise, Bernard Rivers will get this story and you'll be covering local mentions ten years from now."

"All right. All right. I'm coming. You had me at big story. Which house?"

"Never mind that. I'm walking on the road. Hurry."

It was one point four miles from Ritchie and Louise's waterfront house to the highway. I'd measured the distance with my pedometer when I walked their dog, Precious. I could make it to the head of the road in twenty minutes if I hurried.

But why hurry? Now that I'd dragged Charlotte into the picture, I'd have to return to the crime scene at Sparrow's Point with her. Then I'd finally be free to get my truck from town, collect my daughter from my parents' house, and go home to cook up a batch of spaghetti for dinner. I set out at a moderate pace, wanting to put distance between Louise Gilroy and me.

Too bad I couldn't dream myself back into town. Or dream myself into a secure financial position. Each month paying the bills was an exercise in creativity.

Roland had been our family's sole means of support. He'd been old-fashioned and wouldn't hear of me working. I'd volunteered in Larissa's school, walked dogs at an animal shelter, and gardened in our postage stamp of a yard.

I'd lived through the military hell of Roland being declared *duty status whereabouts unknown* from his Special Ops mission. His status had since been changed to *killed in action/body not recovered* two years ago.

Numb with grief and flat broke, I'd come home to Sinclair County.

Masses of bureaucratic red tape snarled the release of Roland's death benefits. To make matters worse, my wealthy in-laws threatened to sue for custody of Larissa after I'd asked them for a loan. Not one red cent of theirs had come our way since Roland's alleged death.

Conversely, my parents had given us the shirts off their backs, but what did we need with more tie-dyed marvels when we already had a closet full of hippie clothes? Without marketable job skills, I was at a disadvantage in today's job market.

Plants and animals I understood.

Humans gave me fits.

A dove cooed, its mournful cry resonating in my soul as I plodded down the winding road. At least I was worrying about survival. Morgan's family had to deal with death. Not just any death. A murder.

Was there a chance Louise was right? That someone had it in for the Gilroys?

The road meandered past the driveway to Sparrow's Point.

Through the dense canopy of oaks and pines, I could barely see the flash of colored lights from the emergency vehicles. Louise might be on to something, especially where her brother-in-law was concerned.

No one had accidentally wandered into Morgan's house and stabbed him. He lived in a sparsely populated section of our county. From Honeycreek Lane, his driveway was as unremarkable as the mobile home park driveway nearer the highway.

If his death was related to a robbery, items would be missing from the house. I hadn't seen any smashed windows or pried-open doors; nothing obvious had been out of place. A flat-screen television dominated the living room. Those things cost a bundle; surely a thief would've lifted that high-end TV.

Did Morgan keep his doors unlocked? Many residents in Sinclair County, like my parents, didn't lock their doors.

His brother locked his doors. I had a set of keys for Ritchie's house in my guise as his dog walker. Someone as successful as Morgan should secure his property. But what did I know about rich people?

I had a high-school education and three part-time jobs. I subsisted on food stamps and bought second-hand clothes at the Thrift Shop. I wasn't one of the movers and shakers of the county. Morgan had been at the top of the heap, changing people's fortunes every time he opened his mouth.

A beeping horn startled me out of my reverie. I glanced up to see a gray sedan barreling toward me. In what seemed like slow motion, I vaulted onto the weed-choked shoulder.

# CHAPTER 6

Adrenaline surged through me like a whirling water spout. I clutched my chest. "You took ten years off my life."

Charlotte smirked at me from her boxy Jetta. A chunky polka-dotted watch adorned her left arm, a matching headband cut a wide swath through the fine hair framing her round face. "Lucky you. Would that we could all be eighteen again. Where's the big story?"

Anticipation glittered in her eyes. I jerked my thumb in the direction of Sparrow's Point. "Morgan Gilroy is dead."

"And?"

"And? Isn't it enough that a man in his prime had his life cut short?"

"You're holding out on me. I can tell. What's the real story?"

"The real story you have to get from the sheriff, who is over there right now taking pictures of the crime scene."

"Crime scene? You mean it?" Charlotte's grin stretched from ear to ear. "Something big happened and lard butt didn't get wind of it first?"

Charlotte had no room to call anyone lard butt. On a generous day, a friend might call her plus-sized; others would be less kind. "I'm looking out for you. You write this story, and Kip will worship the ground you walk on."

She whooped with joy. The car sputtered forward, almost crushing my booted foot. I jumped out of her way again. "Sheesh, don't maim the messenger. I'm willing to hang around a little longer while you do your girl-reporter thing, but then I need a ride back to my truck."

She hit the door-lock release, and the locks shot up. "Hop in. Hot damn. This could make my career. I could end up in Savannah or Atlanta, even. Look out, CNN."

Charlotte claimed she wanted to see the world, but she hadn't pursued employment outside of Sinclair County. She still voiced her dream, that of being a big-time reporter for the Associated Press, but I doubted she'd leave home if she had an engraved invitation.

Which suited me just fine. I wanted her to stay here. I'd done the see-the-world thing and learned that there was no place like home. Since then, I'd planted my roots back into the sandy soil of coastal Georgia. I wouldn't search out the bright lights again.

The world could have the bright lights.

I had a daughter to raise.

Charlotte floored the accelerator, and the four-cylinder engine jolted us forward. I fumbled with my seat belt as we fishtailed through an S-curve. "You're driving too fast."

Sunlight glinted off her trendy glasses and brought out the freckles on her nose. "I'm so excited. Bernard Rivers will turn lime green when he learns I'm covering another murder. This story will be in the year-end summary he does, the one that never lists any of my features."

She whipped into the driveway, the sudden motion locking my seat belt. It brought me up short as I shot forward. My fingers dug into the armrest, my gut awash in fear and adrenaline. I'd survived a skirmish with the sheriff, Louise's angry rant, but Charlotte's unbridled enthusiasm might just kill me.

"What are the deets? What did you see?"

I carefully chose my words. "A man murdered in his home. People will want to know why he's dead. If we have a serial killer running around here, I've got to take extra precautions. I don't want anything to happen to my family or friends."

Sparrow's Point came into view. The flashers atop the police cruisers bathed the historic tabby structure in an eerie wash of blue pulsing light. The shadows in the oyster-shelled stucco added to the ghostly effect. The retired coroner's vintage convertible rode high on the lawn, nosed into the heirloom azaleas bordering the house. Dr. Bo Seavey claimed the vibrant color kept his car from being in an accident.

The red paint helped all right. When anyone saw Bo coming, they got out of his way. My father, the newly minted coroner and retired dreamwalker, had probably asked Bo along as a professional courtesy.

The front door of the mansion opened.

Ronnie Oliver and Virg Burkhead emerged, solemn foot soldiers in their Class A uniforms, carrying a gurney down the stairs. My gaze snagged on the lumpy bag crowning the wheeled bed. Morgan's body was in there. Beside me, Charlotte rasped in a long breath.

A quick glance at her pale face confirmed she'd seen the body-laden gurney as well. "Left!" I shouted as an oak tree loomed in front of the bumper. "Turn left."

She swerved, narrowly missing the wide expanse of tree trunk, and slammed on the brakes. My heart stuttered in fits and starts. Blood roared in my ears. I fought for my voice. "Christ, Charlotte. You'd think you'd never seen a dead body before."

"Not. Never. I mean, I've never seen anyone dead before."

Her ashen face worried me. "What kind of reporter are you?"

"I'm the light reporter. Bernard hogs the good stuff."

The sheriff and the coroner followed the gurney out. I nodded in their direction. "Go on up there, before they leave."

She didn't budge. "Why does it have to be a dead body? Why couldn't Morgan win the lottery?"

This was not the time to wimp out. Charlotte's window of opportunity was closing fast. Anger sharpened my voice. "Get out of the car, Charlotte. Do it now or I'm going to get mad."

Her face reddened. "Why are you so touchy?"

"I'm entitled. I've had a crappy day. I want to go home. Get the story or write fluff for the rest of your life. Your choice."

With that, she bolted from the tiny car. "Oh, Sheriff!"

I followed at a leisurely pace. Across the lawn, the sheriff scowled at me. He was having a pretty bad day, too. Murder truly did suck the joy out of everything.

Daddy's ashen face nearly matched his ponytail. He wore the same outfit as me, tie-dyed shirt and jeans. Instead of my work boots, though, he wore flip-flops.

Bo Seavey's head swiveled at the lilting feminine voice. He was tall and thin, bordering on skeletal, with horn-rimmed glasses perched atop his beak of a nose. He broke into a broad grin and glided to intercept Charlotte. "If it isn't the purtiest gal in the county. Come give Dr. Sugar a big kiss."

Charlotte ignored his outstretched hand.

Good girl, I thought. No telling where those hands had been. At best, they'd been on Morgan Gilroy. At worst, they'd had a date with his privates, another well-known vice of his.

I skirted around Bo, stopping beside my pale father. I gave his hand a quick squeeze. "You all right?"

His mouth tightened, but he nodded and squeezed my hand in return.

"Sheriff, I'm here representing the *Marion Observer*," Charlotte said. "What can you tell me about Mr. Gilroy's death?"

"I know what you are, Charlotte." The sheriff skewered me with a nasty glare. His broad chest puffed up like a blowfish. One hand rested atop his holstered gun. "Baxley. I told you to keep your mouth shut. Why'd you bring the press out here?"

# CHAPTER 7

Sheriff Wayne Thompson could kiss my big toe. I'd had it with people pushing me around today. My chin lifted. "I called my best friend for a ride home. So what if she's a reporter? What would it hurt to give her the official statement?"

"I planned to phone Bernard from the office." Wayne flinched when Charlotte snapped his picture. "Don't push your luck."

"Bernard's not here." It felt good to vent my anger. "Charlotte is, and she's a fine reporter. Give her the details."

"You sure this is okay with Rafferty?" Wayne glanced sideways at Charlotte as she stashed her camera in her pants pocket.

"Kip Rafferty is fine with this." Charlotte's tri-colored pen poised over a narrow pad of paper, her expression locked in serious mode. "What can you tell me about Morgan's death?"

"This is an ongoing homicide investigation." The sheriff barred his arms across his chest. "I can't tell you any more without compromising the case."

"That's it? How'd you know to come out here?"

Atta girl, I thought. Charlotte would stubborn the facts right out of Wayne, then I'd be off the hook. Mercifully, Dr. Sugar moved to Wayne's other side.

"I responded to a nine-one-one call," the sheriff said.

"Oh?" Charlotte stopped writing. "Who called? His brother?"

"No comment. I won't jeopardize my investigation because you want Bernard's job. My concern is to see that justice is done. Leads will be followed. Morgan's killer will be apprehended." Wayne pinned me with a sharp glare. "If there is anything else in this story, anything at all that shouldn't be there, I'll know where the leak is. I can't emphasize enough how serious this is. Don't piss me off, either one of you."

His nasty tone infuriated me. Did he think I was a blabbermouth? Hadn't I kept his secret all these years? I glared back at him, wanting to light into him, but knowing he was trying to do his job. My back teeth ground together.

The strobing lights illuminated his face, a face I'd once cherished above others. Beneath that exterior had been a sensitive boy, one who sought solace in the pleasures of the flesh, one who had endured a hellish childhood.

What would it hurt for me to be big here? I didn't have a feud with him; indeed, I was glad he'd quit trying to date me in high school and I'd ended up with Roland Powell. My late husband had been the better man.

Wayne had remained here in Sinclair County, and being sheriff was the pinnacle of his aspirations. I swallowed my hot retorts. "I understand."

He studied my face for a bit longer than necessary. "Good."

"May I see inside the house?" Charlotte started up the steps.

Wayne blocked her. "Think again. It's a crime scene. Go home. I'll call you if I have anything else I want in the paper."

Charlotte turned to Daddy, pencil poised at the ready. "Do you have a comment for the *Observer*, Mr. Nesbitt?"

"No comment," Daddy said.

In that moment, I nearly burst with pride. Daddy was handling himself like an old pro even though this was his first official call as coroner.

"Is there anything about Morgan Gilroy that you could comment on for the record? How was he killed?"

Dr. Sugar surged forward, eagerness on his thin face. "This is a homicide, plain and simple. The murder weapon was left at the scene, and the mode of death is obvious to anyone with half a brain. Say, you ladies want to have a drink with me at the Fiddler Hole on the way back into town?"

"Bo is no longer our coroner and should not be quoted in the paper," the sheriff said.

After being fired from his job as coroner, Dr. Sugar had taken the job as head bartender of his favorite watering hole. I hoped someone was making sure he didn't drink up all the profits.

Charlotte turned to the sheriff. "You have the murder weapon?"

Never let it be said that my best friend was a slacker reporter. She'd honed right in on that slip of tongue. The corners of my lips kicked up.

Wayne groaned. "We have no further comment. I repeat. This is a murder investigation. Don't go sticking your nose in police business. Let us do our jobs."

"About that drink?" Bo persisted, oiling closer. "I'd be delighted if you lovelies joined me for a drink. My treat."

I backed away, catching Charlotte's pudgy arm and tugging her along. "Sorry. I've got a child waiting for me, and Charlotte has this story to write. But thanks for the invite."

"Wow. Another homicide. Who'd a-thunk it?" Charlotte chortled as we zoomed down the road. "Bernard will be all over Kip because he missed out, but I don't care. The television news crews from Jacksonville or Savannah already know who I am. Should I consider a new look so that I'm more camera ready?"

Distractions were Charlotte's biggest problems. She was often lured down dead ends by thoughts of an elusive butterfly. But it was this same creative mind-set that endeared her to me. She was the queen of possibilities, the champion of every underdog. Great qualities for a friend, but extreme challenges for a serious reporter.

"Don't worry about your clothes. Stay focused on the story," I said. "Do this right, Charlotte. Get your byline on the story." My blood iced. I hadn't considered the possibility of her high visibility on the killer's radar. "On second thought, hand this off to Bernard. I don't want you to get killed."

"Not on your life." She brushed off my belated concern, nearly poking me in the eye. "Bernard can write obituaries and classifieds for the rest of his natural life. I'm hopping on the glory train." She shot me a questioning look. "About that stuff you know that can't go in the paper, what is it?"

I sucked in a half-breath. I wanted to tell her. I really did. "You heard the sheriff. I can't tell."

"Yeah, but you can trust me. I won't put it in the paper. What's the deal?"

I shifted in my seat. "No way. Last time you wheedled information out of me, things got out of hand. We have to do this right or both of us will be out of jobs. And keep me out of the story. I don't want any publicity."

"I don't have much. Hardly enough for an article. You've got to give me something."

She would hound me unless I sidetracked her. I wracked my brain for ideas. "Nose around in his life. Talk to people who knew him at the bank or in the community. Find out if anybody gives a damn that Morgan Gilroy is dead."

Her fingers tapped a rapid beat on the steering wheel. "Only if you come with me."

"I'm no reporter."

"Yeah, but you're better with people than I am. I'll write this much up tonight, after I call my boss, and tomorrow we'll make the rounds of his acquaintances. Can you make it to the paper by nine?"

Emotions warred in my head. Charlotte wanted this murder story, but she didn't have the courage to do it alone. But helping her would put me in the limelight, a worrisome thing since I wanted to protect Larissa. The only saving grace was that people were used to Charlotte and me palling around together.

Going with her wouldn't stick out as abnormal behavior. In fact, people might wonder if I didn't accompany her. I could watch out for the both of us. "I can help you for a little while tomorrow, but I've got other jobs scheduled. I'm pet-sitting for the Browns, plus I have an estimate in progress. The mayor wants new landscaping now that election season is coming around."

Charlotte patted my jeaned thigh. "Great. It will be like old times with us canvassing the town. Remember when we sold yearbook ads? I bet we run into the same people in those same businesses."

I scrubbed my face with my hands, hoping I'd made a good choice. "God, I hope not." Marion was a backwater all right, but was it truly stagnant?

Couldn't be. Something major had changed in Marion. One of its leading citizens had been stabbed to death.

A killer walked among us.

A killer named Bubba.

# CHAPTER 8

Larissa bounded over to my truck when I pulled into Mama's yard, her golden braid swishing behind her like a puppy's tail. Splashes of neon paint dotted her peaches and cream complexion. "Mom, you've got to come see what I did. Mama Lacey says it's the best looking alligator she's ever seen. Ever. It's just so cool."

My mother refused to be called any variation of grandmother. She said she already answered to two names, and that was her limit. Conversely, my father loved being dubbed Pap by his one and only grandchild. I hoped Daddy would be along soon. I needed to speak with him about the strange dreamwalk I'd had.

Larissa's happiness bubbled through me, dispelling the icy chill that had settled in my bones. "Good to see you, too, sweetheart. Sorry I'm late."

"I've had the most fun here with Mama Lacey. Can we move in with them, Mom? Then it would be fun, like twenty-four-seven."

Her innocent remark brought a tidal surge of dismay. I wanted to be the fun person in her life, not the homework nag or the chore-master. "We'll stay where we are for now. I'm glad you enjoy visiting your grandparents."

She latched onto my arm and hauled me around to the side of the small concrete block house I'd been raised in. Grinning back at me was a fluorescent pink alligator, one with impressive, slime-green teeth. Yellow birdies soared in a blue sky over a purple lagoon.

Maternal pride soothed my ruffled feathers. I caught my daughter up in a spinning hug. "It is beautiful. You did a great job."

Larissa beamed. "Yeah. Mama Lacey said if she'd known I was going to nail this design, she would've let me paint the front instead."

"There's always next time," I said.

Mama walked around the house, trailed by three cats. It still shocked me to see her gray hair. Like my father, she was stick-thin.

"Look who's here," Mama said. Food stains dotted her acorn-brown jumper; ragged holes accented her yellowed canvas sneakers. She wore her long hair braided, like my daughter.

She hugged me, enveloping me in the familiar scents of home. Soup, homemade bread, and a hint of sage. "You get those Gilroys straightened out?"

I soothed a strand of her hair away from her face. "I tried. There wasn't much I could do. Morgan is gone. Ritchie and Louise are inconsolable. I know what that's like."

Larissa's breath hitched, and she burrowed into my arms. I hated bringing more bad news into her world. Seemed like death was stalking us these days. I held her close.

"Yes, you do, though I hate that," Mama said. "I wish Roland was here, right now. I wish fate hadn't taken him."

Her questioning gaze burrowed under my skin. Fate had indeed taken Roland, but what had fate done with him? I couldn't find him among the living or the dead.

My lips tightened. "Until we know more about what happened on Honeycreek Lane, you need to keep your doors locked."

Her gaze shuttered. "We don't have locks on our doors."

Mama and Daddy's open-door policy was known throughout

the county. Anyone could crash on their sofa in the front room. During my childhood, we'd had overnight guests from every stratum of society. I'd always felt safe living here, but the world was a different place today.

A killer walked the streets of Sinclair County. Until I knew which Bubba had murdered Morgan, I had to insulate my daughter from harm.

"I'll get the locks installed," I offered, even though I could ill afford the expense. "I want you to be safe. I want Larissa to be safe when she's visiting."

"No locks," Mama repeated in her no-nonsense voice. That tone meant she wouldn't budge. That tone always made me dig in my heels.

This time was no exception. "You're forcing my hand. No locks means Larissa can't stay over here."

"You can't keep our granddaughter from us." Mama's hand went to her heart. The air around her snapped with emotion. "That's illegal. And immoral. And irresponsible. And totally out of the question."

This was like a bad flashback to my childhood. Mama trying to guilt me into doing things her way, Daddy steadfastly refusing to listen to reason. The only hope to move forward was a compromise on my part.

"You can see Larissa all you want, over at my house," I said.

Larissa lifted her head from my chest. Tears glittered in her eyes, eyes that were the same vibrant green as her father's. "Mr. Gilroy's gone, Mom? Like my friend June?"

I stroked her back, wishing I could shield her from the world's meanness. "Not the same as June. Morgan wasn't in a boat. He died at home."

"Mrs. Gilroy said June will come home one day," Larissa said.

June and Larissa had become best friends during last year's

spring break. They'd decorated each other's sneakers with acrylic paint so that June's right shoe matched Larissa's left shoe and vice versa. Larissa still fit in her painted shoes, but she wouldn't wear them until June returned.

I cleared my throat softly. "Mrs. Gilroy wants that to be true, but you shouldn't get your hopes up. June's capsized boat was found too far out. If she was alive, she'd have been found by now. I'm sorry."

Larissa's breath hitched. "Promise me that you won't die. That Mama Lacey and Pap and Grandma and Grandpa Powell won't die either."

I could fill her head with fluffy platitudes, but truth was better than lies. "I can't make that promise. Each of us makes our own way through life. And everyone stays with us in our hearts forever. June is there, right next to your dad."

My daughter clung to me. Her quiet sobs floated on the cool evening air, reminding me of the fragility of life. I massaged her back, wishing I could do more.

Mama touched my shoulder. "Enough of this morbid topic. How about you and Larissa join me for dinner? I've made a pot of soup, and Tab baked a loaf of bread."

Denial rose in my throat. I wanted to go home, lock my doors, and unwind in my own space. Larissa looked up with pleading in her watery eyes, and my resistance melted. "Sure. We'd love to stay," I heard myself say. "Let me help you in the kitchen, Mama."

"How about cleaning up the paint brushes, Larissa-girl?"

Larissa swiped her cheeks dry. "Okay."

I walked beside Mama, not an easy task when she was moving fast. "Don't you frighten my baby girl like that," Mama said out the side of her mouth.

Uh-oh. I hadn't expected this. My shoulders squared for battle. "I didn't frighten her, Mama. I offered her comfort and let her grieve. I mean what I said about the security around here. With a killer on the prowl, I have to make sure she's safe."

"Nothing will happen to her here. We're surrounded by positive energy."

I wished that was all it took. "I respect who you are, and the choices you've made. But Larissa is my daughter. I make the choices for her safety. I hate that her friend died. I hate that Roland is gone. We have to deal with reality."

Mama halted by the front porch swing. "Listen to yourself, Baxley. Negative energy is bad for you. Focus on the good and the rest will fall into place."

"I want the security of a home for Larissa, and the ability to provide for her. I've lost too much already. I won't lose her."

"You keep thinking like that, and you'll end up like Morgan Gilroy. He focused on material things and didn't put his family first. A person without family is a dandelion seed in the wind."

The passion in her voice put me on alert. "Do you know something about Morgan?"

She huffed out a breath of indignation. "His daughter needs a kidney transplant."

"I hadn't heard that." My maternal instinct surged. Poor Connie Lee. "Maybe that's why Morgan was obsessed with money. Transplants cost a fortune."

"If he'd stayed true to his family, she would have been strong. His self-doubt and pursuit of the wrong goals weakened his energy, leaving her vulnerable. His bad chi caught up with him."

Years of free love and purification ceremonies had distilled my parents' personal philosophy. I'd rebelled against their ways, saving myself for Christianity and a normal marriage, which I'd had with Roland.

"If you say so." There was no point in arguing with her. Family was important. Hadn't I come home to feel centered again?

"I know so. Be true to your inner self, Baxley. That will

protect Larissa better than any locks or guns or security system."

I disagreed. "A killer is on the loose in Sinclair County. If you believe Louise Gilroy, Bubba Wright has it in for her family."

Mama snorted and continued inside the concrete-block house. "Louise Gilroy is grasping at straws. Bubba Wright is a family man, a good provider. He doesn't have it in his heart to hurt anyone. Louise lost her way years ago. Her energy is so blocked, she's lucky to be alive."

Mama's assessment of Louise's character hit the mark. Louise seemed to be without a rudder, floating on the tide of life from one crisis to the next. Each successive wave of trouble took her farther out to sea. Ritchie had his hands full with her.

All this talk about Bubba Wright whetted my curiosity. He fished and ran a small business on the waterfront. If Louise had inadvertently discerned the killer's true identity, I didn't want to be blindsided by it later. I was all the protection my daughter had.

It was high time I visited Bubba Wright and took his measure in person. I added him to tomorrow's to-do list.

I filled glasses with water and placed them on the table. "I was hoping Daddy would come home soon."

Mama dished up three bowls of soup. "He'll be here when he gets here. There's a lot of paperwork with his new job."

With any luck, Larissa would be a few more minutes. Just in case she was within hearing distance, I lowered my voice. "I tried to find Morgan today, right after his death, and something weird happened. Angry spirits mobbed me. I didn't banish them because I needed to question them. I got away by using my necklace."

"Leave it with me, and I'll recharge it tonight," Mama said.

I touched Roland's gift protectively. "I don't like to take it off."

Mama opened the pot holder drawer and handed me a small muslin drawstring pouch. "I had this made for you."

I set aside the napkins and spoons I was carrying and withdrew the necklace. Pink and green stones met my gaze. Pink amethyst and moldavite. The pendant was similar in style to the necklace I wore. It hummed in my hand, brightening my mood.

"It's beautiful. I hardly know what to say. Thank you."

"It will center you when I'm recharging your moldavite necklace. We can't have the county dreamwalker going around unprotected, can we?"

Mama fastened the clasp of the new necklace around my neck, discreetly tucking the other one in her pocket. At my sad look, she smiled. "I'll take good care of it. I have a feeling you're going to need constant coverage for a while."

Worry tinged my joy over the new necklace. "Do you sense something?"

"Nothing you can't handle, dear."

Since I was still learning the dreamwalking ropes, her well-intentioned words put me on edge. When Mama felt strongly about something in the future, it generally came to pass.

What the heck was coming my way?

# CHAPTER 9

Peaches and Babyface slobbered on my T-shirt first thing the next morning. I'd become the boxers' best friend ever since the Smiths' first grandchild had been born. This was the third time in the last two weeks that they'd traveled up to Statesboro and I'd taken care of their pets.

I don't know what the dogs thought of the arrangement, but I loved it. Taking care of animals was second nature to me, and if I didn't need the money, I'd have done it free of charge. As it was, I pocketed fifteen dollars for each visit.

It wasn't a business I'd get rich at, but in a good month with several clients, it brought in about five hundred dollars. Which was five hundred dollars more than the nothing I'd have had without doing something I loved. Plus, I already had bookings lined up for the summer. I'd found a niche here with pet-sitting, a niche that would hopefully continue to provide income.

Charlotte bubbled with happiness when I picked her up at the paper. In her crisp maroon pantsuit and flawless makeup she looked camera-ready. "Bernard is beside himself," she crowed. "He's been in Kip's office three times this morning, trying to steal the story from me."

I turned off River Drive onto Main Street. "Since you're smiling, I'm guessing Kip didn't cave. You must have really sold him."

"Sure did. He told Bernard it was time to shake things up at the paper. Can you believe it? Bernard's out back right now,

54

chain-smoking, trying to decide if he'll have a job tomorrow."

I shot her a sidelong glance. "Kip wouldn't fire him. He didn't mess up."

"Bernard's been Kip's go-to guy since I've been there. It was understood I was the junior reporter and Bernard was top dog. But now there's a new world order. Bernard's loss is my gain."

I was happy for her, but success was a two-edged sword. A trickle of unease flowed through me. "If Bernard's that upset, it may get ugly around the paper. He outranks you, and he's going to be on your case on every little thing. You ready for that level of scrutiny?"

"Bring it." Bracelets jangled on her arms as she gestured. "I'm ready to revitalize the news industry in Sinclair County, coastal Georgia, and the entire southeast. I wouldn't mind if the story took me up a notch or two on everyone's radar screen. I might end up writing for the Associated Press. This is my see-the-world ticket."

I chewed on my thoughts as I motored into the bank parking lot. Charlotte had no idea of the pressure she was letting herself in for. I'd never forgive myself if my meddling jeopardized Charlotte's career. "Have you considered sharing the byline with Bernard for this story? That might smooth things over for you at the office."

She pushed her glasses back up her freckled nose. "No way. That glory hound would claim he'd broken the story. This puppy's all mine."

"This could be trouble. Don't say I didn't warn you."

Her jaw dropped. "I don't believe this. You're supposed to be my friend. My best friend."

"I am your best friend. That's why I'm cautioning you not to burn any bridges. You can still ride this wave to glory, but I'm worried, too. If Bernard doesn't play fair, this could turn out badly. Are you prepared for that?"

"I'm prepared to kick reporter butt. That good enough for you?"

I couldn't hold in my smile. Charlotte had her game face on. I should shut up and let her do her thing. "Yeah. It is." I nodded toward the bank. "Go get 'em, tiger."

Her brows knit together. "Aren't you coming in?"

"I'm right behind you."

In my day-glo orange T-shirt, ponytail, and faded jeans, I wasn't dressed for success. I plucked a few stray dog hairs off my shirt. There wasn't anything I could do about the dried doggie drool.

The Marion Bank had been a major player in the world of high finance during the timber heyday in the late 1800s. Ever since then, the bank and our town had been clinging to the ghost of its former glory. The marbled bank entrance was sophisticated enough for Atlanta, and every person in this county was proud to have something so grand here.

Charlotte hurried over to Palinda Lively's desk. Palinda stood, a solid column of charcoal gray. With her mannish suits and her too-short hair, she reminded me of somebody's uncle.

"What can I do for you ladies today?" Palinda asked.

Though Palinda was an import, she'd opened my bank account when I returned. She'd transferred here from another bank in the more affluent county to our south.

Charlotte handed Palinda her *Marion Observer* business card. "I'm here in an official capacity today, Ms. Lively. What's your reaction to the death of Morgan Gilroy?"

Palinda's smile dimmed a few watts, and she sank into her seat. "I'm sad, of course. He was the president of the bank. I can't believe he's gone. I spoke with him yesterday."

"You did?" Charlotte asked. We sat in the padded chairs in front of Palinda's clutter-free desk. "What did you talk about?"

"He'd asked me to plan the company's anniversary party."

Her voice caught in her throat. "It was going to be at his house."

Sparrow's Point was gift-wrapped in crime scene tape right now. No way would the bank be toasting their yearly successes at a dead man's house. I glanced around the bank, aware that every employee seemed to be looking our way.

Gosh, now that Morgan was dead, who owned his house? Was it his brother? His ex-wife? His daughter? Or someone else altogether?

Charlotte shot me a desperate glance. I'd expected her to carry the interview and me to be the moral support. Now it seemed she'd stalled. I needed to jump-start the conversation.

I thought about the kind of quote Charlotte needed to round out her article. "Will Morgan be missed at the bank?"

"Oh, yes," Palinda said. "We'll all miss him. Mr. Gilroy knew everyone by their first name. We have over thirty employees who work at the bank." She leaned a little close to us. "My boss at my last job never got my name right. Kept calling me Belinda. But Mr. Gilroy, he kept track of everyone and everything."

"What do you mean by that?" I asked.

She leaned forward and lowered her voice in a confidential manner. "If the money didn't add up each day, he made everyone stay until it did."

"Oh?" I wasn't a reporter, but this was good stuff. Charlotte's pen scribbled furiously on the pad. "Tell us about it."

"May I help you?" Lowell Ward hurried toward Palinda's desk. His tailored three-piece navy-blue suit told the world he was in the upper tier of the bank management pyramid, and my guess is he'd noticed we weren't conducting any banking business.

I glanced behind us where two people waited to see Palinda. I stood uneasily. "Sorry, we didn't mean to monopolize Palinda. Charlotte's gathering information for a newspaper article on Morgan Gilroy."

Lowell shot Palinda a frown and beckoned us with his hand. "Come with me."

Charlotte glowed. I wasn't nearly so optimistic. Especially when Lowell didn't guide us to the executive offices.

He stepped into the foyer alcove where the half-empty water jug squatted. "I'm surprised Bernard didn't come to me. I handle the bank's publicity."

"I apologize for not knowing the correct protocol at the bank," Charlotte said. "Is there an official statement you'd like to make as the bank's publicity representative?"

Lowell straightened. "The Marion Bank deeply mourns the loss of our president and chief executive officer. Morgan Gilroy was a leader in our community, a sure hand guiding the helm of our bank. We extend our deepest condolences to his family. Gilroy's leadership over the years has been instrumental in bringing commerce to Sinclair County."

My gaze fell on a nearby scale model of the development Morgan had been working on. Sunrise Towers would provide a sweeping change to our landscape. The plans specified the entire waterfront to be studded with handicap-accessible condos. Morgan's subsidiary company had been drumming up support for the active senior community he planned to build on the Marion River.

Trouble was, some locals wouldn't sell. They preferred keeping the waterfront to themselves. Fancy that.

"What about Sunrise Towers?" I asked as Charlotte continued to write. "Will that development effort stop with his passing?"

"Construction of the first unit will begin in a few months as scheduled. Earlier this week, Mr. Gilroy reported that one of the three remaining families had agreed to sell to Blue Skies Development Corporation."

"Who caved? Kinsley? Fields? Or Wright?"

He frowned in my direction. "Fields, but that's off the record until settlement. Is there anything more I can do for you ladies?"

That left Kinsley and Wright as holdouts. Bubba Wright. Hmm. I couldn't think about that coincidence right now. Not when I was helping Charlotte. The statements from the two bank employees would be good, but was it enough to flesh out her story?

"How about a picture?" I asked.

"Feel free to take a picture of the outside of the bank," Lowell said.

"I've got a better idea," I said. "How about if Charlotte takes a picture of you lowering the flag to half-mast?"

I could see the publicity wheels turning in his head, see him thinking how the bank could use this. Lowell nodded. Moments later, we had a great picture and were once again on the road.

"Where else you want to go?" I asked.

"You're good at this," she said. "That photo was positively inspired. What should we do next?"

If I wanted to be a reporter, I'd have tried that career out already. Charlotte's move to the big time would be wearying if I had to do her job, too. "I don't know. His church? His business partners? His fishing buddies? His ex-wife?"

"Yes."

"Yes?"

"All of them. I want to talk to as many people as possible."

I hung with her through the church interview. His ex-wife wasn't home. Luckily, Charlotte had Patty's cell number. "I secretly copied it from Bernard's address book," she confided. "I've got his personal contacts in my cell directory now."

Charlotte dialed Patty from her empty driveway and switched the call to speaker phone. I lowered the truck windows and turned the motor off. It was warm for early spring, warm enough that the mosquitoes were out in full force. I squashed one that landed on my arm.

The ringing ceased in mid-ring. "Hello," Patty said.

"Patty? This is Charlotte from the paper. I'm calling about Morgan's death. I have you on speaker phone." Charlotte placed the phone on the dash and picked up her pen. "Can you hear me?"

"Yes, but I'm not sure what you want from me." Patty's voice barely carried through the line.

"What's your reaction to the news of Morgan's death?" Charlotte asked.

Patty's booming voice startled me. "He was a sorry SOB, and I'm glad he's gone."

# CHAPTER 10

Charlotte exchanged a smug glance with me. "Tell me more."

"That bastard quit paying child support months ago." Patty's voice filled the cab of my truck. "He did it to hurt Connie Lee and me. He was punishing her because she wouldn't live with him at the Palace. As if that was a fit place for a sick child."

Connie Lee at seventeen was nearly an adult. She was however, genuinely ill. As a single parent myself, my heart went out to Patty and the burden she shouldered alone.

"All that man cared about was fishing and screwing," Patty continued. "Sometimes he cared more about screwing than fishing, but most times he just took off in that boat of his. If that joker belongs to me now, I'm going to torch the damned boat. I don't care if I have to eat pork and beans for the rest of my life."

Charlotte scribbled madly. I glanced down at her pad and couldn't decipher her cryptic notes.

Talking about Morgan's assets had me wondering about his heirs. Greed was a common motive for murder. If Morgan hadn't changed his will after his divorce, Patty and Connie Lee would most likely profit from his death. But there was no way either of them was a Bubba.

I couldn't stop thinking about the murder. Who killed Morgan? Which Bubba had done it? Curiosity honed my interest in Patty's words.

"What are the funeral arrangements?" Charlotte asked.

"Don't know and I wish I didn't have to be involved. Ritchie and Louise asked me to meet them at Wallace Brothers after Connie Lee's dialysis today. I said I'd do it, but I want to park that bastard in the cheapest coffin there is, then I want to spit on it."

Wallace Brothers Funeral Home was the premiere mortuary in our region. Roland's parents had insisted on selecting a coffin for him at Wallace Brothers two years ago. We'd buried it empty because his body hadn't been recovered.

I shivered in the bright sunlight. Death was never easy.

Poor Patty. With Connie Lee so sick and her negative feelings for Morgan, how would she endure the funeral?

"Do you have a date for the service yet?" Charlotte asked.

Patty sniffled into the phone. "We were talking about next Saturday, to allow out of town family time to get here. We still have to get with Father Thomas at St. Luke's to see if that fits in his schedule."

"I'll touch base with Wallace Brothers tomorrow," Charlotte added. "About the obituary, how do you want to handle that?"

"God. I don't know. Ask Ritchie."

"Kip wants me to do a feature story on Morgan's life."

"Do not make him sound like the best thing since sliced bread or I will hurt you. You hear me, Charlotte Ambrose? I know your mother, and I will be on your case if you cross me."

"Yeah, yeah. I got it."

"And don't put any of that stuff I told you in the paper. Connie Lee would be mortified if my ongoing feud with Morgan ended up on the front page."

Charlotte stopped writing, a pained expression on her face. "You've got to give me something."

"Just say anything. There must be some standard drivel you can quote from me."

"Like the family of the deceased asks for your prayers, that kind of thing?"

"That sounds good. You can put this, too. Morgan's success lay in the fact that he focused exclusively on achieving his goals."

The call ended and Charlotte flipped back through four pages of notes, her bracelets jangling together. "I've got a gold mine here," she chortled.

"Patty said you couldn't use most of that," I warned.

"She didn't say that until the end. Everything she said before that disclaimer doesn't count."

"Think again. This is a small town. You're going to see the Gilroys everywhere you go for the next fifty years. Do you want them to hate your guts?"

She batted her expertly mascaraed eyelashes, the very picture of feminine innocence. "I can't see why they would."

A rattletrap of a car went past on the road; rap music blared from its radio. "Don't be stupid, Charlotte. Patty has a sick kid, maybe even a dying kid on her hands, and the whole town expects her to hold it together. Ritchie and Louise are devastated by Morgan's death, so Patty will be the only one with a clear head. Odds are, she'll have to pick out the funeral readings and everything. It's not something I'd wish on anybody."

Charlotte's expression softened. "I forgot you went through all of that with the Colonel and his wife."

"It's not something you forget." I shuddered in remembrance. "All that money the Powells spent for an empty box in the ground."

"In Morgan's case, there will be a body in the casket. You'll go with me to the funeral, right? We can scope the crowd for the killer."

As much as I loved Charlotte, I had to draw a line. I had other considerations that had to take priority. "We'll see. I've got to make arrangements for Larissa first. She doesn't need to attend, and I might need to leave early, depending on my schedule that day."

"We'll work it out."

I cranked the truck and circled back through town. "Okay if I drop you back at the paper now?"

Charlotte frowned. "I hoped we could go to lunch."

"Sorry. I can't spare the time today. I've got two pet clients and a landscaping client. And I need to swing by the hardware store to see about rekeying my locks."

"Next time then."

After dropping Charlotte off, I glanced at my watch. Bonnie Chapman's cat could wait a few more minutes. Ever since Louise's outburst against Bubba Wright, I'd wanted to talk to him. I drove directly to his seafood shop on the waterfront.

The lights were on inside of Shrimp 'n' Stuff, but it was deserted. I poked my head in the door to double-check. "Hello? Anybody here?"

The freezer case hummed in the silence. Harvested fish and shrimp lay in a bed of crushed ice, sightless and cold.

Bubba and his wife often fished on the dock behind the shop. Maybe they were there now. I circled the building and sure enough, Eunice was fishing.

With care, I stepped over the thick ropes tying up the aging shrimp fleet. The smell of diesel fuel, yesterday's catch, and salt air filled my lungs. Though Eunice had a rod in one hand and her line in the water, her shoulders slumped.

"Eunice?"

She turned at the sound of my voice. Beneath her turbaned head, tears brimmed over her rounded cheeks and dripped off her ebony jaw. Her bright batik print shirt contrasted with her despondent mood.

"What's wrong?" I asked.

Her chin quivered. "The po-lice done took my man."

# CHAPTER 11

Eunice's hands trembled, and she swayed on her feet. I guided her over to the wooden bench. "Tell me," I said.

"They carried him from the house in his pajamas," Eunice said. A choked sob came out as she sat. "Didn't even let him put shoes on his feet. I was down at the jail this mornin', and they wouldn't tell me a thing. I ax you this, what am I going to do without my Bubba?"

My heart raced. The sheriff had made an arrest? Of all the Bubbas, kind-hearted Bubba Wright was an improbable suspect, in my opinion. What new evidence had the sheriff uncovered?

Eunice wept copiously, her shoulders heaving with the strain. I dropped down beside her on the wooden bench. "Eunice, it can't be as bad as all that."

"I told him and told him that it don't do no good to stick your neck out for nobody. Bubba don't pay me no never mind, just goes off and does what he wants. Says it's the code."

"The code?"

Her work-thickened hands fluttered through the air. "The one in the holy book. That *do unto others* rigmarole. I told him you gotta do unto yourself first. Then you do unto others with what's left over." She shook her head. "He just looks at me with those sad eyes and tells me to hush up. Now my man's locked up and I cain't even fuss at him. What am I gonna do?"

I wanted to help her, but I wasn't supposed to tell anyone about Morgan's dying words. Did Eunice know more than she

65

was telling? "Why is he being held, Eunice?"

"They says he kilt a man. My Bubba? He wouldn't kill a flea. They's got the wrong man, but who's gonna listen to little ole me?"

He killed fish and shrimp for a living. His seafood shop was a testament to his fishing prowess, but being a good fisherman wasn't the same as being a cold-blooded killer. Not in my book.

There had to be more to it. "Why do they think he killed someone?"

"That highfalutin' vindictive Gilroy bitch accused Bubba of killin' her little girl because he found her boat nine months ago. I told him he shoulda left it in the high marsh, but no, he has to go and be the hero and call the Coast Guard and everything. Lost one of his good fishing boots in the marsh for his trouble, too. And now look at the mess he's in. He ain't never gonna see daylight again. He ain't never gonna be on the water again." Her voice broke off into a wail.

Her pain washed over me. "We need to get him a lawyer."

"Cain't afford no lawyer. We got this shop and that raggedy shrimp boat and nothing else."

Hmm. They'd be appointed a lawyer in that case, but truthfully, having Jerry McMillan as your lawyer was worse than having no lawyer at all.

I still couldn't quite believe the sheriff had acted so decisively. "When was Bubba supposed to have killed someone? And who was it?"

"They say somebody kilt Morgan Gilroy yesterday. Kilt him right through his black heart. That banker man don't know nothing 'bout no code. He's been cuttin' the fool his entire life, hustlin' this one and that one, shamin' his family. We don't have no truck with him, but he run afoul of somebody. It weren't my Bubba."

Bubba Wright needed an alibi to clear his name. "Where was

Bubba yesterday?"

"Said he was tired of fishin' from the dock. He took my son-in-law's little johnboat and went fishin' in the creek. Caught a coupla nice trout over by Doboy Island."

"What time was that?"

"He went out mid-morning and came back in a little piece before two. Why?"

The tidal creeks interconnected. It was possible Bubba had boated over to Morgan's and killed him. Possible but not very probable. "Did anyone see him?"

She wiped the tears from her chin. "I don't rightly know."

"Eunice, did Bubba have any reason to kill Morgan?"

"He ain't kilt nobody." She started wailing again, and her fishing pole clattered to the dock.

I caught it just before it fell in the Marion River. The pole had been duct taped together twice and the reel was rusted. I gingerly placed it in the PVC fishing sleeve on the dock.

The Wrights barely eked out a living. Like Mama had said, they were good people. Sunshine beat down on my head and shoulders. A dove called in the distance, the plaintive restful sound at odds with the chaos Eunice must be feeling. How could I help her? I couldn't afford to pay her lawyer bill either.

I gently cleared my throat. "Listen, I know it isn't much, but I'll stop in to see the sheriff and put in a good word for Bubba. Meanwhile, maybe someone will come forward who saw Bubba fishing in his boat."

Eunice's sniffles quieted. "That what he need? Somebody to have see'd him fishin'?"

"That would prove he wasn't over at Morgan's house."

"Hallelujah." With that, she reeled in her line and hurried back into the shop.

I studied the river. Bits of marsh grass floated on the ebb tide. The detritus would decay, releasing nutrients into the estuary, nutrients that fed the young marine life that had put Sinclair County on the map as having the tastiest seafood on the coast.

Eunice's sudden mobilization worried me, but I had only spoken the obvious. Any armchair detective knew Bubba needed an alibi.

I stopped over at Bonnie Chapman's house to take care of her Maine Coon cat. Sulay wasn't so spry anymore. In fact she rarely moved out of her cushy down-filled bed. But her food bowl was always licked clean each day, and her litter box showed signs of use.

Poor Sulay. Bonnie had gone in for a knee replacement, thinking to be home in a few days. Instead, she'd had a heart attack under anesthesia, prompting open heart surgery. Her out-of-state children had stashed her in a nursing home for her recovery.

Through slitted eyes, Sulay watched me move around the cottage. I refilled her water bowl, emptied the litter box, and filled the food bowl with fresh kibble.

I was of the philosophy to let sleeping cats lie, but I believed in the personal touch as well. Bonnie adored this cat, and Sulay had to be lonely in her owner's absence. This was my second week of caring for this feline, her second week of only having a few moments of human contact a day.

Should I call Bonnie or her daughter to see about moving Sulay to my house for the duration of her convalescence? I hated to change her environment, but it couldn't be good for her to be in solitary confinement for so long. I made a mental note to check on Bonnie's progress and see if she'd be receptive to my boarding Sulay at home in her absence.

Sulay allowed me to stroke between her ears and under her chin. I made a fuss over her and she purred. Yeah. I definitely should see about springing this kitty from solitary confinement.

A quick stop by the hardware store put me in reverse. Re-keying my locks was expensive. But that wouldn't secure my house. None of the windows had locks.

Crap. Safety was expensive. More money than I could afford right now, but I spent the money anyway. I bought ammo for my grandmother's shotgun, which I'd also inherited, and until now, kept locked in my bedroom closet. Roland had taught Larissa about gun safety from the cradle, and she knew guns and knives were weapons as well as protection. At ten, I trusted her not to play with either. With a killer running loose in the county, I had to keep my daughter safe.

I also bought up the leftover plant stock from the hardware store. At half price, they were a bargain. They'd thrive in my little greenhouse out back.

It would be nice to find a beat-up old boat for Dottie Thompson's flower garden. That would elevate the plants above ground, making it easier for her to view them from her sickbed. I'd seen an abandoned boat recently, if only I could remember where.

I had two more stops before I could go home. The first was at the jail to talk price with the sheriff and to get a down payment from him for his wife's flower bed.

Tamika buzzed me into the inner sanctum of our new jail right away, since I was a police consultant now. I couldn't help but notice the waiting room was crammed full of people.

"You having a fire sale?" I asked the sheriff after I entered his office.

He rose in a fluid, predatory movement. His dark eyebrows aligned in one angry slash. "I knew you couldn't keep your mouth shut."

# CHAPTER 12

I bristled. "I don't know what you're talking about."

He stalked over and closed the office door. His crisp trousers looked freshly pressed, leading me to wonder if he ironed his own clothes. "Every citizen out front swears they saw Bubba Wright fishing yesterday. They say he couldn't have killed Morgan Gilroy."

I sat down as if I owned the place. "That's good news for Bubba, right?"

He leaned across his oversized desk, planting both palms in the center of the glossy surface. "I had this case wrapped up, and now it's busted wide open again. Why? Because you visited Eunice Wright this morning. I ought to lock you up for obstruction."

I wasn't going to take his criticism sitting down. I sprang to my feet. "Hold up. I didn't obstruct anything. Eunice said she couldn't afford a lawyer. I suggested that if someone saw Bubba fishing, he'd have an alibi."

His head popped back at my explanation. He straightened and studied me. My palms dampened. No matter how innocent I was, Wayne was still the town's top law enforcement officer. He could slap me in jail for interference if he wanted. He'd never been arbitrary or capricious in the past. I clung to that assurance.

"The entire congregation of the First African Baptist Methodist Church is in my lobby." He rubbed the back of his neck.

"They swear Bubba Wright is innocent."

I tried for a casual shrug. "If that's the case, I don't see the problem. You have the wrong man. Better to find that out now than after an expensive trial."

"Where the heck is Bubba Powell? Did you warn him off?"

I didn't like this change of subject. "I didn't tell my brother-in-law anything, but he didn't kill Morgan. You know that. How many times have you gone hunting with Roland and Bubba over the years? You know Bubba Powell's not twisted or mean."

"He wasn't home this morning. I put an APB out on his truck, and my deputies report he's not on the roads in this county. Which suggests you warned him and he's fled. I can arrest you for obstruction. I should hold you here in a cell until he turns up."

My gut tightened. Why did Morgan have to implicate a Bubba with his dying breath? Why couldn't he have been killed by a David or a Michael? My brother-in-law, Bubba Powell, couldn't tolerate close scrutiny.

And I wasn't going to jail for something I didn't do. "Wait a minute. I didn't say a thing to Bubba. There was no need. I'm telling you. My brother-in-law wouldn't kill anyone."

The sheriff huffed out a breath as he sat in his leather chair. "I wasn't too worried about him being missing this morning until my case against Bubba Wright went south."

I released the breath I'd been holding and sat as well. The best defense for my brother-in-law was a good offense. "What about the other Bubbas in the county?"

He snorted. "I've got a deputy stationed at Pax Out. Bubba Paxton is conducting his healing service this morning, and I'm not about to interrupt him. I don't want two congregations down here. At least I know the First African Baptist Methodists didn't bring any snakes with them."

Bubba Paxton's church was a pretty sharp turn off the road

of mainstream religion. Attendance at Pax Out grew weekly, and people eagerly lapped up his message of salvation. Thursday was his day for healing, and reports through the grapevine indicated that new snakes had been added recently to the healing unctions.

But what else would you expect from a crackhead evangelist?

"What about Bubba Jamison?" I asked.

"Jamison's neighbor said he and his wife drove up to see her sister in Savannah this morning. Unfortunately the neighbor doesn't know the sister's name. I put out an APB on his Lincoln Town Car." He stared at me, a frown etched into his tanned face. "I did not need my day blowing all to hell and back like this."

I swallowed around the lump in my throat. I hoped he wasn't thinking about locking me up in jail again. "This mess isn't my fault. You're conducting a murder investigation. There's bound to be a few glitches along the way."

His steely gaze narrowed. "Where is Bubba Powell?"

"I don't know. I'm not his mother."

"You think he went down to see the Colonel and Elizabeth?"

Bubba avoided his parents like three-day-old fish. "I didn't say that. I don't know where he is."

"You didn't warn him?"

"Believe it or not, my life does not revolve around screwing up your investigation. I came here to get a deposit from you on that flower bed for your wife. If you want me to do it, I need one hundred dollars today. Right now, or you can forget the whole shebang."

"All right. Here," he whipped out a checkbook from his desk and wrote me a check. "Take the money. Put the flowers in. The sooner the better. I can't have chaos at home and work. A man needs peace and quiet in his life."

I pocketed the check, feeling better than I'd felt all day. If

Wayne needed my landscaping skills, chances were good he wouldn't lock me up in a jail cell. "I'll finish drawing up my plans today. I'll mix perennials with annuals to give her lots of blossoms."

He waved in a dismissive manner. "Whatever you think; just get it started."

My cell rang. I dug it out of my pocket and muted the call. A glance at my phone display window showed it was Ritchie Gilroy on the line. I couldn't help him right now. I let the call go to voice mail. "Sorry, I forgot to mute my phone when I came in. I didn't think I'd be here this long."

Wayne studied my phone with great interest. Awareness dawned on his rugged face. "You got Bubba Powell's cell number in there?"

My stomach turned to dog pooh. I briefly considered lying. "Yeah."

"Call him."

"He could be in a business meeting. I don't want to interrupt."

The sheriff leaned forward again. "Call him or I'm confiscating your phone. Put him on speaker, so I know you're not tipping him off."

If he took my cell, I'd be out of business. I hated being pushed in a corner like this, but I had no options. My cell was my only phone. Bubba answered on the second ring. "Where are you?" I asked.

"At the hospital having tests run." His voice sounded strained.

Worry trotted in my head. I ignored the sheriff's glare. "You sick?"

"I'm healthy, but I can't talk about it right now." Bubba sighed. "They'll be back any minute for another test."

Wayne snatched the phone from my hand. "Powell? Where are you?"

"That you, Thompson? What are you doing with Baxley's phone?"

"I've got her in my office, and now I've got your cell number. One of my deputies will come to the hospital and pick you up. Stay put."

"Listen here, Turtlehead, I'm not going anywhere with you or your deputies," Bubba Powell shot back. "Leave Baxley alone. If you're sleeping with her, I'll rip your head off."

"You're wanted in an ongoing investigation," the sheriff snarled. "You will come peaceably with my deputies, or I'll lock you up in jail so fast you won't know what hit you."

Menace dripped from Wayne's voice. I had no doubt he'd arrest Bubba without a qualm. His intensity reminded me of his high-school glory days as the football quarterback. For all intents and purposes, he was still calling the plays.

"God, Roland was right. You are an ass," Bubba said. "What the hell kind of charge you got on me?"

"Murder," the sheriff said.

I heard a rapid intake of breath and realized it was mine. I wanted my phone back, and I wanted out of this building, out of this nightmare.

"Murder? This is a joke, right? My life isn't crappy enough already?" Bubba's voice warbled. "Christ. Murder. What in the blue blazes is going on, Baxley?"

"I know you didn't kill anybody, Bubba," I said, trying to smooth the troubled waters. "But the sheriff has questions about a case he's working. He was concerned when he couldn't find you this morning. He thought you skipped town."

"Where would I go?" Exasperation riddled Bubba's response. "Sinclair County is my home. I'm over here getting tubes crammed in every possible orifice. Crap. I can't leave the hospital right now. It took a month to set this up. You have to wait, Thompson. I'll answer your questions as soon as I'm done here. Who am I supposed to have killed anyway?"

"Morgan Gilroy," the sheriff said.

"God, I wish I had killed that arrogant pencil neck," Bubba said. "He made my life miserable in more ways than one."

"Stay put, Powell. One of my deputies will be right over."

# CHAPTER 13

I understood my brother-in-law's reaction exactly. Frustration pretty much described how I felt every time I encountered the sheriff. He could take a fairly decent day and foul it up with the most pungent manure in a matter of seconds.

What had I ever seen in him back in high school? Wayne Thompson was a control freak driving a runaway train, hurtling into the future at breakneck speed, not caring who he railroaded.

My fingernails bit into my palms. "Bubba Powell didn't do it."

"I've got a dying man's testimony that he did," the sheriff countered. Light gleamed on his gold badge as he leaned forward.

His offensive strategy only made me dig my heels in and stand my ground. "Bubba's just getting back on his feet after losing the election. A false accusation could destroy his new business."

Calculation lit in Wayne's knowing gaze. "So, that's where your affections lie these days?"

His accusation stung. Outrage churned in my gut. "I am not interested in him that way. Bubba Powell is like a brother to me. Trust you to take genuine caring and make it sound like sex."

"Get over yourself, Baxley. Everything is about sex. Some people are better at hiding their needs."

This felt like high school all over again, with Wayne pressuring me to sleep with him and me clinging to the shield of my moral compass and refusing him. He'd been right about sex being fun, but he'd been dead wrong about him being the man for me.

"I am not having this conversation with you." I rose to leave his office before I said anything to jeopardize my police consultant status.

He mirrored my action, skirting his desk, stopping less than a foot away from me. A hint of his woodsy aftershave wafted my way. I wrinkled my nose as he studied me, his shrewd hunter's gaze ruffling the hair on the back of my arm.

"Why are you so determined to clear all of my suspects?" he asked.

His accusation zinged me. I couldn't have been more disoriented if I'd grabbed an electric fence. Thoughts jumbled in my head, whispers slid around the edge of my mind. I fought for equilibrium.

Triumph blazed in his eyes. Wayne Thompson was a bona fide jerk, but he excelled at detecting weaknesses. I wasn't prepared for him to examine my motives regarding this case.

Heck, I wasn't even sure of them myself.

"I don't want to clear all the Bubbas. Only my brother-in-law," I said evenly. "He's innocent. So is Bubba Wright. You've known both these men your entire life. They aren't killers."

"People come in here and lie to me all the time," he said. "They think because I grew up in this backwater town that I'm a stupid hick. Ain't nothing wrong with my brain. Sure I'm a redneck, but I'm proud of it."

He wasn't telling me anything I didn't know. "What's your point?"

"My point, sugar, is that you don't know what you're talking about. People put on one face to the world, but they act like animals when their backs are to the wall. Even you. If danger threatened your family, you'd fight back. Admit it."

A lump formed in my throat. I glanced uneasily at the distant door. Where was he going with this? "Yes. I would protect my daughter. What parent wouldn't?"

Darn him. He'd made this personal again. I'd come here to discuss the case. "You're rushing to judgment with these accusations. How can you stand there and paint one or two or ten men with suspicion in hopes that the murder charge will stick?"

"I'm doing my job. Someone, some *Bubba,* crossed the line with Morgan. I'm going to nail the SOB, even if it is your Bubba. No one commits murder in Sinclair County and gets away with it."

His words blew through my head so fast I mentally replayed them to read between the lines. "You're letting Bubba Wright go?"

"Thanks to you, I can't hold him. But he remains a person of interest. I'm continuing my investigation, and you're staying away from my suspect pool." With snake-like quickness, he caught my chin in his hand. He leaned in close enough for his warm breath to brush my cool cheek. "Don't get in my way, Baxley."

My mouth went dry. I'd forgotten how fast he was. I batted his hand away, but I didn't step back. "Are you threatening me?"

Something dark flashed through his eyes. "Take it any way you want. When I run out of leads and ask you to come in here and examine the evidence, then you're on the case. Until then, keep your sweet nose to yourself."

"You are threatening me. I can't believe it."

"Believe it. I have the authority to arrest you right now for being a thorn in my side. However, your incarceration would delay my wife getting a flower garden. I'm using officer discretion to overlook your alibi suggestion slip-up with Bubba

Wright, but this is the only time I'll be so generous."

I could go toe-to-toe with him over this, but I had Larissa to consider. There wasn't any point in taking Wayne on and showing him how much smarter than he I'd always been. Was that why he was acting like a bully? He didn't want me thinking circles around him?

I almost smiled. "Lucky me." With as much dignity as I could muster, I swept out of his lair down the tiled hall, past a harried Tamika at the reception desk. I'd gotten what I wanted, a down payment for the flower garden, but I'd also gotten a bonus. A stern warning to steer clear of the sheriff's investigation.

I greeted everyone in the crowded lobby again as I hurried through. Outside, fresh air filled my lungs, but the oppressive weight in my chest didn't ease. The sheriff meant what he said. He would lift every rock in these Bubbas' lives, and my life, too, if I crossed him. I was no saint, and I needed my rocks to stay right where they were.

Bubba Powell couldn't withstand close scrutiny either. He'd been through a succession of jobs in recent years, each of them less illustrious than before. His wife had left him and moved the kids out of state. The Colonel didn't want anything to do with his eldest son because he was such a screw-up, and Elizabeth Powell went along with whatever her husband wanted.

But Roland had always championed his brother.

As Roland's widow, I'd inherited that responsibility.

If that put me on a collision course with Sheriff Thompson, so be it. The sheriff was wrong about Bubba Powell. He was a decent man who'd had nothing but sour luck. With my changed circumstances, I saw how easily that could happen.

How in one minute all could be right in your world and the next it was the most mangled up car wreck in the junkyard?

Was that what happened to Morgan?

Had he caused someone else's life to turn to crap? My

thoughts wandered to those last two holdouts in the block of land slated for the new condo development, Sunrise Towers. Did Morgan apply extra pressure to make those people sell to him?

I made a mental note to drive by the Marion waterfront and check out the lay of the land. But first I listened to my voice mail message from Ritchie Gilroy.

"Baxley, please take care of Precious this afternoon and tomorrow morning," Ritchie said. "After Louise and I visit the funeral home, I'm taking her over to the Jekyll Island Hotel for the evening. We need to get away from this nightmare. I know you'll take good care of our dog. We'll be home by evening time tomorrow. Just add this to my tab."

Crap. How would I get everything done this afternoon? I scooted home with the *Spiraea*, Black-eyed Susans, and coneflowers I'd purchased and added some wild indigo, Carolina lupine, and *Fothergilla* from the greenhouse to take over to the Thompsons. I backed up to the compost pile, and half-filled the truck bed with dirt.

That was when I remembered the location of the torn-up boat I wanted to form the basis of the container garden. I'd seen it at the dump. On my way to pick it up, I phoned Bonnie Chapman at the rehab center and received her permission to move her cat to my house. I pulled in the Quick Mart for a diet soda, a granola bar, and twenty dollars worth of gas.

If I hurried, I could deposit Wayne's check, install the plants, pick up the cat on my way home, and still meet the bus. Larissa could come with me to walk Precious.

Events progressed on schedule, except Dottie Thompson insisted on me coming inside to speak to her during the plant installation. With a heavy heart, I wiped my dirty hands on my jeans and trudged into her stuffy mauve bedroom.

Dottie lifted up on her elbows, her wild hair going in every direction. Her slitted amber eyes added to the scary picture, reminding me of a snake-headed Medusa. I hoped to God she didn't strike me dead with her terrifying glare.

"Tell me who my husband is screwing," Dottie demanded. "Is it you?"

# CHAPTER 14

"I know he's cheating on me." Desperation tinged Dottie's shrill voice. Her lacy black nightgown looked as if it had been slicked on with a paintbrush. "He never buys me a damn thing unless he's guilty as sin. Is it you? I need to know. You screwing my man?"

I was screwed all right. Screwed for taking this landscape job in the first place.

No amount of money was worth this degree of aggravation. But I had cashed Wayne's check and paid for the materials. Unless I gave the sheriff a refund, I was jolly well stuck. Refunds were bad for my bottom line. Only one good option here: suck it up.

"Wayne wanted you to have something nice to look at," I soothed. "He hired me to plant a flower garden you could enjoy from in here, something that would add cheer to your day."

"What would cheer me up is learning who's been catting around with my husband." She eyed me speculatively, her stubby fingers mangling her floral coverlet. "He's always had a thing for you, ever since high school."

Heat crept up my neck, staining my cheeks. Dottie was not well, I reminded myself. If she needed half the pills in the mound of containers by her bedside, she was a very sick woman. I needed to stay on the high road here.

It would help a lot if it weren't so warm in here. Or if it didn't smell like a sick room. Poor Dottie stuck in this tomb all the time. No wonder she fretted so about Wayne. She had nothing else to do with her time.

"That was a long time ago, Dottie." I gentled my voice. "Another lifetime."

"Don't matter. I know my man. He's not screwing me, which means he's screwing another woman."

"That's between the two of you."

Her head lifted from the pillow. "You're damn right it's between us, and it's gonna stay between us. I've got four boys that need their daddy to come home every night."

I understood that sentiment. I'd give anything to have Roland help me raise Larissa. But that option wasn't available. "As a mother, I respect your maternal instinct. Trust me, I'd never get involved with a married man."

She huffed out a breath as she rested her head. "Wayne's a smooth talker. He can talk a woman into just about anything."

Was she talking about the time when Wayne ran her embroidered pink panties up his car antenna for everyone to see? *Saturday* had flown high for about a week before it disappeared.

Nah. It had been too long since high school. Wayne must have talked her into something else recently. I shuddered. I did not want to know details of Wayne and Dottie's married life.

"I'm sorry, Dottie."

"It's just awful." She burst into tears. Her voice hitched. "He doesn't come home at night. Sometimes he'll stop in here to get a shower on his way to work. That's when I smell *her* on him. That's when I see that just-been-laid look in his eyes."

Nearly paralyzed by her outburst, I handed her a tissue. Her flare-up rang true. Roland had had a sated look after we'd been intimate. It was his all's-right-with-the-world vibe. I'd felt pride at seeing that look, pride and love. We'd made each other happy.

Dottie was unhappy. She'd landed herself an unfaithful man. Thank goodness I'd trusted my instincts and waited for Roland.

"I thought I could change him." Dottie dabbed at her moistened cheeks with the tissue. "I gave him what he wanted and more, but it's never been enough. I screwed him in every room of this house, in every cell at the jail, and in our boat. Now I've got four hellion boys and a bad back."

Lordy, this was way too personal for me. I gazed through the filmy curtains at my lovely boat planter. "Maybe he's distracted right now because of the Gilroy murder investigation."

"Morgan Gilroy?" Dottie waved dismissively. Diamonds sparkled on her sausage-like fingers. "Give me a break. I could solve that case in a day with my hands tied behind my back."

Her boast intrigued me. "Who did it?"

"You're kidding, right?"

"No. I'm not. I'm interested in your take on the situation."

"I haven't seen Morgan Gilroy in the three years I've been stuck in this room, but he's always been a taker. Mark my words, he screwed somebody, somehow. Somebody that played for keeps. Morgan got killed for stepping in the wrong rose garden."

"Wayne had Bubba Wright in for questioning this morning."

She snorted. "Bubba Wright didn't kill anyone."

"You seem certain."

"Of course I'm certain. It doesn't pay to be halfway about anything. If Wayne is looking at Bubba Wright, he needs me to help him analyze the clues."

"Have you helped him with other investigations?"

"Yeah. He discusses his work after making love."

Hmm. If Wayne was sleeping around, he might blow his own case with pillow talk. Who would tell the sheriff to keep his lips and his pants zipped? Not me. I cast about for another topic.

"What about Morgan's business partners?" I asked. "You think one of them did him in?"

"Morgan owned most of the county. He brokered deals with outside people. It was an outsider. Had to be. Unless . . ." She slanted her eyes over to me. "Unless Wayne interviewed the wrong Bubba."

"What do you mean?" My heart raced. Did she know about the victim's last words? Did she know about the four Bubbas?

"If I had to pick a man that wanted Morgan dead, I wouldn't pick Bubba Wright. I'd pick the man who was shagging Morgan's ex-wife."

Her accusation stung. Bubba Powell and Patty had been an item long ago, but they'd married other people and moved on with their lives. "Patty divorced Morgan. He wouldn't care who Patty saw, er, socially."

"Wayne's not like that. If we divorced and I took a lover, he'd kill the other man."

Bile rose in my throat. "What a hypocrite."

Dottie lurched forward in her bed, her wild hair gyrating. "I knew it! You *know*. Who is he screwing? Tell me and I'll solve the case for you."

"I don't know anything, and it isn't my investigation. It's your husband's case. Wayne made a big point out of telling me I wasn't a consultant on the Gilroy case." I forgot and took and deep breath and wished I hadn't. I made a show of glancing at my watch. "Look at the time. I've got to get going or I'll miss Larissa's bus. I'll check your garden periodically to make sure the flowers are thriving."

Dottie waved my business card at me. The one Wayne had pocketed at the beginning of this disaster. "I've got your number."

I was afraid she was right.

# CHAPTER 15

Sulay did not come peaceably. The cat mewed pitifully. I'd placed one of Bonnie's shirts in the carrier to ease her transition, but not even her owner's familiar scent comforted Sulay as we waited for the school bus.

Larissa jerked her thumb toward the carrier as she bounded into the truck. She lowered her blue bookbag to the floor mat. "Whose cat? Is it ours?"

The wistful note in her voice tugged at my heart. Though I loved animals, I found it hard to justify the expense, when we were scrambling to pay for the basics. However, I didn't mind pet-sitting at home, which is what this would be. A temporary arrangement. "I'm taking care of Sulay for Bonnie Chapman. She's still recovering from surgery. Since the rehab is taking so long, I offered to move her cat to our house to keep her socialized and Bonnie agreed."

"Cool. I've always wanted a cat." She studied the cat. "How come she's so fluffy?"

"Maine Coons come that way."

"I want to hold her. Can I let her out of the cage?"

"She stays in the cage until I release her inside our house. I don't want her to get loose and run away while I'm responsible for her."

"Are we going somewhere else?"

"I've got another pet-sitting job this afternoon, and I want to talk to you about it."

Larissa hadn't been back to the Gilroys' since her friend's death, though we had taken care of Precious at our house during some of that time. My plan had sounded so inspired earlier when I'd made it. Taking Larissa with me to walk Precious made perfect sense. Larissa loved animals, and she'd always adored June's Lab. But now, seeing how whole and animated she was, I worried about the potential negative impact.

She had finally put June's death behind her. The news another Gilroy had died already had Larissa thinking about her friend again. Would this afternoon's outing do more harm than good? I gripped the steering wheel tightly and prayed for guidance. Parenting would be so much easier if there was a rule book for these delicate situations.

"So? What's the deal-i-o?" Larissa asked.

I hovered on the brink of indecision for a second longer, then I plunged into the abyss. "The deal-i-o is that the Gilroys asked me to walk and feed Precious this afternoon. At their place. I wanted to give you the option to come with me."

"Oh."

I couldn't read her shuttered expression. Was I pushing her? Making her grow up too soon by having to face death head-on? "You can always stay with Mom and Dad while I go out there, but I hoped it wouldn't make you too sad."

Larissa sat there. Sulay mewed softly in the backseat. An eternity of seconds ticked by until my daughter spoke in a quiet voice. "I miss June. I miss Daddy too. Why do people have to die?"

I wished I'd taken a keener interest in religion. My parents had instilled in me a love and respect for all creation, but the part about the hereafter was fuzzy. Unless you counted dream-walking. "I don't know the answer. People live and people die. It's the cycle of life."

"You make it sound like a science fair project. That's not

what they taught at Vacation Bible School. Not that I believed them anyway. Believing in God didn't save June."

"Whatever you choose to believe, that's up to you. Faith is personal, no matter what they told you in church. When bad stuff happens, it's up to us to deal with it and go on with life."

"Is that what you did, Mom? Did you get on with your life after Daddy died?"

Woo-boy. My blood flashed iceberg cold and volcano hot in the space of a heartbeat, steaming up my orange T-shirt. My deodorant was working overtime today. How'd we get to this conversational black hole? Much as I wanted to, I couldn't sidestep this question. Larissa needed answers. Unfortunately, my answer vault was bone dry.

"I'm not the same person I was before, when your dad was with us," I said. "I miss your dad terribly. Not a day goes by that I don't think of him. But I have responsibilities in the present. I have to take care of us. That motivates me to not spend my life looking at what I've lost, at what could've been. I want to be a good parent, so I put one foot in front of the other. Sometimes that's all it takes is that first step. Once you do that, you at least have the appearance of living again."

My daughter stared at her hands. I wasn't sure if my words from the heart had helped her. In that moment, I was willing to learn every religious tenet there was, if that helped her cope.

"I want to see Precious," Larissa said.

"You don't have to go. I don't want you to feel that I'm pushing you. I just wanted to offer this chance for you."

"I get it, Mom. And I want to do it."

"You sure?"

She nodded, her freckled face a tight mask. "Yeah. I'm sure."

★ ★ ★ ★ ★

Precious ran away as soon as Larissa took the leash. One sharp tug and the flat-coated retriever bolted into the woods. I padded after the dog. "Coming?" I asked Larissa.

She jogged at my side, a frown on her face. "I thought she was happy to see me."

"Believe me, she was happy. She doesn't get that excited to see me."

"Then why did she run away? If she likes me, why didn't she stay with me?"

At ten, Larissa was too young to ask such a cosmic question. Why did anyone run from the people who loved them? Strength came from love. Running made troubles worse.

Beyond the woods was Sparrow's Point, Morgan's house. Farther out was the highway. I hoped the dog would stop to chase a squirrel or something because I didn't want to hand Larissa another dose of death-based reality today.

"June's house felt too quiet. Too still. Sad even," Larissa said. "All of her pictures were gone. Even the refrigerator magnet she made at Sunday school wasn't on the fridge."

I hadn't noticed the absence of pictures. Roland's picture was prominently displayed at our house. I wanted Larissa to feel her father was still a part of us. I wanted her to remember his face. But a parent wouldn't forget a child's face. Louise and Ritchie Gilroy hadn't needed the daily reminders of their missing kid. They felt that loss with every breath they took.

"I'm sorry this is hard for you." I seemed to be apologizing to everyone today.

"I'm sorry I dropped the leash. Precious sure can run fast."

"We'll catch her." The doggie treats in my pocket boosted my confidence. "Do you see her?"

"I think she went down into the drainage ditch."

I groaned. "Great. Tromping through smelly mud would be a

fitting end to this perfect day."

Larissa laughed. "Bring on the mud. I love getting dirty."

We pulled up at the edge of the ravine, and there was Precious, digging for all she was worth. Every few minutes, she'd stick her nose in the mud and snuffle. Then she'd dig some more. Mud clung to the curly hair on her ears.

"What's she after, Mom?"

"I have no idea. She smells something, that's for sure." I eased around the poison ivy lining the sloping bank. "You stay up here. No reason for both of us to get muddy."

"Yes, but I like getting muddy." She circled me. "Please can I get her?"

I wanted to cushion her from the muck of life, but she needed to make those baby steps of progress. Besides, her clothes and shoes could be washed. "All right."

I followed her down, sliding a little, holding onto roots and shoots to stabilize my descent. The bank showed numerous shallow indentations. The area where Precious was digging seemed to have caved into the creek.

"Gotcha!" Larissa said, brandishing the slimy leash. Precious turned and licked her face, sending the two of them tumbling in the goop.

"Looks like bath time to me," I said, shepherding them back up the ravine. Together Larissa and I washed the dog with a hose and pail. I enjoyed my daughter's happy squeals every time Precious decided to shake.

"We're having fun, aren't we, Mom?" she asked, her green eyes brimming with joy, globs of mud caked in her honey-brown hair.

I met her gaze with a smile. "Yeah. We are definitely having fun." Warmth spread through my veins. I felt at peace for the first time in a long while.

Larissa and Precious romped along the Gilroys' waterfront

lawn playing fetch afterwards. I settled into a wooden swing to watch.

Beyond the lawn, the wide expanse of vibrant green marsh and a ribbon of tidal creek stretched out to the sea. What must it be like for the Gilroys to see that breathtaking scenery day after day and wonder if it was the last thing June saw?

Now tragedy had struck their family twice. A man named Bubba had killed Ritchie's brother. But which Bubba? It was maddening not to know.

My phone rang. Charlotte's name flashed on the display window. What did she want?

"Baxley, the sheriff has Bubba Powell." Charlotte gasped in a ragged breath. "What are we going to do?"

# CHAPTER 16

Larissa wanted to help rescue her Uncle Bubba, but I put my foot down, immediately falling from the pedestal of fun-Mom to uncool-Mom. She could pout all she liked; the jail was no place for a ten-year-old kid. Mama welcomed Larissa with open arms and surprised me by insisting Daddy accompany me.

"You gonna be all right with this?" I asked, leaning in so that he could hear me over the air noise from the truck's open windows. There would be guns aplenty at the police station. Neither Mama nor Daddy had any tolerance for weapons.

Daddy gripped and regripped his hands. "Nope. I'm not all right with this. But I'm learning to cope with the downside of my new job."

The quiver in his voice alarmed me. I couldn't rescue Bubba if Daddy fell apart on me. "Let me turn around and take you home."

"Don't bother. Lacey said I needed to be at the jail," Daddy said, his voice sounding stronger. His head came up. Wisps of gray hair escaped his ponytail and fluttered in the breeze around his thin face. "Bubba Powell never hurt anyone. Wayne made a big mistake."

"Wayne won't welcome your opinion."

Daddy snorted. "That's not an opinion. That's the truth." He cleared his throat and held out his hand. "Your mom fixed your necklace. I have it for you."

"Thanks." I pocketed it. "I'm glad we have this time together.

I need to run something past you. Yesterday, I did a dreamwalk, and it got all messed up. I couldn't find Morgan and angry spirits mobbed me. That ever happened to you?"

"I've had my share of troubles, but mobbed? No. Can't say that's ever happened."

"I could've banished them but I needed to talk to them. One of the leaders, a tattooed woman, said she was watching me. What did she mean by that?"

"It means you should be careful until you find out what she wants."

"She said something about her sister needing money from a bank robbery. Like I'm going to help criminal spirits."

"One thing I've learned about dreamwalking is to never say never. Spirits sometimes take offense to us being in their world. We run a risk each time we dreamwalk."

I chewed on that for a moment. "I didn't understand what was happening at first. It sorta snowballed and they all came at me. But then I stood up to them and they backed away. Now I'm worried about going back. What should I do?"

"They can't take dominion over you unless you give it to them, but they can mess with your head. Stay focused when you dreamwalk. You're strong. Much stronger than I ever was. You'll be fine."

"Thanks for the vote of confidence." I only wished I felt that confident about it. Sooner or later the sheriff would ask me to find Morgan, or I'd get another dreamwalking client walking up to my back door. I had to face my fear and get past it.

Charlotte met us in the parking lot, her reporter bag slung over her squared shoulders like a strap of ammo. A fire of injustice blazed in her eyes. The slanting sunlight glinted off her chunky silver watch, nearly blinding me. Her ice-blue skirted suit was coordinated outfit number two of three in her plus-sized dress-up wardrobe, and she'd go broke trying to look the part of a major news anchor if her moment in the sun didn't come soon.

I gestured toward her reporter gear. "You think that's a good idea? To go in with guns blazing?"

She nodded rapidly, dislodging her glasses and then shoving them back up her nose. "My readers need to know about this gross miscarriage of justice. We have freedom of the press in this country. Wayne can't do a damned thing about it."

"You go in there and threaten Wayne with freedom of the press, and Bubba Powell won't see daylight for fifty years," I said, hoping she'd follow my cautionary lead. "We've got to be smart about this."

Charlotte swore and stomped her foot, the heel of her ice-blue pump clomping loudly on the pavement. "I want to stick it to him, Baxley."

"Wayne has that effect on people. We've got to get past that kneejerk reaction. We've got to have a plan."

She nodded toward my father as he leaned up against my truck. His eyes had gone all glassy and unfocused. "Is that why your dad's here? He's part of your strategy?"

I jerked my thumb in my father's direction. "Daddy wants to spring Bubba just as much as we do. I don't have a plan, but among the three of us we should come up with something."

My stomach clenched at the sight of the concertina wire looped atop the chain-link fence next to the squat brick building. I'd always thought of our jail as a secure depot for crooks who broke the law. I'd been comforted by the austere, locked-down look of our local law enforcement facility. People who broke the law should be behind bars.

Bubba Powell couldn't be guilty, but he was penned up in that fortress. Locked up with drug addicts, drunks, wife beaters, and the overflow federal prisoners we housed. The dark clouds gathering to the west added to my feeling of hopelessness.

We had to get Bubba out of there.

"We could hide a jail key in one of Mrs. Paul's Cocola cakes," Charlotte said, shielding her eyes from the sun. "Bubba could enjoy the homemade treat and sneak out when everyone went to sleep."

"We have no key, and we're not wasting a good cake like that," I said.

Daddy blinked and joined us. "I could give the guards free herbs for life. It would be worth it if they let Bubba go."

"No," Charlotte and I chorused together.

Charlotte shook her head, her bobbed locks swinging freely. "Using a bribe is a bad defensive strategy, Mr. Nesbitt. They'll put you in jail."

"We're not going to bribe anyone." I spoke firmly, trying to assert my leadership. "Bubba Powell is in deep trouble. We've got to come up with another idea, one that isn't illegal."

"I know!" Charlotte snapped her fingers. "I'll tell Wayne that Bubba Powell spent the night with me. I'll be his alibi."

It had always been Charlotte's wish that we marry brothers so that we'd never drift apart. Bubba Powell had never looked her way, but she still carried a torch for him. "Charlotte, we can't lie. That's perjury. You can go to jail for that."

Her cherubic face fell. "It would make such a great ending to the story."

"Get serious. This is Bubba Powell's life we're talking about. The only way we can clear his name is to figure out who killed Morgan Gilroy. We can't trust the sheriff to stumble upon the truth."

"Mag idea, Baxley." Charlotte sparkled with excitement. "I'd love to beat Wayne at his own game. It's about time he got a reality check. And you seem to have a knack for investigation."

I studied the windowless building. Now that I thought about it, I'd love to be the one who solved this case. As long as it didn't endanger my family. "I think living with Dottie is a fairly big reality check for Wayne, but he sure seems anxious to close this case before he has all the facts. He isn't acting right."

"It wasn't easy for him growing up in this town," Daddy interjected. "That boy had a lot to overcome."

He couldn't guilt me into feeling sorry for Wayne, not when Wayne so obviously had the wrong Bubba. "I hope you didn't come along to stick up for the sheriff, Daddy. He's pig-headed stubborn and we're going to tell him he has to let Bubba Powell go."

Daddy clapped a hand on my shoulder. "Right on. That's my girl."

I bent down to speak in the small holes in the thick glass barrier. "We have to see the sheriff. It's very important," I told the receptionist.

Tamika buzzed us into the admin area. She wore a navy polo today, with the sheriff's logo over her heart. She wrinkled up her nose at me and my posse. "He's not going to like this."

I suppressed a shiver. My chin went up. "Too bad."

"Yeah, too bad," Charlotte echoed.

Wayne looked up from a stack of paperwork when we trooped into his office. His casual uniform of polo and tan slacks looked rumpled, his thick head of hair a bit mussed. He groaned aloud. "Not again. I told you to stay out of this."

"I can't do that," I said, walking right up to his cluttered desk. "It's all over town that you've arrested Bubba Powell for Morgan Gilroy's murder. Daddy, Charlotte, and I know you charged the wrong man. He's innocent."

Wayne tossed his pen on the desk and leaned back in his chair. He studied me. "Can you prove it?"

"Well, no, but he didn't do it," I insisted.

"Let him go." Charlotte stepped forward. "You've got the

wrong man."

His lips pressed together in a thin line. "Don't waste my time. Powell's got no alibi, plus everything points to him."

"Less than six hours ago you thought another man killed Morgan Gilroy," I said. "How can you be sure Bubba Powell killed Morgan?"

"Powell's family, Wayne." Daddy came up on my other side. "He doesn't have a mean bone in his body. What do you have on him?"

Wayne focused on Daddy. "Tab, he told me he hated Gilroy, that he hated him enough to kill him. That's motive in my book. I've hunted with him, and he definitely knows his way around a knife. That cinches it for me."

"Every man in this town knows how to use a knife and probably all the women, too. That proves nothing," Charlotte said.

"It's no secret Bubba Powell hated Morgan," I said, continuing Charlotte's voice-of-reason argument. "He's hated him for twenty years. Why wait so long to kill him?"

"I'm satisfied I've got the right man," the sheriff said.

"You're a stupid-head." Charlotte leveled a finger at him. "And I'm going to put that in the newspaper. Enjoy your last term in office. I'm going to be on you like stewed tomatoes on rice."

A muscle twitched in Wayne's thick neck. "All I have to do is pick up the phone and Kip will fire you in a bug-sucking minute. You don't understand how the system works, do you, Charlotte? Ever wonder why Bernard gets the plum assignments? He works within the system. You move outside the boundaries and you rock the boat."

Charlotte stood a little taller, a wintry storm in her eye. "Are you threatening me? Because it sure sounds like a threat."

The sheriff didn't flinch. "Call it what you will. It's the truth."

This was getting out of hand. Charlotte and Wayne would

both get fired at this rate. I had to do something. Anything. But I only had one thing left. One thing that I wasn't supposed to mention.

I cleared my throat and recklessly plunged ahead. "What about the others?"

Wayne leveled his sharp gaze on me. His dark eyes narrowed with menace.

Charlotte took the bait I'd offered. "Yeah, what about the others?"

Confusion filled Daddy's face. He glanced my way. "What others? What are you talking about?"

"Baxley," the sheriff growled.

"There have to be other suspects." I wished my heart rate would slow down. "That's what I was asking about. Have you cleared the other suspects on your list?"

Wayne shrugged. "There are other people I'd planned to question, but with Powell virtually giving us a confession, there's no need."

"There's every need." My fingers coiled into tight fists at my side. "Your evidence is circumstantial at best. My brother-in-law is innocent. If you lock him up, you force us to take action."

Though the sheriff was sitting down and I was standing, he made me feel small. "Go back to your plants and pets, Baxley. Leave the investigating to us professionals."

My anger rose a notch. If he was a professional, we wouldn't be having this conversation. "What about bail?"

"The judge will set bail in the morning." He motioned toward the door. "Now, please, everyone, go home. I've got work to do."

"I can't do that." Daddy's voice sounded loud and strong.

I was slap out of ideas to spring my brother-in-law. And I didn't want Daddy mentioning his "herb" stash to the sheriff. "Sure you can. I'll drive you."

Daddy's breathing transitioned from fast and shallow to slow and deep. He glanced around the room with purpose as if he were memorizing landmarks. "Nope. I'm staying right here until Bubba Powell is a free man."

"You can't stay in my office," Wayne said.

"Peace, man." Daddy sat down on the floor and zoned out.

Wayne lurched to his feet. "Tab, you can't sit there."

My heart tanked. "Let's go home, Daddy." I tugged on his bony arm.

Daddy didn't respond. The lights were on, but his mind was elsewhere. He'd perfected the transition over the years so that he could literally plunge right into a dreamwalk. It made for a speedy result for his former clients, but it sure put me in a bad spot now. My palms dampened. Was Daddy going to find Morgan? Would the angry spirits come after him?

"Let the games begin," Charlotte cheered and snapped Daddy's picture.

Wayne grabbed my arm. "Outside. Now."

# CHAPTER 17

"Tab can't stay there." The sheriff stopped outside his office and glared at me. "He's interfering with my investigation. I can't work with him in my office."

I wrenched my arm free, rubbing the sting from the tender flesh he'd gripped. Mortification lit my cheeks. Trust Daddy to pull a stunt like this and Wayne to lecture me. Competitive instincts swirled through the glut of emotion, warming the chill from my bones, invigorating me.

Wayne might be top dog here, but I was not giving up. "You said the investigation was closed."

"My deputies will move him into the interrogation room." The sheriff shot me another angry look before he strode off, his footsteps echoing down the wide corridor. "Wait in the lobby."

No way. I edged into the office doorway. I wasn't leaving here without Daddy. Which reminded me of an issue I had with Charlotte. I turned to her. "You can't print that picture of Daddy meditating."

"Yes, I can. Thanks to freedom of the press." Her saucy smile made me cringe. "This is like an old-timey protest movement. Your father is demonstrating against the injustice in this county. That's breaking news. That will sell newspapers."

Charlotte's press credentials were irritating the crap out of me. If she didn't outweigh and outmean me, I'd take the camera from her right now. "Daddy does not need a spotlight on his lifestyle."

My friend waved away my protest in a swirl of ice-blue fabric. "Cops aren't overly concerned about marijuana use these days. It's a misdemeanor. If he was dealing crack cocaine, you'd have to worry."

My gut clenched. Charlotte had stars in her eyes. She had her eyes on the prize and not on our friendship. "I do worry. Except for Daddy's new coroner job, they have no steady income stream. Somehow there's always soup on the stove." Now that I'd inherited the dreamwalking business, I understood about the free vegetables. Sacks of them had appeared at my back door. But how did my parents pay for electricity or car insurance?

Charlotte tucked her notebook in her reporter bag. "Hey, whatever works."

Easy for her to say. I longed to ask Mama how they made ends meet, but what if the answer was something illegal? Could I accept that? When Roland was alive, I routinely sent them money. Now I could barely feed myself and Larissa.

How did they survive?

A door slammed down the hall. The noise washed down the empty corridor with the intensity of a shock wave. I tensed. Were Wayne's goons coming to haul Daddy away? Would they lock him up in a jail cell? My mouth went dry. I shouldn't have allowed Daddy to come.

"Put Paxton in the interrogation room, Virg." Wayne's voice carried down the hall like a Hail Mary pass.

"Roger that." I recognized Deputy Virgil Burkhead's deep voice. He'd done some radio work at one time and now he announced the football games for the high school. We'd had a run-in on the last case, one involving a Taser, so I stayed out of his range if I could.

A crash sounded. The sound reverberated as if someone had run head-on into a wall of plexiglass. I glanced in the direction of the noise, not sure if I should bolt for cover or watch the show.

"You can't hold me," a man bellowed. "I didn't do anything."

Virg, Wayne, and Bubba Paxton rounded the corner, an unholy trio if there ever was one. Wayne looked strong and tall, confident in his ability. Virg's brown and tan Class A uniform tested the strength of its buttons. Rumor had it that Virg could bench-press more than his substantial weight. I had no doubt he could flatten the scrawny preacher with one hand. Bubba Paxton's haggard face was lit up by anger. His arms were behind his back. I saw the handcuffs on him when Virg shoved him into a room and closed the door.

Virg thrust his beefy thumbs in his belt. He nodded our way. "You want me to stay with him, run a sweep through the hall, or tend to the problem in your office?"

I gasped silently. Bubba Paxton was a murder suspect, implicated by Morgan's last words by virtue of his first name. It couldn't be coincidence he was here. Hope flared in my heart. Maybe my brother-in-law could go home tonight after all. Maybe the case against him wasn't airtight.

"Stay with Paxton," Wayne ground out. "The other situations can wait." He strode past us into the office, stepped around Daddy to reach his cluttered desk, and retrieved a stack of thin files.

"Get him out of here," Wayne flung over his shoulder as he hurried up the hall.

Courage made me bold. "No can do. Free Bubba Powell first," I hollered after him. "Daddy won't budge until he knows Bubba is clear."

"How bizarre!" Charlotte whispered. "He's got Bubba Powell locked up in jail and Bubba Paxton handcuffed in the interrogation room. Is this a Bubba convention or what?"

The answer burned in my throat, but I'd promised to keep

mum about the Bubbas. I feigned ignorance and whispered back, "It's something all right. What's the deal with the crackhead evangelist? Why is he here?"

The overhead fluorescent lights buzzed, a low frequency rumble at the edge of my consciousness. I'd asked those questions to keep Charlotte from saying them to me, but hearing them aloud, I realized how much I wanted to solve this puzzle. I wanted to know who'd killed Morgan Gilroy, not just to clear my brother-in-law or to protect my family, but because I needed to prove to myself that I was still smarter than Wayne Thompson.

Very grade-school of me, but it was the truth.

An inconvenient truth.

Charlotte tapped three fingers on the side of her freckled face. "Maybe he roughed up some Beanies. Word on the street is that they're siphoning off the members of Pax Out. I remember from way back that Pax didn't like to share his crayons with anyone."

The Beanies. Was that "Angels of the Lord" cult moving into our county? Did Bubba Paxton go all wild man on them? What did that have to do with the murder investigation? "I remember Bubba being stingy with those crayons. Tell me more about the trouble at his church."

Charlotte leaned in and dropped her voice. "I don't know all the details, only what my sources told me. Beanies have been hanging around the laundry mat, the liquor store, and the dollar store, offering to lend people a hand with their packages."

I didn't see the connection. "That doesn't sound dangerous to me."

"On the surface, no. But they put religious tracts in every package they tote. Plus they give a little pep talk offering to free the people from their financial burdens."

The Angels of the Lord had been dubbed "Beanies" in a

newspaper editorial last year due to their propensity for eating dried beans. The nickname had stuck. And now the Beanies were coming after Bubba Paxton's congregation. Trouble indeed.

I couldn't tell Charlotte about the four Bubbas, but if she reasoned it out for herself we could brainstorm about the homicide. "A religious turf war doesn't justify bringing Bubba Paxton into the police station."

"Do you think his presence has anything to do with my murder story?"

"It might." I hadn't broken my promise to Wayne. My curiosity revved up. "Should we sneak down the hall and listen? Daddy will be all right in Wayne's office for a few minutes."

Charlotte nodded eagerly, the bright fluorescent light dancing off her glasses. "No need for both of us to go. You stay here with your father. I'll go into sneak mode. That way you can get me out of jail if I get caught." She took a step and froze. "On second thought, you go. I have freedom of the press behind me to publicize your arrest if you get caught."

Satisfaction purred inside me. This was perfect. I could eavesdrop and only Charlotte would know. There was no real risk here. "I won't get caught. I'll be right back."

I tiptoed down the hall. Tamika's hearty voice carried down the corridor from the reception area around the corner. Dang. Was she coming this way? I stopped for a moment, fiddling with my shoe, and listened harder. The receptionist was talking a mile a minute and laughing. Probably on her cell with a friend. I crept forward.

Faintly, I heard Wayne's voice through the wall. "Where were you yesterday?"

I pressed my ear up to the seam between the door and the door jamb, praying that no one would open the door in the next few minutes. "I don't know, man. I don't keep track of every hour of the day. I'm in ministry. Every day is different."

"This is vitally important." Danger edged the sheriff's voice. "Do you have an appointment calendar we can check?"

"It's all in my head," Bubba Paxton shot back.

There came the screeching sound of a metal chair sliding on the bare floor. "It better be in your mouth, moron."

"Look, I don't know, okay?" Bubba Paxton was talking fast. Had Wayne or Virg grabbed him? "Our service times at Pax Out are aired on the local television channel. I know I was in church for the mid-morning service."

"What about after that?" Wayne asked. "What did you do in the afternoon?"

"That's what I'm trying to tell you. I do church work. I go to people's homes and minister to them as they need it. It's a free service I provide."

"You fleecing these people out of their Social Security money?" the sheriff snarled.

"There's no fleecing in my church. We're a reputable organization, which is more than I can say about other religious entities in the area."

"You talking about the Angels of the Lord?"

"Yes, I'm talking about those Beanies. Those gutless wonders are bad to the bone."

"Come on. Where were you yesterday? Give me names and addresses."

"Can't. My visitations are confidential."

"Can't or won't?"

"The people I see, and the things they confide in me, are private matters." Bubba Paxton sounded smug. That was a bad sign, him hiding behind his virtual ministerial collar. Would Wayne let a confidentiality arrangement halt his line of questioning?

Wayne swore aloud, followed by a loud thump. "You're screwing 'em, aren't ya?"

A gasp slipped from my lips. I clamped a hand over my mouth and tried not to retch. I couldn't get the image out of my mind of skinny Bubba Paxton being naked with his congregation.

"Like I said, I provide a reliable service for my members," Bubba Paxton said.

"What was your relationship with Morgan Gilroy?"

"The dead guy?"

Charlotte joined me at the door, her ice-blue pumps in her hands. I'd been so intent on listening that I hadn't noticed her tiptoed approach. I held a finger to my lips to remind her to keep silent.

"You are not pinning this on me." Bubba Paxton's voice rose an octave. "I didn't kill anyone. I am not a killer."

"But you are a druggie and a known felon. You could have gotten coked up and killed Morgan Gilroy."

"I can't believe you. I've been clean for eighteen months now. I'm making restitution, keeping my nose out of trouble. As a minister, I'm a valued member of society."

"About that minister thing, what sort of official training do you have for that?" Wayne's voice sounded deceptively soft.

"I don't need any training to hear what's in a person's heart. I can tell you right now that yours is black and full of bullet holes."

I inhaled sharply. Bubba Paxton was dead in the water if he thought he'd earn brownie points by psychoanalyzing Wayne. He seemed as headstrong and passive-aggressive as my father. The realization stunned me. Bubba Paxton was acting just like my father. I didn't want them to have anything in common. My father was neither a known felon nor a wild man.

"Shut up, piss ant," Wayne said.

"All right. I will be quiet, but only because I've decided to meditate."

"Ah, hell. Don't do that." Through the door came the scrambling sound of metal furniture being scooted out of the way. "Wake up, Bubba. This isn't funny."

At the sudden silence, I exchanged a worried glance with Charlotte. Bubba was more like my father than I thought. Was he a dreamwalker? Would he seek Daddy out in the astral plane? I couldn't quite picture it.

"Christ. How the hell do they do that?" Disgust riddled Wayne's voice. "This couldn't get any more messed up if it tried. Now I've got two loonies zoned out. Wake him up, Virg."

"How?" Virg asked.

Alarm flared through me. I grabbed Charlotte's arm and ran down the hall, not caring about the telling slap of our footfalls on the floor.

"What?" She huffed between breaths when I stopped outside the sheriff's office.

I nodded toward the interview room. "Wayne's coming out."

She propped her butt on the wall to step into her shoes. "How do you know that?"

"I'll bet you a million dollars that door opens in the next five seconds."

"Deal."

The words were barely out of her mouth before the door opened.

# CHAPTER 18

Wayne started down the hall, saw us standing outside his office, and stopped. "What are you jokers still doing here?"

"I'm not leaving without my father," I said.

"I'm not leaving without Baxley," Charlotte echoed.

The sheriff jerked his thumb towards the exit. "Both of you, out in the lobby. I can't do my job for tripping over civilians."

He could make us leave, but Daddy was in a vulnerable state while he dreamwalked. If he was moved, he'd be severely disoriented when he came back to full consciousness. I had to protect him. "You lay a hand on my dad and I guarantee you'll have bad karma for the rest of your life," I warned as I headed out.

He ran his hand through his thick hair and managed a little half laugh. "You think I'm having good karma now? I am not having a good day. Bad karma would be a step up from where I am right now."

Virg oiled past us in the hall. His broad shoulders took up most of the corridor. He was as big as a tank, probably as strong as one, too. His resonant voice boomed loudly. "Ronnie's on his way in with the other one, Sheriff. Where we gonna put him?"

Charlotte and I minced along at a snail's pace. I didn't know about her, but I wanted to hear who they had coming in. I strongly suspected it was the final Bubba, Bubba Jamison. He must have returned home from Savannah.

"Figure something out," Wayne said. "Let's move the crackhead into my office with Tab Nesbitt. I've got a feeling Jamison will start screaming about due process once he gets here. We've got to do things by the book with him. He's connected to some powerful Atlanta people."

I faked tying my shoe again at the corner, glancing over my shoulder to see them enter the interview room. I exhaled a sigh of relief. Thank goodness they weren't moving Daddy. We'd learned the hard way that any additional spatial disorientation after he'd zoned out was extremely debilitating. I didn't care if Bubba Paxton got disoriented from being moved. His well-being wasn't my concern. Besides, I didn't know if he was truly meditating or if he was faking it.

"Y'all leaving?" Tamika asked as we passed her desk.

"Not just yet," I said. "Daddy and Wayne are working on Bubba Powell's release."

"This place is like Grand Central Station today." Tamika stood and stretched. "I can't remember when we've had so many people in here. The Coke machine is sold out. That's never happened before."

Charlotte bristled. I touched her arm, silencing her. "We'll be in the lobby if you need us," I said.

We passed through the air lock of doors and entered the tiled lobby. Four molded plastic chairs lined one wall; three others flanked the vending machine. Bail bondsman ads dotted the few tables in the room. Wanted posters filled the bulletin board over the chairs. One fluorescent light flickered overhead.

"Where do they find these people?" Charlotte's nostrils flared. "The empty Coke machine isn't headline news. Nobody cares about that."

I glanced at the humming machine wistfully. "I do. I could use a Coke right now."

Charlotte plopped down in a chair. Her hand tapped a stac-cato beat on her leg. "Get over it. We've got to figure out what these morons are doing. Something big is going down. Except for the time they arrested Daniel Huxley and all the Save the Marsh folks for trespassing, they've never gone after so many locals. What is it about the Bubbas?"

Before I could sidestep her question, a well-dressed woman hurried up the sidewalk. Anticipation skittered through me. "Here comes trouble," I said.

Muriel Jamison arrived in a flurry of gauzy skirts, clanking bracelets, and windswept brunette locks. Her exotic eyes were pinched tight with worry. She sailed past us, stopping at the windowed barrier. She leaned down into the speaker and spoke in ringing tones. "I'm Muriel Jamison. I demand that you release my husband, Sloan 'Bubba' Jamison, at once."

"Ma'am, I don't have any information on your husband," Tamika said. "If you'll take a seat, I'll check on his status."

"You do that." Muriel jabbed her index finger against the clear barrier. "You find out and get Bubba out here right now, or I'm going to bring in the biggest hornets' nest of lawyers from Atlanta that you've ever seen. I'll sue everyone in this place. You'll wish you'd never crossed me or my daddy."

Charlotte and I froze as Miss High and Mighty paced the small room with a prowling gait. I didn't want to call attention to myself, not when Muriel was in pit-bull mode, but curiosity worried at my gut. Would she really sue the sheriff and his staff?

Muriel's spiky heels clacked on the tiled floor. With each successive lap, she slowed to glare at the spot where Tamika should be sitting. When Tamika finally returned, Muriel rapped authoritatively on the window. "Well?"

"He's been Mirandized, and he's in processing," Tamika said. "He's not available for release."

Muriel whipped out her checkbook. "I'll pay the bail right now. Any amount. Just tell me a number."

"Ma'am, bail is not an option right now. There's nothing

further I can tell you at this time." Tamika's voice still sounded upbeat, but there was a steely thread throughout. Good girl, I thought. Don't let this pushy woman get the best of you.

"I'll see about that." Muriel walked over to the door and made a call on her cell. "Daddy? They've got Bubba in the Sinclair County Jail. They won't let me talk to him. I can't find out any information."

Charlotte flipped her pad open and jotted down a few notes. I didn't know the Jamisons well, but Muriel's father was the real deal in Atlanta. I mentally thanked Wayne for kicking us out here. This was more entertaining than the Paxton interview. I couldn't wait to see what would happen next.

How were Morgan Gilroy and Bubba Jamison acquainted? Was there bad blood between them? Or had Bubba pissed off the sheriff in one of his anti-establishment newspaper editorials? Either way, it appeared that this was an unusual situation. My pulse kicked up.

"All right. I'll wait for your call." Muriel ended the call and sat across from us. Tears glistened in her eyes.

It had cost her to make that phone call. This was getting more and more interesting. Did Muriel fear her powerful father?

Muriel's chin quivered. Her hands shook. With that phone call she'd gone from confident and assertive to defeated. The blankness of her dark eyes reminded me of the despair I'd felt about Roland's death. Unwanted emotion welled up inside of me.

"It'll be okay, Muriel." Sympathy tinged my voice, but the sentiment didn't reach to my heart. If Muriel's Bubba was cleared, then the murder suspect pool was wide open again. Which was bad for my brother-in-law.

"You're the pet-sitter girl, aren't you?" She looked down her thin nose at me.

I wondered if her thick lips had been collagen enhanced. "I

own a pet-sitting business and a landscaping business. I'm Baxley Powell and we met a few months ago. This is my friend, Charlotte Ambrose."

"Nice to meet you," Muriel muttered, as if the politeness police would know if she didn't acknowledge my greeting.

What was proper etiquette for the waiting room at the jail? Miss Manners hadn't prepared me for the complexity of this situation. Was fraternization encouraged?

"I'm sorry your husband is having trouble." Crap. I'd apologized again. I had to stop doing that.

"Me, too. Darn Bubba's sorry hide," Muriel said. "I told him not to drink those martinis at lunch. Bubba can't have another DUI on his record."

Muriel's remark put an odd spin on an already bizarre day.

Charlotte eased her notebook open and jotted surreptitiously.

They'd brought Jamison in for DUI? Not for the murder investigation? That was not good news.

No matter how you looked at it, we were running out of Bubbas.

# CHAPTER 19

Charlotte nodded toward the glass door. "Coke break. Let's go."

For all my big talk about needing a soda before, my craving for caffeine paled beside my need to stay near my father. With a quick glance to Muriel across the room, I shook my head and spoke in a confidential tone. "I can't leave. Not while Daddy is inside."

"You sure?" Charlotte's freckled nose scrunched up. "It'll be hours before they figure this mess out."

Muriel's chin came up. She slitted her exotic eyes our way. "What mess? What's going on in there?"

Her pupils narrowed with feline intensity and her plumped upper lip curled to show a hint of teeth. Muriel's moment of vulnerability was over. If Charlotte and I weren't careful, we'd be dinner.

"The sheriff has his hands full, that's what." Charlotte uncrossed her legs and crossed them the other way, away from Muriel, her ice-blue pump swinging wildly. "We came here this evening because the sheriff is questioning Baxley's brother-in-law, Bubba Powell. By the time we arrived, the sheriff was interviewing Bubba Paxton."

"That skinny preacher kid?" Muriel asked.

"Yeah, that's the one." Charlotte elbowed me. "Jump in any time, Baxley."

"You're the hotshot reporter," I said. "You tell the story."

Charlotte paused to shove her glasses up her nose. "As I was saying, when we got here, he had the two Bubbas. The sheriff refused to let Bubba Powell go, prompting Baxley's dad to stage a sit-in protest. Very new age and retro at the same time."

"He wasn't arrested?" Muriel glanced over at me. I could almost see the gears turning in her well-coiffed head.

"He's sitting on the floor of the sheriff's office," I said.

"Good strategy," Muriel said. "That way he can hear everything the sheriff says."

"I doubt he's paying attention to the sheriff," I said. "Daddy's regular senses shut down when he sits and meditates. He can meditate for hours at a time."

"And your father is?"

"Tab Nesbitt."

"I've heard of him." Muriel snapped her fingers. Interest enlivened her face. "I've been meaning to talk to him about getting a message to my late aunt, but no one would give me Tab's address. Didn't he retire from his dreamwalking job?"

"Yes, he did."

"Hmm." She studied me. "You took over for him, didn't you?"

My stomach lurched. "I did."

"I'll be around to see you once this gets resolved."

"As you wish." Though I couldn't imagine who she'd want to boss around in the afterlife. Good thing she didn't ask me to dreamwalk today. I couldn't concentrate on anything, not with Daddy off on his own, somewhere between this world and the next.

"You know, I've never done a story about our resident psychic," Charlotte mused. "I should interview you. Especially now that I'm the lead reporter. This murder investigation is doing great things for my career. I'll schedule you next, just in case the *Atlanta Journal* comes a-calling and wants other examples of my work."

"You'll do nothing of the sort." I bristled at her absurd suggestion. "We don't need to call attention to anyone in my family being outside the realm of normal."

"Wait, back up a moment." Muriel leaned forward in a flurry of jangling bracelets. "Murder investigation? What murder investigation?"

"The one Sheriff Thompson is conducting," Charlotte said. "Morgan Gilroy was found dead at his home yesterday. Wayne's been interviewing suspects. We know he's talked to three Bubbas—Bubba Wright, Bubba Powell, and Bubba Paxton. It *might* be coincidence that Bubba Jamison is here now, but I wouldn't bet on that."

"Morgan Gilroy? Murdered?" The color drained from Muriel's face. Her mouth flapped soundlessly a few times. "My Bubba worked with him on that waterfront deal in town. Everything went to hell because the stupid fishing-shop man wouldn't sell."

"That would be Bubba Wright," I said. "That's very interesting. There *was* a connection between Bubba Wright, Morgan Gilroy, and Bubba Jamison."

"Connections don't mean anything." Muriel settled back in her chair.

"They mean something all right." Charlotte flipped open her notebook and scribbled a few notes. "They mean your Bubba will be questioned about the murder of one of the town's leading citizens."

"You have a lot of nerve implying that my husband is a murder suspect." Muriel's voice rose to an uncomfortable level. "I assure you that my father, the lieutenant governor, won't stand for that. Bubba didn't do anything. He's completely innocent."

God forgive me, I didn't want him to be innocent. I wanted

him to be guilty so that I could take Bubba Powell and Daddy home. Fortunately, Bubba Jamison wasn't squeaky clean. There was that DUI charge he'd been brought in on. Probably small potatoes for the lieutenant governor to clean that up. However, not even a big wheel like the lieutenant governor could sweep a murder under the rug.

I fingered the gold chain at my neck, pulling it out until I touched my new amethyst pendant. Like my moldavite necklace from my missing husband, the stones in this one helped center me. Roland wouldn't cave in this situation. He'd get his brother out of jail. I'd do that, too. Even if it meant I was uncharitable in my thoughts about the other Bubbas.

Despite Muriel's protests to the contrary, Bubba Jamison advanced to the top of my suspect list.

# CHAPTER 20

Charlotte, Muriel, and I looked up at the opening snick of the metal door. Like Pavlov's dogs we salivated for the treat of good news. Wayne stepped through the opening, and his icy glare settled on me. The air temperature in the impersonal lobby dropped noticeably.

A stranger in a strange land couldn't have felt more ill at ease. Whispers flickered at the edge of my mind. I wanted the comfort of home, about a gallon of macaroni and cheese, and a lifetime of get-out-of-jail-free passes.

The sheriff beckoned me forward with a terse flip of his large hand. "Get your dad."

I allowed myself a small breath. Whatever fury he'd been battling when he sighted me hadn't been directed my way. His voice had been curt and imperious, but definitely not hostile. I rose from my seat, aware that Charlotte and Muriel remained planted in theirs. Momentum restored my courage.

"No point in my doing anything if you're not releasing Bubba Powell." I wasn't trying to be a smart aleck. I was quite serious. Daddy wouldn't leave until he'd gotten what he came for, the release of my brother-in-law.

Wayne stepped back, inviting me through the doorway. His shiny gold sheriff's badge caught the light as he moved. "You can have him, too. I want everyone to clear out."

I sensed the other women rising. Before I could hoof it back to Wayne's office, Muriel asked, "What about my husband? Is he free to go?"

I halted as Wayne once again filled the doorway. The cold fury pouring off him chilled me thoroughly. I got the distinct impression he did not care for the Jamisons.

The sheriff's rugged features hardened into a tight mask. "We'll release him, ma'am, just like the lieutenant governor requested. But he's my guest for the next twenty-four hours."

"Bubba wasn't weaving or anything," Muriel said. "He shouldn't have to go before a judge. Fine him and send him home."

"Can't do that, ma'am." Cool steel laced through his words. "There's that little matter of resisting arrest. One of my deputies needs his face stitched."

My blood raced. Bubba Jamison fought the cops? If Jamison got angry and violent when cornered, that lack of emotional control could lead to murder. Very bad news for Muriel, but a needed ray of sunshine for my brother-in-law.

"He only resisted because you weren't listening to him." Muriel dismissed Wayne's explanation with a flick of her manicured fingertips, as if her husband's violent actions were of no consequence.

Wayne matched her look-down-the-nose posture. "When cops pull you over, you need to listen to us. Bubba Jamison didn't." He glanced my way again. "You coming?"

I hurried toward him. Charlotte came, too.

Muriel trailed us to the door. "You can't keep my husband locked up in there with common criminals," she said.

Wayne stepped aside so that Charlotte and I could enter the administrative area. He blocked Muriel's entry. "I take offense at your remark. There's nothing common about our criminals."

Over my shoulder, I saw Muriel had gone ghostly white. I shot her a sympathetic glance. Muriel was on her own.

"I'm calling my lawyer," Muriel shrilled.

"Suit yourself," the sheriff said.

The door slammed behind us, echoing ominously down the tiled corridor lined with dark-colored file cabinets, fraying my taut nerves. I had had my fill of being in this institutional box with its artificial lights and its negative energy.

Wayne hurried past me. I lengthened my stride to keep up. With shorter legs and a heavier frame, Charlotte fell behind. "You were rough on Muriel," I said.

"I hate outsiders," he said. "These damn Atlanta people come in here and act like they've discovered Sinclair County. I got news for them. We've always known right where we were."

"How come you're letting everyone go?"

"Because I can't make the murder charge stick. Yet." His voice dropped. "I know it's one of the Bubbas. I just don't know which one."

"It isn't Bubba Powell. He's too nice a guy."

"Given the right motivation, Bubba Powell could kill in a heartbeat."

I did not want to hear this. "Gee, you sure know how to suck the fun out of things."

He shot me an indecipherable look. "Fun is fun. This is work."

His terse tone irritated me. Darn it, Bubba Powell wasn't capable of killing anyone. He couldn't be. I wouldn't let him be.

That thought wobbled in my brain like a tire out of round. What if Wayne was right and my brother-in-law had done the unimaginable? How would we face that? What would drive a well-intentioned goof like Bubba Powell to take another man's life?

I couldn't answer that question.

Wayne was right about me being a mama bear. I'd protect Larissa with my life. If someone came after her, they'd have to go through me. Was it possible Bubba Powell had a similar Achilles heel?

Was that weak point the dead man's ex-wife?

The certainty of Bubba's innocence dimmed, adding to the weight of my thoughts. No wonder Wayne was Mister Doom and Gloom. If I thought the worst of people all day, I'd be miserable.

Wayne opened his office door. Inside, Daddy and Bubba Paxton sat cross-legged on the floor. Neither man heeded our arrival. Two blue-jeaned warriors off on a mental jaunt.

From past experience, I knew Daddy couldn't hear us, but I wasn't so sure about Bubba Paxton. He didn't seem to be under as deeply as Daddy. There was a tangible energy to him that was lacking in Daddy. That observation depressed me further.

Why did Daddy have to do this here? Why couldn't he restrict his meditations to home where he was away from prying eyes?

With a deep sigh, I turned to Wayne and Charlotte. "I need to do this in private."

"Just get them out of there," the sheriff said and retreated.

I stepped inside the office, closed the door, and locked it. I'd never actually recalled Daddy from a dreamwalk, but I'd seen my mother do it time and again. I touched my father's shoulder and whispered in his ear. "Time to wake up, Daddy."

Stepping back but still touching him, I monitored his breathing. Still the same slow rise and fall to his chest. No discernible level of external awareness was apparent. I tried again. "Wake up, Daddy. We have to go home now."

Still no response. My pulse thundered in my ears. How was I going to fix this?

I'd done what I'd seen Mama do, used my voice and my touch to draw him back. Only it hadn't worked. Beads of sweat formed along my hairline and trickled down the channel of my spine. I never should have allowed Daddy to come.

Pulling a high visibility stunt like this had repercussions. If medical people got involved, Daddy might get locked away for the rest of his life. They'd believe his ramblings were those of a crazy man.

My gaze skittered over to Bubba Paxton sitting next to Daddy on the floor. Was it possible that he dreamwalked, too? I didn't like the idea of a reformed crackhead being one of Daddy's associates in any way, shape, or form. I'd much prefer Bubba Paxton kept his Holy-Roller self on the other side of the county, away from my family.

But if he could help my father, I would overlook my prejudice for the moment. I touched Bubba Paxton's shoulder. "Wake up."

His eye movements increased under his eyelids and his breathing pattern shortened. I clapped my hands next to his ear. At the sudden noise, he startled awake, his eyes rounded with anxiety. He was only a couple of years older than me, but his glowing skin gave him the appearance of a younger man.

Guilt immediately assailed me. Even if I didn't care for Bubba Paxton, I didn't mean to frighten him. "It's okay. You're in the sheriff's office."

Bubba blinked, looked around, and stretched. He rubbed the back of his neck. A five o'clock shadow darkened his austere features. "Man, that's some serious mojo."

My stomach tightened. "What are you talking about?"

"Tab went over the bridge." Bubba scooted closer to my father. He touched Daddy's lifeless hand and murmured something in Daddy's ear.

"What was that? I didn't catch it." Worry spun through my body. Daddy had been adamant about not ever crossing the bridge. It was a barrier he always respected. I'd always steered clear of the bridge.

Dread gripped my heart. "What are you talking about?"

"I caught up with Tab in the dream world and we looked for Morgan. It was a brilliant plan but we kept missing Gilroy.

When we couldn't locate him, Tab started looking for someone else."

Icy fingers of dread brushed the length of my spine. "Bring Daddy back."

"Don't you get it? He went over the bridge. That's not supposed to happen. I can't bring him back. I already tried. But you could do it. Let me take you to him."

My fear swelled to monster proportions. I edged back. "I've never been over the bridge. But it's too risky. Angry spirits are after me on the other side."

Bubba stretched each arm and then each leg, massaging them in turn. "Tab needs an anchor by the bridge to pull him back. His connection to you will draw him near enough to hear you."

I shook my head so fast my molars snapped together. "No."

"He wouldn't come back for me. I've been calling him to no avail." A fevered light filled Bubba Paxton's dark eyes. He focused the full force of his charisma on me. "I need you. He needs you."

The thought of letting a former crackhead accompany me on a metaphysical journey was downright ludicrous. I shouldn't seriously consider it. But I couldn't abandon my father either. Daddy needed me. If I didn't help him, would he get back home? Terror welled in my throat.

Before I did anything with Bubba Paxton there was a question I had to ask. "Did you kill Morgan Gilroy?"

His sharp teeth flashed before my eyes. "No. Someone else beat me to it."

I shook my head, not wanting to believe him. "This is nuts."

"It's the only way to get Tab back. Do you trust me?"

"No."

"You'd better. Stay physically near me during the dreamwalk. I'll take you to the bridge and then you command your dad to come."

Crunch time. Trust that Bubba Paxton was a dreamwalker and he wanted to help? Or run the gamut of angry spirits by myself?

There was a problem with the second option. That left Bubba Paxton awake and aware in the room with us. Not a good plan. That left me dreamwalking with Bubba. I swallowed around the lump in my throat.

I was doing this for my father. I wasn't trying to be Bubba's friend. And if he turned out to be a stone-cold killer, I'd have to deal with that later. Bringing Daddy back was my top priority here. And Bubba could help anchor me if I ran across trouble.

"All right. Let's do it," I said.

Bubba and I sat cross-legged in front of Daddy. We linked hands with each other and with Daddy. I'd seen the crystal bridge once, and I summoned that image. Focusing inward and then out. Light and shadow alternated as we whirled into the spirit world, landing at the base of the bridge.

Though it was twilight on our side, the other side was pitch black. Relief sighed through me. I hadn't lost my touch for directionality. I'd done good. Even better was the lack of angry spirits. This could be a very precise extraction.

"Wait here," I told Bubba.

"That was slick," he said. "No wonder Tab retired. You got jets, Bax, that's for darn sure."

Gotta love a priest who uses the word darn as a compliment. "I've got a missing father, and I'm going over the bridge to get him back."

"Don't step off on the other side. That's how I lost Tab."

"Why'd he cross over?"

"Said he wanted to look for someone else."

"Who?"

"Dunno."

Bits of this and that shimmered randomly in the bridge's

facets. I crept over, knowing that the airy bridge had held my father's weight, not sure how it would hold up to two people on the return trip. But then, I wasn't myself out here; I probably didn't weigh much of anything.

As I crossed the bridge, the light thinned to nearly nothing. I lifted my hand in front of my face and I could barely see it. Whispers and rustlings grew with each step, filling me with dread. I reached for the handrail and hung on.

I edged forward, heel to toe. I stopped because I ran out of hand rail. I clung to it for my life. "Daddy! Daddy! I'm over here. Come toward the sound of my voice."

My name threaded through the whisperings. The rustling sound was on all sides of me. I glanced back over my shoulder. "Bubba. You there?"

"I'm here. Right where I'm supposed to be," he answered.

His response comforted me. I wasn't alone in this scary place. But Daddy was. I called for him once again. "Tab Nesbitt. I command you to come to me."

My eyelids grew heavy. The darkness shimmered. Sleep beckoned. "Just let go," the whispers urged. "Come to us, Baxley."

"I'm not going anywhere. Not without my father. Daddy! Listen to my voice. Mama and Larissa are waiting for us. We have to go now. Listen and follow the sound of my voice."

The darkness stirred, and something tugged my arm. "There's a price for being here," a husky alto said. "You willing to pay it?"

Tattoo woman. I couldn't see her, but I recognized her voice. "I want my father."

"We all have wants. What are you willing to pay to get your father back?"

"My father isn't for sale, neither am I."

"Your father wandered into the abyss. He can't hear you."

The abyss? Is that what the utter darkness was? Fear gripped me hard. "Why should I believe you?"

"Nobody's making you do anything. I'm just doing a little business."

"What is it you want?"

"My sister's in trouble. I want you to help her."

"What's your sister's name? Where is she?"

"Raymondia LaFleur. She's in Tampa."

"She got a phone?"

"Don't know. But she was plugged into the online community. If you can't find a phone number for her, try those social networking sites."

"So if I agree to contact your sister, you'll bring my father to me?"

"Yes." The *s* sound drew out in a long hiss.

I shivered even though I wasn't hot or cold. Daddy wasn't coming. That much was obvious. I didn't want to help tattoo woman, but I wanted my father. If I stepped off the bridge, I'd be lost, too.

"Okay. What's your name?"

"Rose Kingsley."

"Deal."

The air shifted. I clung to the handrail. Would tattoo woman be successful? Would Daddy return from the abyss?

How could I face Mama if I failed? I couldn't. Failure wasn't an option. I'd do whatever it took to bring Daddy home.

Without warning, something shoved into me. I kept my grip on the bridge rail and tried to figure out what hit me.

"Take him," Rose said.

"Daddy?" Disbelief tinged my voice.

"Baxley?"

I felt down his arm for his hand, pulled it to me and inched backward. "Thank you, Rose."

"You tell Raymondia the proof's in the pudding."

As Daddy and I inched back, the darkness thinned. "Rose? You coming?"

"Can't. I'm on this side of the bridge now. There's a price, remember?"

My gut hollowed. Rose had paid a price to help me. "I'll be in touch with your sister right away."

We crept toward the right side of the bridge, step by step. Daddy's features came into view. Dark circles ringed his eyes; his parched lips were cracked and bleeding. He looked like he was running on fumes.

"Just a few more steps, Daddy." I glanced over my shoulder. "Bubba, you there?"

"Yeah. What took so long?"

"It took as long as it took."

"You got him?"

"I do."

I heard steps running toward me from behind. Bubba, I hoped. And it was. He caught Daddy just before he collapsed.

"Take us home, Baxley," Bubba said.

I wrapped my arms around the two of them and pictured Wayne's office. We whirled. Lights flashed. Then we were on the floor of the sheriff's office. I blinked into awareness.

The hollow feeling in my gut didn't ease. Daddy lay toppled to one side. I pulled a bag of crystals out of my pocket, placed them in his hand. Moments later, his eyes opened.

His enlarged pupils slowly contracted in the brightly lit office space. His face was ghostly pale, but he was there. I took a few deep breaths, studying him as he strengthened.

"We're back in the land of the living," I said. "Thank goodness."

Daddy gripped my arm, his bony fingers manacling my wrist. Tears welled in his eyes. "He's not there, Baxley. Roland's not there."

# CHAPTER 21

Even though I'd come to the same conclusion about my missing husband, Daddy's pronouncement socked me in the gut. In some ways it would be easier if Roland were dead. At least then I could ask him what happened. Not that I wanted him dead. Quite the contrary.

"I know, Daddy."

"You do?"

"I've looked for him in my dreams."

"What's going on?" Charlotte pounded on the door. "Baxley? Let me in."

"We gotta get Tab to a hospital. He doesn't look good," Bubba Paxton said.

"No hospital," Daddy and I said in unison.

"Mama knows what to do," I added. "Can you walk, Daddy?"

"Get me to my feet," he said.

We levered him up. Daddy pitched forward, and Bubba caught him. With our arms supporting him, we left the office.

Charlotte bounced around us like a new puppy. "What happened in there? What's wrong with Tab? Why didn't you let me in?"

"Not now, Charlotte," I said. "I'll fill you in later. Run interference for us, okay?"

Her eyes widened knowingly. "Sure thing."

The sheriff rounded the corner. "Everything all right?"

"Peachy," Charlotte said, standing tall. "Where's Bubba

Powell? We're not leaving here without him."

Wayne jerked his thumb toward the door. "Just missed him."

Anger surged. Bubba Powell should have waited for us. But I couldn't waste concern on him while my father's health hung in the balance. "I have to get Daddy home. Excuse us."

The sheriff skirted Charlotte and corralled us. "Good God almighty, Tab, what did you do?"

Daddy gathered himself. "Chased a foolish dream."

"You look like death warmed over."

"We really need to get him home," I repeated.

"Hell." The sheriff lifted Daddy like he was a child. "Where's your truck?"

"Front parking lot." I hurried after him out the side door, drawing in deep breaths of honeysuckle-laced evening air. Daddy was back on this side of the veil, and Bubba Powell was free. Mission accomplished.

I fumbled in my pocket for my key fob and unlocked the truck doors remotely. Wayne deposited Daddy in the truck and buckled his seat belt. "Take care of him," the sheriff said as he walked away. "I want a full report in the morning."

"Me, too," Charlotte whispered.

I couldn't handle Charlotte's expectations right now. "We'll talk later. Daddy's in trouble."

"You get him fixed up. Then we'll talk about my suspect story."

"Wait. What suspect story?"

"The sheriff's suspect pool of Bubbas. I may be dense, but I'm not stupid."

Worry arced through my thoughts. But with Bubba Paxton standing nearby, I had to be careful what I said. I pulled Charlotte to the side and lowered my voice. "You don't have all the information. You could ruin people's reputations and piss off the sheriff. This is an active investigation."

Charlotte swore fluently. "I've got a career-making story bust-ing loose all around me, and you want me to skimp on details?"

Bubba Paxton watched me intently. I couldn't deal with him right now, not until I'd defused Charlotte. "I know you want to beat Bernard Rivers at his own game. Learn from his example. See how he worded active investigations. He did it right, or he wouldn't have lasted this long."

Charlotte groaned in frustration, the overhead parking-lot lights glinting off her trendy glasses. "You've made your point."

With that, she hopped in her Jetta and peeled off, leaving me with the crackhead evangelist. I did not want to be in debt to a man who had writhing snakes tattooed up both arms, but he'd helped me bring Daddy back. "Thanks."

"Take care of him." Bubba Paxton stared after Charlotte. "Your reporter friend. Is she going to write about me?"

"I hope not."

"If the elders at my church hear that I'm a murder suspect, I will lose my job. They hired me on the condition I keep my nose clean."

I blinked. "I thought Pax Out was your church."

"I'm the front man. Investors own the church. I'm already in the doghouse because the Beanies cut into our business."

I'd never thought of a church as a business, or that attendance would matter so much financially, but it made sense. "Ya don't say?"

"Three of my families joined the Beanies and renounced their worldly ways." He jammed his hands in his pockets. "The elders want more money, but I'm out of doors to knock on. We need new people in Sinclair County."

I shot him a sympathetic glance. "Sorry about your situation. Thanks for helping with Daddy. I've got to go."

He glanced to where Daddy sat, eyes closed, head propped against the window. "You need help unloading him at his pad?"

"I can manage. Thanks for your offer though."

Bubba hesitated. I sensed he was waiting for something. I nodded toward my father. "Daddy appreciates what you did for him. Thank you for being his friend."

"Tab's special. I know he isn't what you wanted in a father, but he's always had your best interests at heart. Peace be unto you." Bubba walked toward the dark highway.

What? How did he know what Daddy thought about my well-being? I didn't understand his remarks, but I let them slide.

I looked around. My truck was the only vehicle in the parking lot. It had to be at least ten miles out to Pax Out.

Remorse tasted bitter in my mouth. How would he get home? "Can I give you a lift?"

He waved my offer off. "I'm good. Thanks. God will provide."

I wished I had his certainty.

# CHAPTER 22

Daddy slept all the way home. Mama helped me tuck him into his waterbed. "What happened?" she asked over a late supper of fish stew.

I recounted events in a sanitized version, conscious of Larissa's big ears. "I'm disappointed in Bubba Powell. He left the jail as soon as the sheriff released him."

"Money. That's the root of all evil." Mama gestured with her soup spoon. "The Powell family worshipped money as those two boys were growing up. Only the biggest and best for Roland and Bubba. The Colonel and Elizabeth didn't teach them family values."

My daughter's chin went out. So did mine. "No, Mama, you're wrong. Roland had his priorities straight. He loved us, and he did right by us. I won't let you drag his memory through the mud."

Mama clucked dismissively. "I respect your right to your opinions, and I expect you to respect mine, too. The Powell brothers needed more home training when they were boys."

Stiffly, I placed my paper napkin on the tie-dyed tablecloth. "It's late. We should go. Larissa has school tomorrow."

"Don't you want to talk about what happened?" Mama asked. "It won't hurt for you two to wait a few more hours. I'm sure your father will be awake by then."

"I've got work to do tonight, plus Daddy's exhausted. I'm sure he'll sleep through till morning. And no, I don't want to talk about it. I know what went wrong."

Her gaze sharpened. "You do? Let's hear it."

My stomach lurched. If I didn't get out of here, I'd be wearing my fish stew. "I'd rather not discuss it."

"Don't keep me in suspense. What happened?"

"Later, Mama."

"Now, Baxley."

"It's a sensitive topic. Besides, Larissa has school tomorrow. We have homework to do."

"About that. I wondered if I could home-school Larissa. It would free up more time for you, and give me more time with my granddaughter."

More time to brainwash her to be like them, totally unaware of finances and responsibility.

I stood, my face frozen into a mask of civility. "Thank you for dinner, Mama, and thank you for looking after Larissa today. I appreciate your kind offer, but Larissa stays in public school."

My daughter padded after me out the door. Her poker face gave nothing away. It was all I could do to contain my emotions. By all rights, my head should've popped off. Steam should be blasting from my ears.

Larissa climbed into the truck with me. "Why are you keeping secrets, Mom?"

"Secrets?" I congratulated myself on sounding so calm, so normal.

"Yeah. It has to do with Dad, doesn't it? He's alive, isn't he?"

"I can't find him on the other side. That's the truth."

"So he is alive. I knew it."

Shadows swirled in the truck cab. I gave her hand a squeeze. "Don't read too much into this. He could be dead."

"But he could be alive."

"I don't want you to get your hopes up. I can't explain what happened to him." My voice faltered. "I don't know where your father is."

"But you don't see him when you dreamwalk."

"No. I don't."

"That's a good sign." Larissa studied the house. "Mama Lacey is wrong about him. He doesn't worship money."

I switched on the ignition and eased away from the cottage. "He took good care of us."

"Is he coming back, Mama?"

"I don't know."

"Will you teach me how to dreamwalk? Will you, Mom?"

A hard edge crept into my voice. "This isn't what I want for you, Larissa. I had trouble in school because I was so different from the other kids. I want you to fit in, to have a normal childhood."

"Normal. Like having two parents and living in the same house all my life? That's so yesterday, Mom. I'm happy here in Sinclair County because I can be myself."

I allowed myself to breathe a little easier. My intelligent-beyond-her-years daughter's head was on straight. "That's what I want for you, baby. To be happy with who you are."

"I'm happy. But I'm curious about new things. Out of all the people I've met, Mama Lacey and Pap are the most down to earth. I feel at ease around them."

"I understand that, I really do. Mama Lacey and Pap are different, and that difference sets them apart in the world's eyes. I had to make a choice. I could either live in their world or be part of the world at large."

"I'm not you. Plus I've seen lots in the world."

I turned off the highway onto our rutted driveway. I held my tongue until I switched the ignition off. "Larissa, you are ten years old. That doesn't make you a world expert."

"It makes me a Larissa expert."

I shook my head at her logic. "You are something else, young lady."

Her green eyes met and held my gaze. "Will you teach me to dreamwalk?"

I matched her intensity. "It's dangerous. I want you to promise me that you'll let this drop."

"I want to do it, Mom."

"I hear you. The answer is no."

"You're not listening to me. I want to help June."

That fish stew congealed in my stomach. "June? What's she got to do with this?"

"I see her face when I close my eyes." Her voice softened. "June's hair is down around her face, but I know it's her, Mom. I want to learn how to talk to her."

Her words chilled me, and I'd been through the gauntlet today. How long had my baby been hurting? How long had she been seeing visions?

"How come this is the first I've heard of it?" I asked, trying for nonchalance.

"I've been feeling Pap out about his abilities, but he won't tell me anything. He said I have to talk to you first."

"Pap is right. You can always tell me anything." I reached across the void between us and brushed her face with my palm. "How long has this been happening?"

"A couple of weeks. I was cleaning out my closet and came across the shoes we painted. I held one and thought about her. An hour went by before I realized it. After that I started seeing her when I went to sleep. I want to see more, but that's all I see."

"Holding the shoe must have triggered the episode. You don't have dreams of anyone else?"

"I don't know any other dead people." Larissa stared at her interlaced hands in her lap. "Except for Daddy. I don't see him."

# CHAPTER 23

During the night, I dreamt. Funhouse-distorted faces flashed before my eyes in rapid succession, along with streaks of fractured light and diabolical laughter. Laced throughout it all, a soundtrack of terrible screams. Heart pounding, I clawed my way up out of sleep. I switched on my bedside lamp, but the soft glow didn't curb my spatial disorientation.

If I'd had the strength to get up and look in the mirror, I'm sure my face would have been ashen and pale. I sucked down gulps of air and clutched a pillow to my stomach. Despair welled up, dredging with it the horrors of the past few days. Tears brimmed in my eyes.

Troubles. I had so many right now, I didn't know where to turn my attention. Morgan—dead. My career as a police consultant—on hold. My brother-in-law—a murder suspect. My deal with Rose the tattooed woman—scary. My allegedly dead husband—somewhere in the land of the living. My daughter—seeing her dead friend in her sleep.

My grip tightened on the pillow.

There had been a point early in my marriage, back when Larissa was a baby, that I'd been troubled by ugly dreams like this. Roland had encouraged me to go to the health clinic on post and get help. For years I'd taken prescription sleeping pills. I'd stopped them when I began footing my medical bills eighteen months ago, but I'd held on to three pills.

For emergencies.

Mercifully, the scary dreams had stopped, and I hadn't used the pills. I thought about taking a pill now. I reached over in the drawer of my nightstand and found the prescription bottle. With a flick of my wrist, the pills rattled reassuringly inside the plastic container.

I glanced at the clock. Four in the morning. If I took a pill now, I wouldn't awaken in time to get Larissa off to school. That wasn't going to happen. I wouldn't let my problems affect my daughter. She was the best thing I'd ever done, and I wasn't going to screw that up.

The pills went back in the drawer.

I picked up my stack of to-be-read books and flipped through them. But even with busy hands, my mind wouldn't settle. There was nothing I could do about Morgan or the sheriff's amateurish investigation. If Wayne wanted my police-consultant services, he could darned well pay me for them.

How would I find Rose's sister in Tampa? Should I drive down there and look for her? It was easily five hours to Tampa. I couldn't get there and back in a day, not with Larissa in school, and I couldn't afford the expense of gas and a hotel. I'd try the library computers. With any luck, Raymondia LaFleur would be in the phone book.

My missing husband floated into the queue next. The U.S. Army said Roland was dead, and we'd buried an empty casket with his name on it. But the Army had yet to release his death benefits.

Where was he?

Why didn't he come home?

Was he in danger?

Why didn't he contact me?

He'd been Special Ops, and his missions had been top secret. He'd been adamant about following the rules. Consequently, I never knew where he was going or when he'd be back. He'd left that last time with the same corny promise he always made: "I'll be back."

I couldn't imagine him not wanting to be with us. Larissa was his pride and joy, and we'd had a happy marriage. The notion of him abandoning us wasn't possible.

Roland loved us. He'd said it every chance he got.

I touched the chain at my neck where I wore the green pendant Roland had given me. I believed in love, and I believed in Roland. Therefore, something had gone terribly wrong in his life.

But what?

How could I even pursue that line of inquiry among the living? Where had he been for two years?

Frustration rolled through me, pounding me like giant breakers on the beach. I fisted my hands in the sheets. I needed to be proactive, not stuck in a mental bog. How could I help my loved ones?

The big cat I was pet-sitting padded into the room and leapt up onto the bed. Sulay's dark eyes glowed with feline secrets. She ambled closer, purring and settling beside me.

I should be able to do something. Who could I help?

My daughter.

A fleeting sense of peace came over me, as if this was the puzzle my subconscious had been trying to solve. I took a few deep breaths. With each inhalation, I became more confident this was the right course of action.

I could help Larissa.

She'd asked me to help her understand her vision. Granted, I didn't want her to be cursed with bad dreams, but I'd had no say in it. She'd had a vision, and that vision kept recurring.

After the nightmare I'd just had, I felt great empathy for her. It was a wonder she was able to close her eyes at night.

Dreams could be interpreted symbolically or literally. What

did Larissa's vision mean? June's body had never been recovered. Once her boat was found by Bubba Wright, a search and rescue operation had ensued, but it had been fruitless. The tide changed every six hours, and with a full three hours of a strong ebb tide, the chances of finding her body in a tidal creek had been negligible.

It had been a miracle her little boat had been found. With the full moon and spring tide, the boat had gotten hung up in the high marsh on the last vestige point before open sea.

I hugged my knees to my chest as I pondered that likelihood. Was it a miracle?

Or something else?

Miracles were few and far between, as far as I was concerned. My friend Daniel Huxley would know about the likelihood of the boat ending up there. In his guise as Coastal Watchdog, he was a tidal expert.

That's what I'd do.

I'd give Daniel a call later today.

Making that decision calmed me. I had something positive to do. I couldn't solve all the puzzles in this world, but I could help my daughter, and I could help Rose.

I stroked the purring cat at my side. Comfort pulsed through my fingertips and up my arm, filling me with reassurance. I was glad of the companionship and took Sulay's presence as a vote of confidence in me.

Bubba Powell owed me an explanation, and I would track him down.

I yawned and settled down into my pillows to wait for dawn.

# CHAPTER 24

The headline of the *Marion Observer* read "Banker's death ruled a homicide." Charlotte's byline snugged up tight under the headline. A photo of the sheriff and the coroner looking grim on the steps of the deceased's home covered three newspaper columns. The story filled the entire top half of the front page.

Charlotte must be dancing on air.

I pushed my tea mug aside and studied the entire page of the weekly paper with rapt fascination. It had been months since I'd seen her byline on the front page, much less above the fold. Bernard pretty much hogged all the front page news. Good for Charlotte.

Holding my breath, I skimmed the article, hoping like crazy she'd avoided mentioning the Bubbas. Relief sighed from my lips as she mentioned that persons of interest were being questioned by the authorities.

Thank God.

The only other item of front page interest was that the new property tax bills had been mailed. Bernard had poured his heart into the piece, making it sound as if the rise in assessments spelled homelessness and despair for every family in the county. While I'm sure that wasn't the case for most of the population, the change was surely bad news for me. Higher property taxes would throw another kink in my tight budget. I needed to convince the sheriff he needed my psychic consulting services for the murder investigation.

Larissa strolled into the kitchen cuddling the fluffy Maine Coon cat, Muffin trotting obediently at her heels. "Can we keep Sulay, Mom? She's such a sweetie."

I loved that Larissa had my affinity for animals. I hated that we barely had a positive cash flow. Regret clanked in my empty stomach. There's nothing I would've liked better than filling our home with furry playmates for Larissa. "Bonnie Chapman wants her kitty back once she comes out of rehab. Plus, Sulay loves her home. She knows this is temporary."

As if she understood our conversation, Sulay twisted, jumped to the floor, and stretched out by the air vent. I got out bowls, cereal, and milk for our breakfast.

Larissa's gaze tracked the cat's motions. "If we can't keep Sulay, can we get another kitty?"

My lips tightened. I shook my head, poured out our breakfast. "We've already got Muffin, and we will board other pets from time to time, but pets are expensive. We have to watch our expenses."

Larissa's face fell. It lit up a moment later. "What if I tell you I dreamed we had a cat? A dainty little yellow one."

"I'd tell you that dreams don't always come true."

"What about Pap's dreams? And your dreams?"

Tricky ground there. I pushed her bowl of cereal across the table and started in on mine. "That's different. Dreamwalks are different from nighttime dreams."

"I believe in my dream about June. It was a night dream."

Mental quicksand tugged at me, pulling me deeper into the stinky mire. I didn't want the dreamworld to be part of Larissa's conscious life. I wanted her dreams to fade upon waking.

My beautiful daughter deserved the best I could offer her, and that was a shot at being normal. I swallowed around a lump in my throat. "Honey, I feel awful about you losing your friend. And I want you to know that I'm taking your dream seriously."

"You are?"

"Since last summer, I've had a good many dreamwalks and developed some investigative experience. I'll ask around, see if there's any light I can shed on her disappearance."

She looked thoughtful, filling her spoon up with milk and cereal and then emptying it out. "Good. I believe June is trying to tell me something."

"This isn't what I wanted for you. I hoped your dreams would be your own, not messages from others. How do you feel about it?"

Larissa shrugged. "It doesn't bother me. I want to help my friend."

"Do you hear anything in your dream?"

"Nothing. There's no sound at all. Just a silent movie of blue water and her hair."

"You know I love you, right?" Larissa nodded, her ponytail flashing golden in the morning sunlight. I cleared my throat and continued. "You can talk to Pap and me about your dreams any time, but promise me you won't tell anyone outside the family about them."

Her green eyes rounded. "Ever?"

"When you're twenty-one, you can decide for yourself. Until then, especially while you are growing up, keep your dreams a secret. Can you do that?"

She wouldn't meet my gaze. "I don't like secrets."

My maternal radar pinged, bringing a small wave of dread. I hated to question her about this, but I couldn't let it go. No mother would. "You're keeping secrets from me?"

"June asked me not to tell her secret."

Her voice was so low I had to strain to make out the words. Did Larissa know something that might be relevant to June's death? "I think it would be okay to tell now."

Her gaze flicked over to me and back to her cereal. "It's about June's mother."

Interest unfurled like a flag in a stiff breeze. I sensed this secret was important. "Louise? Did she have something to do with June's disappearance?"

"No, nothing like that. She used to cry a lot. She'd argue with June's dad and then go cry in her room."

Her statement puzzled me. "What did they argue about?"

"Kids. She wanted more kids. Only something is wrong, and she can't have any more. She wanted to adopt but Mr. Gilroy said no."

"You heard them arguing?"

"He said he wouldn't raise another man's cast-offs." Larissa chewed her lip and slowly lifted her gaze to mine. "What's a cast-off?"

I wanted to march over to Ritchie Gilroy's house and yell at him. Instead, I took a moment to compose myself so that my anger didn't leak into this conversation. "He was talking about orphans or kids with no dad."

"Everyone has a dad."

"Everyone has a biological parent, but not everyone has a dad."

Larissa fooled with her spoon some more. "I don't understand."

"Ritchie Gilroy's a jerk. Poor June. It must have been tough hearing her parents argue."

"June used to cry, too." Larissa put down her spoon. "She thought she wasn't the kid her mother wanted. That's why she tried so hard to please them all the time. She wanted her mom to stop crying, to be happy to have her for a daughter."

Anger flared again, bright and fiery. It wasn't just Ritchie who deserved my ire. Louise had contributed to her daughter's anguish. And June had been such a great kid. She deserved better parents than the Gilroys. No wonder Larissa had kept her friend's secret.

My heart went out to my daughter who had borne this secret for so long. "I'm sorry their argument upset you. Despite what you and June overheard, the Gilroys loved her, and they were very glad to have her, just like your father and I are glad to have you in our lives."

Larissa thought on that for a minute. Her gaze filled with speculation. "Why don't I have any brothers and sisters?"

So much for light breakfast conversation. My accessible, approachable style of parenting had serious drawbacks, especially after a sleepless night. But it was too late to change tactics. Truth and honesty were what I believed in, values I hoped to impart to Larissa. "We traveled too much at first. We kept thinking once we got settled somewhere we'd expand our family. But we never stuck for long in any one place. The time slipped away from us."

Whatever she'd seen in my gaze must have satisfied her. She went back to staring at the soggy cereal. "June and I pretended we were sisters."

"I used to do the same thing with Charlotte."

Larissa stirred her cereal in an offhand fashion. "Will you get married again, Mom? Will I have a real sister or brother?"

I worked to unclench my fingers. Why did conversations with Larissa always veer into uncharted territory these days? I took a deep breath. "I'm not thinking about remarrying. I'm not even dating anyone."

"But you could be. That Watchdog guy in town. He'd like to take you out."

Was her observation based on longing or observation? Here I thought I'd had a good handle on parenting, and now I realized how little I knew of what went on in my daughter's head. I'd missed June's suffering, Larissa's, too. What else had I missed?

My pulse kicked up a notch. "How do you know that?"

"I've got eyes. He acts different around you."

I didn't believe her, didn't want to believe her, but when I visited Daniel's office later that morning his eyes lit up with masculine interest.

Darn. Larissa's observations were right on the mark.

# CHAPTER 25

"Baxley. You're just what the doctor ordered." Daniel Huxley's hand closed around mine just a tad longer than necessary for a handshake. Smile lines wreathed his tanned face.

Startled by the extended contact and the jolt of lust on the sensory plane, I stared at him, seeing him clearly for the first time. Graying at the temples of his collar-length hair made him look ten years older than me. His cream-colored cotton shirt was dotted with tan fishes. Below that were brown shorts and upscale sandals. A sense of quiet authority and masculine approval emanated from him.

My pulse thrummed in my ears as I boosted my sensory protection. Even with the forewarning from Larissa, I was stunned by Daniel's marked interest in me. How had I missed seeing his attraction to me before? Was I giving off some feminine "I'm available" vibe?

I kept my tone neutral. "The doctor? Are you sick?"

"Heck, no. I'm as healthy as a horse." He squared his broad shoulders and flexed his biceps. His jaw worked on a stick of gum. "I meant it as a complimentary figure of speech. You always brighten my day."

I averted my gaze to the nautical charts lining his cramped office. "You might not feel so generous in a minute. I want to ask you some questions about the tides."

"Go right ahead. I'll buy you lunch if you stump me."

I hesitated. Daniel was an outsider, brought in by the regional conservationists ten years ago. His Coastal Watchdog salary came from funds raised by a lobbyist group. It hadn't occurred to me until this very second that his loyalty might be bought and paid for. Would he lie to protect his job?

If he lied to me, I'd know it. Part of my extrasensory set of skills helped me read between the lines of what people said. My spidey-sense didn't always work; if a person believed his lie, I couldn't pick up anything.

Daniel seemed like a straight arrow. I didn't get a sense of him having a hidden agenda. I brushed aside my concern. I had enough problems to solve without adding new ones.

"I'm counting on your discretion," I said.

With a laugh, he clutched his heart. "The suspense is killing me. I never knew you were such a tease. Give it up."

"I want to know about the tides on a certain day last summer. The day when June Gilroy went missing."

His genial expression instantly sobered and his broad chest became even broader. Something flickered across his brown eyes, something I hadn't seen before. Were my earlier thoughts about his loyalty warranted? My gaze narrowed.

"What's this all about?" he asked.

"I've been thinking about June lately, wondering how her boat got that far up in the marsh, wondering why her body was never found."

"Where are you going with this, Baxley?"

His caution irritated me. Was he protecting someone?

I'd never had thoughts like this before I married Roland, but my husband had taught me a lot about human behavior. He'd taught me to be observant and to watch for tells. And I'd always had an extrasensory ear for the truth. Before this conversation, I'd never wondered about Daniel's loyalties or agenda. Now those questions burned in my gut.

"My daughter was June's friend," I said with practiced

patience. "She's still grieving over the loss. I thought if I better understood what happened, I could help her get through this."

Daniel leaned back against his old wooden desk and crossed his brawny arms. "The Gilroys have enough going on right now without someone bringing this tragedy up again. All those people calling them with June sightings trying to collect that ten-thousand-dollar reward nearly did my cousin Louise in."

"I didn't know you were related to Louise." Disapproval came through loud and clear in his voice, but his claim rang true. He earnestly wanted to protect the Gilroys.

"My uncle married her aunt twenty-five years ago. We're not blood relatives, but family nonetheless. I've known Louise most of my life. She recommended me for this job."

That answered how he got here. Plus, he owed the Gilroys for his job. Loyalty was a desirable trait. I could work with that.

"I'm not after the reward." I infused my voice with maternal concern. "Like I said, I'm trying to help my daughter gain closure. I know the basics about the tides, that there are two high and low tides each day, but I've never heard of a boat being caught in the high marsh before. That's what I want to know. How did the boat get up there?"

He stared out the adjacent window for a long, prickly minute. "The Department of Natural Resources concluded the wind blew the boat across the marsh at flood tide."

"I heard that. Was the tide high enough for that to happen? What about the river currents? Wouldn't the current determine a boat's location?"

"The strongest currents follow the water channels." His brow furrowed and his words came out deliberately, as if he were picking through a vegetable bin of tomatoes. "The current flows toward the mainland on the incoming tide; it flows out on the outgoing tide. We have about a six-foot difference in volume in the creeks between high and low tide."

Nothing new there. Even someone as boat-dumb as me knew those tidal basics. How could I get him to open up? I needed to know what he knew if I wanted to make any headway. "Would you mind going through that day from your perspective? I was hoping I might come up with something helpful by looking at this a different way."

His tone sharpened. "I really don't see the point of this."

"Please. I'm not sure it will help either, but I'm willing to do anything to help Larissa get a good night's sleep. I'm hoping you can help us."

He stared at his moss-green, strappy sandals. I thought he wasn't going to say anything. Then he spoke in a low voice. "Louise told me that she'd called Morgan to okay June's coming over to his place to swim. June left home in mid-afternoon. When she didn't return in an hour or two, they assumed she was still at the pool with her uncle. No one knew to look for her until dinnertime. By then the tide was ebbing, draining our tidal creeks. The sun was setting."

"Why didn't Morgan call her parents when she didn't show up?"

"He assumed she'd changed her mind. Apparently that had happened before, when June arranged to swim and didn't show up. He didn't think anything of it. That's what he told us."

"There are sandbars throughout the creeks leading out to the sound. Why didn't the boat get stranded on one of them? I don't understand how it got so far up in the high marsh."

"That lightweight aluminum boat skimmed across the water surface, even with June in it. With a strong westerly wind, it is very probable that the boat would end up in the marsh. Look at the huge rafts of marsh rack that get deposited there on a daily basis. The wind pushes floating material across the water, and when the tide retreats, it gets stranded up there."

Dang. His explanation sounded so plausible, and he believed

every word of it. I'd been sure there was something investigators had missed. "What about the fact that the boat was filled with water? Wouldn't that have made it less easy to float into the high marsh?"

He chewed on his gum, his dark eyes once again searching my face. "It could have hindered the boat's momentum, but the truth is, we don't know when the boat filled up with water. That back plug wasn't tight. The boat was discovered on a high tide the next morning. It could have filled then."

I inhaled sharply at the revelation. "The plug was loose? How do you know that?"

"Because I went up in the high marsh to get the boat after Bubba Wright radioed it in. Louise and Ritchie didn't want it known that June had made such a rookie mistake of not securing the drain plug."

"This is news to me. I was there at the house with Louise, waiting for news that morning. She never mentioned the drain, not once."

"Like I said, after we found the boat, we concentrated on finding June's body. I combed all through the marsh from the boat back to shore while the shrimpers trawled the creeks. I believe her body was most likely swept out to sea."

Something tugged at the edge of my thoughts. If I were here to fish for alternate ideas, I had to think outside the box. "What are your least likely ideas?"

"Pretty much the span of the rumor mill. Abduction, runaway, foul play. I've got nothing new."

His last statement didn't ring as true as his others. His voice sounded off a smidge, tighter, maybe. I sensed he was holding back. "But you are thinking of something else."

He didn't say anything.

"Tell me. I need to know."

He briefly met my gaze. "I don't want this getting back to my cousin. She's not a strong woman."

My throat constricted. Fear and anticipation tripped across my nerve endings, whispering of bad news to come. "You have my word," I managed to squeak out.

"I came across six full-sized gator wallows in the high marsh. If June had boat trouble and tried to walk home through the marsh, she might have run across a gator."

I shuddered.

I couldn't help it. No mother needed that image of her child's last moments. "Good God. I hadn't thought about that. A gator would explain why the body was never found."

"I agree, which is why I never mentioned the possibility to Louise." He rubbed his squarish jaw. "You know what bothers me?"

"What?" I couldn't believe how airy my voice sounded. The shock of a possible death by gator echoed inside the sudden chasm inside my head and wouldn't turn me loose.

"June knew her way around a boat. Why didn't she drop anchor, seal the plug, bail the boat, and come home? If she had engine trouble, she could have anchored and waited until the shrimpers went out in the morning. I don't understand why she left her boat."

I silently agreed with him. There weren't any good reasons for her to abandon her boat. Only bad reasons, unless she'd had an accident or a medical emergency. "Do you think she fell out of the boat?"

"Anything is possible, but we'll never know, especially since her motor wouldn't run after being submerged. If someone took her for anything other than the sex trade, they'd have ransomed her by now. Louise and Ritchie would have paid anything to get her back. She wasn't the type to run away either. We've never had an abduction here for nefarious purposes. Therefore, I believe June is dead."

I exhaled heavily. The horrible choices he threw out weren't any I'd considered before. "I believe she's dead as well, but the loose ends bother me."

June's very pink bedroom flashed into my thoughts. Louise had left it intact all this time, ready for June to come home. How hard that must be, to walk in that room, listening for her child's presence and hearing only the ache of silence.

"What about your daughter? Does Larissa believe June is alive?"

Larissa's vision of June floating in the water flashed into my head. "In her heart, no, but she still clings to the hope of a miracle. That June will walk into our house and laugh in that infectious way she had, and they will be best friends again. The girls pretended they were sisters."

"I wish I could help her. What about on a therapeutic paddle through the rice canals? I could put your daughter in a two-seater kayak with me."

"Thanks, but since June's disappearance Larissa won't go on the water at all."

He exhaled heavily. "I'm sorry to hear that."

"Me, too, but I understand her apprehension." I gathered my thoughts and stepped toward the door. "Thanks for humoring me today. I won't hold you up any longer."

Daniel moved with me. He leaned in close enough for me to smell his mint-flavored gum. "How about lunch? The pizza place around the corner serves a mean pepperoni."

I edged closer to the exit. "I can't today. I've got a full schedule."

"You going to Morgan's funeral on Saturday?"

I swallowed thickly. "Yeah."

"See you there."

# CHAPTER 26

Remembering my promise to the spirit named Rose who brought Daddy back from the bridge, I drove to the library and procured a computer with Internet access. Moments later, I had my answer. There were no phone listings for Raymondia LaFleur in Tampa. None at all. I tried searching for mobile phone listings, but came up empty-handed. Now what? I plugged her name into a search engine and found nothing related.

The cursor blinked at me, awaiting instruction. I tried social networking sites. The library firewalls blocked my access. Darn it. I had no idea how to find Rose's sister. And even less of an idea how she'd react to the message I was supposed to impart.

With that, I exited the building and sought the butterfly garden I'd installed there. Technically maintenance of the garden was the city's responsibility, but I liked to stop in each week, pull a few weeds, and enjoy the restful space. The trickling waters of the little fountain played out their soothing melody as I yanked dollar weed and Virginia creeper out of the butterfly weed and *Spiraea*. Afterward, I sat on the wooden bench amidst fluttering butterflies, sunny coneflowers, and vibrant red-leafed *Fothergilla*. The warm spring sunshine chased away the last of the chill embedded in my marrow.

How could I help Rose? I had to think of something. She'd sacrificed to help me get Daddy back. I couldn't burn bridges in the spirit world, or I'd have a very brief career as a dreamwalker. I let my mind drift, and it meandered around to Daniel Huxley.

My visit to the Coastal Watchdog office had been productive. I now had two new bits of information. Daniel was related to Louise Gilroy, and the drain plug had been loose in June's boat.

Three bits of information, if you counted the presence of gator wallows in the high marsh. I shuddered.

What did they mean?

June had been a responsible child. She wouldn't normally forget about the drain plug, but I forgot stuff all the time. Just last night I'd put the margarine in the pantry instead of the refrigerator. Distractions were a fact of life. June could have had a boating mishap if she was upset.

Had June decided to run her little boat through the tidal creeks out to the sound and back before going to her uncle's for a swim? The idea seemed plausible now that I knew of the strife in her family. I could easily see her running wide open across the water, feeling the ocean breeze ruffle her hair, distancing herself from the harsh edge of her parents' bitterness.

With Larissa's dream of June floating in the water, I strongly believed her friend had drowned. That outcome had been one I'd long suspected anyway. Even so, that line of thought brought up another question. Was her drowning an accident?

How maddening to be no closer to an answer.

Nothing I'd learned today would help Larissa find closure. I couldn't solve June's disappearance any more than I could clear Bubba Powell from suspicion of murder.

Why didn't my brother-in-law wait for us last night? Charlotte had told him we were there. He should've waited. His inconsiderate behavior worried me. That wasn't like him one bit.

And it didn't add credence to his innocence.

I tried him again on my cell.

He answered with "Powell here."

"Powell here, too. Why didn't you wait for us last night?"

"Places to go, people to see."

His breezy attitude annoyed me. He wasn't acting like himself. Was his odd behavior indicative of something more sinister? "Where are you?"

"I'm headed to the bank. I've got a hot lead on a new idea to dredge up sea shells from the ocean floor and supply them to road builders. I want to lock in on a low interest rate right away."

"You're asking the bank for another loan?" My heart sunk. Bubba the dreamer was back. When would he learn there were no shortcuts in life?

Roland and I had bailed Bubba out of two prior get-rich-quick schemes. I didn't have that luxury now, not when I was struggling to keep a roof over my head.

"Thought I'd try to get this loan outright since Roland isn't around to co-sign with me." He hesitated. "I wasn't going to bother you with it."

Dread rolled through me. I wasn't in a financial position to bail him out. If he got overextended this time there could be serious consequences. "Bubba, this isn't a good idea. Let's get together and talk about this."

"No can do. I'm on a roll. Things are finally going my way, and I'm cashing in on Lady Luck while she's smiling. I'm finally going to be the man my father can be proud of."

Poor Bubba.

At forty he was still trying to earn his father's approval. The Colonel was a mean SOB. Nothing Bubba accomplished would ever cause him to shine in his father's eyes. Bubba had committed the unpardonable sin of not joining the military. He would never measure up to the Colonel's high standards.

Just as I had never been good enough for the Colonel or Elizabeth. I was a Nesbitt, one of those crazy hippies from the wrong side of town. Definitely not good enough for their golden boy, Roland.

I'd always understood Bubba's feeling of being second best. Unlike him, I didn't keep trying to please his parents. I was too busy living my life, something Bubba should have learned to do years ago. I wished he'd find something else to fill that hole his parents had left in his heart.

I gentled my voice. "Bubba, we've talked about this before. You've got to live your life for you."

"And for Patty."

A chill slid down my spine. Bubba and Patty? If he was back with her, he was on a collision course with the law. "Good Lord, Bubba. Didn't you learn anything at jail last night? Now is not the time to renew your affair with Patty Gilroy. The sheriff and his deputies are grasping at straws trying to find Morgan's killer. They'll charge you with murder if you so much as wink at Patty."

"Too late. I've winked at every square inch of her lovely body."

The warmth of the sun on my back cooled. "Bubba, her husband was murdered."

"Her ex-husband."

"Small distinction in this town. Everyone knows her as Morgan's wife. Stay away from her until the dust settles on the homicide investigation. Please, I beg you. Keep your distance from Patty."

"I love her, Baxley. I thought you of all people would understand that love is enough. It has to be enough. That's why I need this loan. I'm going to make something of myself. I'm going to be the man Patty needs to take care of her and Connie Lee."

His voice broke as he spoke. Air whistled between my teeth. I hated to burst his balloon, but someone needed to talk sense into his head. "Trust me on this. Patty needs time to process

Morgan's death, too. With you moving in on her so soon, her emotions are still fragile. She could truly love you. Or she could be using you."

"She's not like that. And I can't stay away from her now. Not when Connie Lee is so sick. Patty needs me. Her daughter needs me. I've been spending more time with Connie Lee lately, and she's a delightful child. There's a way she moves her hands when she talks that reminds me of my mother." He sighed. "Now you know I'm a lovesick fool."

He wasn't listening to me. Patty and her daughter consumed his thoughts now. Nothing I could say would change that. I was wasting my breath.

With a sigh, I gave him the encouragement he sought. "You're doing a good thing being a friend to Connie Lee and Patty."

"More than that. I'm giving Connie Lee a kidney if I'm a match."

I shot to my feet, sputtering. *"What?"*

"You heard me. I've got two kidneys. I don't need them both, not when Connie Lee needs one."

"I know you want to help, but organ donation? Isn't that extreme? Plus, chances are astronomically slim that you will be a match."

"Doesn't matter. Even if we're not a match, I want to donate my kidney. They can give her drugs to make it all right. Hell, now they have these databases where someone else can give Connie Lee a kidney if I give their kid one."

We were venturing into uncharted waters. If Bubba wouldn't listen to me, I had one last resort. "Have you talked to your parents about this?"

"Why would I do that?" Disgust tinged his voice.

Birds chirped overhead. "This is a big decision, one that will affect your health for the rest of your life."

"My mind is made up, Baxley."

That famous Powell mindset; how well I knew it. Everyone saw it in the Colonel's rigid attitudes, and he'd passed the legacy on to his sons. When Roland had made up his mind about something, he'd been inflexible. His brother appeared to be just as pig-headed stubborn.

"Fine."

"No more badgering?"

"You won't hear it from me. It would be a waste of breath."

I heard the rapid clacking of heels behind me on the library sidewalk. I glanced over my shoulder to see Muriel Jamison bearing down on me. What did she want? "I've got to go. Let me know about your loan."

"I will. And Baxley?"

"Yeah?"

"Thanks for coming down to the jail last night. Without you and your dad believing in me, I'd still be behind bars."

The tightness in my heart eased a bit. "You're welcome."

I clicked off the phone. Bubba Powell was heading for trouble at the bank, with Patty Gilroy, and with the sheriff. There was nothing I could do to avert the upcoming disaster.

"Yoo-hoo, Baxley!" Muriel called breezily, as if we were best friends. Her silken pantsuit of burgundy with swirls of gold embroidery looked quite warm. Bracelets jangled as she hurried my way.

I donned a professional smile. "Muriel. Hello."

"I wanted to ask you about this garden. I didn't realize you'd created it until recently, and I wasn't able to bring it up last night at—" She faltered briefly, closing her exotic eyes. "At that institution. Anyway, I'd like you to come out to our place at the north end and build this on a bigger scale."

"You want this garden?" I couldn't believe my luck. A paying customer had dropped into my lap from out of the blue. Imagine that. Thank you, wheels of fate.

"Yes or something very much like it. I have several gardening magazines I've been studying, but none of the gardens are as picturesque as this."

I clipped my phone back into my belt holster, my mind whirling with scheduling details. I needed my planner from the truck before I locked in on a time. "I'd be happy to set up an appointment for an estimate tomorrow. Let me get you my card from the truck, and we can talk about a convenient time to meet and discuss this at length."

She walked along beside me, her spiky heels clacking on the sidewalk. Her floral perfume blotted out the fresh air, dosing me heavily with roses. "It has to be morning. Are you free early in the day?"

"One moment while I check my availability." My calendar was clear as the blue sky overhead. I studied the blank page for a few moments, striving to appear a successful, busy landscaper. "You're in luck. I have an opening late tomorrow morning. I'd be delighted to come out to your home before lunch."

Details of fountains, plants, and butterflies danced in my head as I scheduled an appointment for ten on Thursday. Muriel drove off in her Lexus and Eunice Wright took Muriel's spot next to my truck. She had a passenger in her ancient Buick.

Her husband.

I groaned.

No matter where I went, I was surrounded by Bubbas.

# CHAPTER 27

I refreshed my professional smile once again and leaned down into the driver's open window. "Eunice. Bubba. Good to see you two. How've you been?"

The alcohol fumes boiling out of the car knocked me back. My breath hitched in my throat. It was barely noon and judging by Bubba Wright's red, glassy eyes, he was sloshed. One strap of his faded overalls listed off his massive shoulders. His grizzled hair was closely shorn, his dark face clean-shaven.

Eunice shook her head sadly. A sense of desperation oozed from her full figure. "Not good. Not good at'all. Every since he got loose from the jail, my Bubba has been on a terrible drunk." She poked her husband in the shoulder. "Tell 'er, Bubba."

His slurred words were at least two-hundred proof. "I didn't do it. I didn't kill the banker."

"Of course you didn't." I glanced over at Eunice. "What's this all about?"

Bubba Wright pounded his fist on the torn center console. "They're gonna get me. I ain't going back to no jail, ain't serving no time for a crime I didn't do." He heaved in a breath. "They always blame the black man."

Worry etched Eunice's face. "Can you help us, Baxley?"

Confusion rippled through me. "I don't understand. What happened? Why do you think I can help?"

"You knows the system and you knows the sheriff. You told us to get Bubba an alibi and we did. But what if they stick it to him anyway? What then?"

My gut clenched and my hands went up defensively. "Wait a minute. I never said to manufacture an alibi. I only suggested that if someone had seen Bubba at the time of the murder, then the cops couldn't hold him. I didn't advise you to tell people to lie about his whereabouts."

"Bubba didn't do it," his wife said. "He's innocent, I tell you."

"I believe you, Eunice, but lying about his whereabouts will blow up in your face. Where was Bubba on Monday afternoon?"

Eunice shook her head rapidly, fear clouding her brown eyes, despair dragging down her shoulders. "Those developers want us out. They're gonna use this to railroad us so they can build those condos up and down the waterfront." She waved a white envelope at me. "Looka here. Our taxes tripled for Shrimp 'n' Stuff. Tripled. How are we supposed to pay dat? Who's gonna pay triple for bait or fish? The good old boys are stickin' it to us 'cause we got what dey want. They cain't have our land."

My brain whirred. I remembered another town where I'd lived and people suddenly faced increased taxes. A solution occurred to me. "Appeal the tax rate. They can't make sweeping changes like this without allowing for an appeal process. I'm not a lawyer, but Daniel Huxley over at Coastal Watchdog is very aware of property regulations around here. He could help you file an appeal."

"An appeal?" Eunice dragged out the word appeal for several seconds, rolling it around her mouth like foreign food. "What good would dat do?"

"It could get the rate overturned. I haven't been to the post office this morning, but if my bill increased, I'll file an appeal too. If enough of us do it, we'll get their attention."

Eunice tapped the thin envelope against the steering wheel. "The Huxley fella? He can fix this tax mess?"

"I believe so."

Eunice momentarily closed her eyes as if in silent prayer. "Praise the Lord. Child, I am so glad you came home. You sure are prettying up this town and helping people with their animals. Your mama and daddy are busting-out proud of you for taking over for your daddy, too."

"Thank you, Eunice."

Bubba leaned around his wife and blasted me with another cloud of cheap booze. "Why don't you dreamwalk and ask Morgan who kilt him so we's can skip all this po-lice nonsense?"

If only it were so easy. "Daddy and I dreamwalked last night, and we didn't find Morgan. Besides, even if we did learn something, a psychic vision won't count as evidence."

"You'd be right surprised about that, little gal," Bubba continued. "Dreamwalking done fixed a boatload of trouble in this town. I've gotta mind to go over dere right now and ask Tab to try again."

Sunbeams surrounded me, but my bones went cold. "I'm looking into Morgan's death. Please don't ask Daddy to go under again. He's taking risks with his life he shouldn't take. I nearly lost him last night."

Bubba scoffed. "Tab knows what he's doing."

I shot him a quelling look. "He's a grandfather, and he's got no business playing messenger from the afterlife."

Bubba burst out laughing. "You're a feisty one. Ain't nobody gonna be tellin' Tab what to do. He's got his own tide table."

Cold slithered across the back of my neck, leaving a slimy worm trail of dread. It oozed down into my collar and beyond, numbing as it went. My head pounded. I searched his face, looking desperately for a clue of what he knew. "What do you mean?"

"I means what I mean."

"Hush up, old coot." Eunice shoved Bubba back onto his

side of the car. "You be botherin' her."

"I ain't botherin' nobody, woman. I'm sittin' in my own car, mindin' my own business."

"You're three sheets to the wind and darn near making a giant fool of yourself," Eunice said. "Baxley's done helped you twice. Why, you'd still be sitting in jail worryin' about goin' up to the big house and worryin' about the tax man takin' our business. Don't you be scarin' her 'bout her daddy. I'm takin' you home afore you land us both in a heap of trouble."

"Guess I better mind my boss." Bubba winked at me. "Come on to the shop this afternoon, Baxley. I got a nice big fish with your name on it."

I straightened, my hand going to the dull ache in the small of my back. "Y'all take care."

"Have a blessed day." Eunice waved as she drove off.

I snorted aloud. The blessings of this life were starting to feel like dog pooh.

# CHAPTER 28

I stopped by the sheriff's office first thing on Thursday, right after the bus whisked Larissa off to school. "Have you decided? Am I on the Gilroy case or not?"

He rose as I entered his office. "What happened last night? Did you and Tab find Morgan?"

"No, we didn't. And Daddy got in a heap of trouble up there. I don't want him working on your murder cases ever again."

Wayne gave a careless grin. "I didn't ask him to do anything. He did it on his own. You were there. No way you can blame me."

"I do blame you. He wouldn't have been tempted if you hadn't fingered my brother-in-law."

"Bubba's a suspect."

"Come on. You know him."

"We've already had this conversation."

"You're right. I apologize." I rubbed my temples. "It was rough last night. Daddy went beyond the safe zone. He crossed over. By all rights, he should still be wandering around in the spirit world."

"How'd you get him back?"

"Made a deal with a spirit. But I can't find the person she wants me to contact, so who knows what will happen next. Can you help me?"

He sat back, studying me as if my face were a football highlight reel. "This is a switch."

"I owe her for Daddy's life. You don't understand. If I burn this bridge, I may as well hang up my dreamwalker spurs."

"Spurs." His eyebrows waggled suggestively. "I like it."

"God. Why did I think you would help?" I turned to go.

"Wait. I can look for a person, that's no problem. But let's make it interesting, shall we? We've finished processing the murder weapon. Why don't you take it for a test run?"

"An even trade?"

He nodded. "Our original deal stands. I pay you for cases you solve. If you can close this case, we'll talk payment."

That was fair. I gave him the details about Rose and her sister Raymondia LaFleur in Tampa. Minutes later he had her cell-phone number.

Impressed, I called Raymondia from his office. The call went to voice mail. "This is Baxley Powell in Marion, Georgia. Your sister Rose said to tell you, the proof's in the pudding."

I grinned at the sheriff. "Thanks. I finally feel like I've done something good."

"You're welcome, and I'd appreciate it if you'd solve this case for me in return."

"I'll do my best."

He sent me down to the interview room while he retrieved the evidence. Mama had both my necklaces, so I had a packet of charged crystals in my pocket. I flexed my fingers and waited. I disliked being part of anyone's dog and pony show, but consulting for Wayne helped pay the bills. Plus, the best way to prove my brother-in-law's innocence was to find the real killer.

Wayne closed the door and placed the evidence bag on the table in front of me. I mentally braced for the disorientation I would encounter from touching an object of violence. Pushing my entire body through a keyhole would be more pleasant.

"Would you wait by the door? Your energy is crowding me. I need space to work."

The sheriff obliged.

With confidence, I picked up the package, intending to open it and hold the hilt in both hands. There was no need. I tumbled into the spirit world, drawn by the anger and rage infused into the knife. I was bathed in Ritchie's despair and anguish. Faces of townspeople flashed before my eyes in dizzying array. Then Morgan.

Only Morgan had a dark spirit glommed onto his face, covering his mouth and nose like a shroud, shielding his eyes. He still wore the bloody shirt with knife holes slashed in it.

"Morgan?" I circled him.

He tugged at the thing on his face, but it wouldn't budge.

"Can you hear me, Morgan?"

He nodded.

"Who killed you?"

Silence.

"It was a Bubba, right?"

He nodded again, flailing at the thing on his face.

"Was it Bubba Jamison?"

Another spirit blocked Morgan from my view. "He can't talk now."

Dark emotions raged and seethed in this spirit. Fear clawed at my throat. Another demon? Why was I having such bad luck on my dreamwalks?

My chin went up. "I need to ask Morgan one question, then I'll go."

"Did you find Raymondia?" the demon intoned in ominous tones.

My head jerked up. "Rose? Is that you?"

The scary shape thinned and re-formed into a familiar tattooed woman with burning red eyes. "What did my sister say?"

Definitely Rose. Sort of. "She was hard to find. I left her a message on her phone."

"You didn't talk to her?"

"I called her a few minutes ago. The sheriff helped me obtain her phone number."

The tattooed woman doubled in size. "The sheriff? You sic the law on my sister?"

"No. He agreed to help me. I'm helping him with Morgan's killer. We have a deal."

Anger and rage roiled around the woman. The red eyes whirred in circles. "You didn't hold up your end of the bargain. Until you have a message from my sister, Morgan is off limits."

I reached for Rose. "Wait. That's not fair. I did my part. You changed the deal."

"My turf, my rules. Just so you don't forget your debt, I'll give you a reminder."

The dark cloud enveloped my fist. Skin burnt. I screamed and tumbled spastically back into my world. My hand. It felt as if acid were eating the flesh from my fingers. Sobs wracked my body.

"Baxley."

The far-away voice sounded familiar. A man's voice. "Roland?" I righted myself in the darkly shadowed world, ignoring the all-consuming stab of pain. Hope grew in leaps and bounds. "Roland, is that you? Where are you?"

Darkness surrounded me, and I whirled to another place and time. A brighter place. Someone grabbed my shoulder. I bolted up, ready to clock whoever had me.

Wayne caught my balled fists. "Easy. You've been out for almost thirty minutes."

I blinked as the room's walls slid into place. Wayne. The jail's interview room. An evidence bag on the table. My memory clicked. And my hand throbbed. I jerked it loose from his grip.

"Easy. I won't hurt you," Wayne soothed.

I held my hand to my face. A crude rose tattoo looked back

at me. I screamed. "Get it off! Get it off!"

Wayne kept his distance. "What?"

"Did you do this to me?"

He glanced at my arm. "A tat? Cool. When did you get a tattoo?"

"Just now. If you didn't do it, Rose did."

"Can they do that?"

"You didn't?"

He shook his head, eyes wide. "Do I look like a tattoo artist?"

I blinked back tears of pain and shock. "What am I going to do? I've got striped hair and a tattoo. If Roland's parents get word of my altered appearance, they will use it against me to gain custody of Larissa."

"Calm down. The Colonel and Elizabeth won't know about the tattoo unless you tell them. What about Morgan? Did you find him?"

"I did. Rose has him. She won't let him communicate with me until I get her a message back from Raymondia."

"You're serious?"

"As a heart attack. She's scary as all get out. And now I bear her mark. I hate this."

"Did you learn anything else?"

"On the way to the spirit world, I sensed Ritchie's despair and anguish."

"Got news for you. I sensed that, too, and I'm not even psychic. The man fell apart in front of us when he saw his brother dead. Anything useful?"

"A whirl of faces from town. No Bubbas."

"Damn Sam."

I stared at my throbbing hand. The skin wasn't broken, so no need to put antibiotic ointment or a protective bandage on it.

The demon's mark wouldn't pose a risk of regular infection. No telling what other infection it might bring. "My sentiments exactly."

# CHAPTER 29

After my tattoo disaster, I needed to clear my head before talking butterfly gardens with Muriel Jamison. I drove over to the Smiths' and walked their boxers. Peaches and Babyface sniffed the length of Lovett Road with joyful abandon, as usual, pulling heavily toward the two deserted homes on the street. After the structured walk, I let them romp a bit in their backyard.

Usually I enjoyed hanging out with them, seeing how excited they were about everything, but today I didn't feel on par with their inquisitive energy. Today I leaned against the white picket fence and let the bright sunshine drowse over me, hoping it would quiet the nagging sense of unease that had settled on my shoulders.

The racing dogs faded from view as latent concerns about the Gilroy family surfaced on my mental chalkboard. What happened to June? Who killed Morgan? The more I knew about the Bubbas, the more sinister each of them appeared.

And then there was my dad. He was no longer a young man who could push the boundaries of life with his mind or his body. I'd nearly lost him. I would have lost him without Rose's help. Of that I was certain.

I shuddered.

It was too soon to lose anyone else. There should be a rule that only one loved one could die in, say, every five years. Panic hit again. No, five years was too soon. Make that ten years, or twenty.

I steadied my breathing and another worry loomed. I'd dreamwalked with Bubba Paxton. And he'd known private information about me beforehand. How did a crackhead evangelist learn of my strengths and weaknesses? We were barely passing acquaintances. Did he spy on me in the dream world?

Dread pulsed into my veins, setting my frayed nerves on edge, activating the whispers that slithered around the corners of my mind. I glanced around, half expecting to see a ghostly legion of ancient soldiers with weapons drawn and aimed at me.

The treetops swayed overhead, serenading me with rustling oak leaves and palmetto fronds. Only the tranquil sounds didn't bring the customary sense of peace I normally felt out in nature. Instead, my unease increased.

Peaches darted past, slinging slobber on my leg as she chased Babyface. The dog's action startled me out of my musings. A glance overhead confirmed the tingling I sensed in my bones. The breeze stirring the treetops accompanied a bevy of dark clouds approaching rapidly from the south. Time to get the dogs in the house and move along.

A storm was coming.

I herded them inside, gave them each a treat, and refilled the water bowls before hurrying back out to my truck. In mid-stride, I paused, assuming an athletic crouch, tense and ready to leap in any direction. The wind stirred my hair, but something else stirred my senses.

A prickling sensation ruffled the fine hairs on my neck. My latent senses brightened to full alert at the realization I wasn't alone. My gaze swept the forested perimeter, the paved driveway, and the quaint cottage behind me. No physical threat was apparent, but I sensed something out there, some energy source that made me stop and take inventory of my immediate surroundings.

I scanned the woods line again, hoping the watcher was human and not something from the spirit world. The woods were the most logical place for a person to hide. Palm trees rustled, more oak leaves swirled past.

Summoning my courage, I called out, "Who's there?"

Doves cooed in the ensuing silence. The prickling sensation at my nape intensified. Someone was out there watching me. I was absolutely certain of it.

Was it friend or foe?

A few months ago, I'd felt someone watching me, and that someone had helped me catch a bad guy. Was this the same helpful person? Was it the killer?

Blood rushed through my ears, deafening me to all but the noisy pounding of my heart. Adrenaline spurted through my veins.

A killer was on the loose in our county. A killer I wanted to expose and send to jail so my brother-in-law would be safe from suspicion. Did the killer know I was looking for him?

The other homes on Lovett Road were vacant. No one could possibly hear a cry for help if I encountered more trouble than I could handle. The only person in earshot was the hidden person.

I didn't much like those odds.

I sprinted the remaining six steps to my truck, cranked her up and roared out of there. I pushed the truck for all she was worth, glancing in my rearview mirror as I sped down the highway. Hoping to see something of interest, something that would help me to understand what just happened.

All I saw was the worry reflected in my eyes and a thin ribbon of empty highway.

Someone had been watching me.

Why?

# CHAPTER 30

"I'm all right," I said.

Mama pushed a cracked mug of green tea into my trembling hands. "Drink this."

I glanced down at the worn kitchen table. What was I doing? Mama didn't need two patients to nurse. I shouldn't have stopped off here on my way to my landscaping appointment with Muriel Jamison. "I shouldn't have bothered you. You've got your hands full already."

Mama sat across from me, a second mug of tea in her hand. Comfort radiated from her person. The soft color of her jumper reminded me of a peaceful stream. "Nonsense. This is right where you're supposed to be. Tell me what frightened you."

I needed to tell someone. That must have been why I drove to my parents' house instead of directly to my appointment at Muriel Jamison's house. I exhaled a long breath. Steam from the tea filled my nostrils, warming the chill from my bones. "Two things. First, I dreamwalked this morning, ran into an angry spirit, and got tattooed."

She studied the tattoo on my hand. "Interesting."

"Did Daddy ever have anything like this happen in the spirit world and have the entity follow him home?"

"No entities, no tattoos."

"Will it go away?"

"Time will tell."

"I feel like a freak. Bad enough I have crazy hair. Now I've got a tattoo."

"Lots of people have tattoos. It's perfectly normal."

"I wish. I've never felt less normal."

"You said there were two things that upset you," Mama prompted.

"Someone was watching me over at the Smiths'. Roland taught me self-defense, but I wasn't thinking about fighting. Not with a killer on the loose in Sinclair County. All I thought about was running. Like a coward."

Mama's brown eyes clouded with concern.

I couldn't meet her intent gaze. I slurped in a sip of hot tea. My thoughts jumbled, worries past and present mixing with worries about the future. The weight of the world hung on my tensed shoulders. "When did it all get to be so hard, Mama? When did the worries and concerns of life become such heavy burdens that I can't even see anything else?"

Mama held her silence. I sipped my tea again, grateful for the beverage diversion. Outside, thunder boomed across the lowlands, the sound reverberating across the flat landscape. Wind gusted through the screened windows, billowing the faded tie-dyed curtains.

Rain fell. Big splatting drops followed by a thick curtain of water. Moisture penetrated the screens, dampening the air inside the small house. Mama made no move to shut the windows. She never did when it rained.

I gestured toward the rain-speckled counters. "How do you do it, Mama? How do you accept everything that happens?"

"I made peace with who I am years ago."

Her inactivity spurred me into motion. I jumped out of my chair and moved the open package of tea bags out of the high moisture zone. "I'm not like you. I can't sit by and do nothing."

She nodded encouragement.

"You're saying that's who I am, a person of action." If it

175

hadn't been for me, all of their staples would have spoiled years ago. I'd collected thrift-shop glass and metal canisters to protect the sugar, flour, grits, and rice. Those same canisters lined her counter today.

"That's part of who you are." Her voice sounded strained. "All we've ever wanted is for you to be who you are."

I glanced at her over my shoulder, worried. "I'm doing the best I can. I've got two jobs, three if you count the dreamwalking gig, and I still come up short sometimes. Life is hard. Too hard."

Her open expression shuttered. "You're not the only one who's ever shouldered the burdens of life. Troubles come at everyone hard and fast. Sure, life can stress you out if you let it. Your father and I made a conscious choice years ago—we don't get consumed by material things. Our treasure is people. That's what we set store in."

My jaw tightened. Old hurts boiled to the surface. "Nothing in this house has changed since I was a kid. It's still a hodgepodge of yard-sale rejects. What did you and Dad do with the money I sent home all those years?"

Mama's face glowed with joy. "We gave it away."

Anger sparked through me like sheet lightning. I paced the tiny room, past the rusted refrigerator, the gold stove with the white oven door, the formerly green table. "That money was meant for you, to better your life."

She smiled. "It did. The friends who received that money had nothing."

I leaned forward, splaying my palms on the table. Pent-up questions surged out. "How do you pay your taxes, Mama? How do you put gas in your car?"

Her smile dimmed. "Life isn't about the money. You don't understand."

In all these years, we'd never had this discussion. We'd danced around the truth, with me playing the role of dutiful daughter and them starring as my parents. Now that I had so many adult responsibilities, I couldn't allow the fiction of their carefree existence to stand without challenge. "Enlighten me. I want to know."

She recoiled as if I'd slapped her. "You know the answer. Be yourself. Put others first."

The room brightened as the sudden shower ceased, but my thoughts darkened. My parents were still free-spirited hippies, living on love with no visible means of support. Except maybe my father's herb farm or his brand new job as the county coroner. Were my parents the local drug kingpins?

My gut twisted at the possibility. I staggered away from the table, unable to ask, unwilling to know the answer to my parents' dubious income stream.

"I don't care for that look on your face, Baxley," Mama said.

I didn't care for it either, but I couldn't make it go away.

A rattletrap car coasted up to the back door. It had come through the grassy tract through the woods. People had been welcome at both our front and back doors for as long as I could remember. But now, the thought of someone approaching from the back lane seemed sinister. Stealth fed right into my worries that my parents might be dope dealers.

"You have company." To my credit, I didn't say she had a drug customer. Oh, but I wanted to say that to see how she would react to that label. But I couldn't give voice to my gnawing concerns. To do so would breach the trust she had in me. It would cause irreparable harm to our relationship.

Mama rose with fluid grace. "Think about what I said. If you stop being afraid, there will be room in your heart for other emotions."

How easy it sounded, to stop being afraid. How hard to implement. "Tell Daddy I came by."

She nodded toward their bedroom. "Tell him yourself. He's feeling much better today. The crystals you carried with you helped speed his healing this time."

One intense chat was all I could handle in a day. "Can't. I'm late for an appointment out at the north end."

Mama's lips tightened. She ambled toward the door and that rattletrap car of her visitors.

I hated to leave here this morning with this tension crackling between us. I wanted to put it right. "Thanks," I said. "Thanks for the tea, and thanks for listening."

Mama paused on the threshold, a genuine smile lighting her time-worn features. "You're welcome."

Her caring smile carried me out the front door. I did feel better. In spite of her needling, in spite of coming here terrified from a faceless threat, I felt much better.

Trees glistened with moisture; the lawn looked greener than it had in days; a squirrel scampered across a power line. Normal things. Normal, everyday things were things I could handle.

I looked forward to talking with Muriel Jamison about the landscaping job. If she wanted a replica of the library garden, it would be the easiest money I'd ever made.

I should have known that nothing about Muriel Jamison would be easy.

# CHAPTER 31

Muriel pointed to the jumble of magazines and catalogues beside the elegant crystal vase of blood-red roses. "That's what I want."

The heavy floral scent in the room smothered the exotic aroma that had greeted me when I first entered this soaring mausoleum. Like everything else in this place, the dining room furnishings were expensive and overstated. What must it be like to live in such a showcase?

I glanced at the oil paintings flanking the gleaming triple-mirrored buffet, the elegantly upholstered dining room chairs, the richly patterned Oriental rug hugging the cold slate floor. Each furnishing demanded a full, lingering inspection, but I had no time to gawk. Not with Muriel hot on the trail of a new garden. Urgency thrummed through my veins. I would build her the garden of her dreams.

But the multitude of glossy design elements pictured on her inlaid mahogany table stopped me cold. Dread flooded my body at the topiary gardens, wildflower jungles, formal courtyards, stepping stones, reflecting pools, soaring columns, shade plants, sun plants, Old World statuary, raised terraces, lily ponds, carved natural stone stairs, and more. It was too much for any one climate zone, budget, or single garden.

"You have excellent taste," I hedged. "If you had to choose one feature you couldn't live without, which would it be?"

"I thought you knew." Muriel's voice turned petulant. "I

want the fountain."

There were no fountains pictured in her examples. I frowned and jogged my memory. "The fountain at the library?"

"Yes. I want that one, only different. With tons more butterflies."

I tried not to sigh, but one slipped out anyway. I covered it by walking over to the French doors to view the acres of rolling lawn and the distant fields of salt marsh.

Nature I understood. People baffled me. With determination, I faced my prospective client again. "Where do you want the new landscaping installed?"

Muriel tapped the side of her face. Bracelets jangled, melodic and discordant. "Oh, the backyard, definitely. Unless you think it should go in the front?"

Her front yard had the acreage for every one of the gardens she'd shown me, but she'd need to hire a full-time gardener to keep everything manicured. Or she'd expect me to come back out here every week and prune it for free. Rich people often expected something for nothing. That wasn't happening.

Landscaping was my job. I couldn't give my services away, not when I had a kid to support.

Wait. What was I doing?

I barely knew Muriel. Worrying about our potential future relationship was a waste of energy. I needed to develop a business relationship with her, and for that, I needed her to sign a contract. From the looks of this place, she could afford anything she wanted.

"Fountains are nice visuals," I began. "If I installed a fountain in my yard, I'd want to enjoy it."

She nodded her coiffed head. I wasn't sure how she got her hair to look windswept and sultry. From her stylish thigh-length, swirled jacket to the Oriental fan–accented necklace in the same pattern as the jacket fabric, this woman had a strong concept of style.

"Like the one at the library." Interest lit her exotic eyes. "I love driving by and seeing the water flowing. I want oodles of wild flowers too, especially bright yellow ones. I want people to stop and take notice as they pass by. The bigger, the better."

Her enthusiasm filled me with dismay. Muriel's ideas for the landscaping treatment were different from mine. My gaze sidled over to my watch. I could spend the entire day hoping Muriel would see reason, or I could give her the tacky, ostentatious garden she wanted.

On the other hand, I had dogs to walk and a murder to solve.

I punted. "While the library's garden is indeed charming, a wildflower garden would be best suited to your backyard space."

Muriel scowled at me, the thin arches of her plucked brows drawing together like twin hilltops. "I'd like passersby to see my fountain."

Guiding a client was risky, but I stuck to my guns. This informal garden belonged behind her formal house. "They will. I'm quite certain your one-of-a-kind butterfly garden will be the rage of the cocktail circuit."

My client-to-be nodded with excitement. "Yes. That's exactly what I want."

I did a mental fist pump. Muriel could be guided. And even better, she could afford her top-dollar taste. This job took on a rosier glow.

"Muriel, where are my brown loafers?" a male voice boomed.

I turned at the intrusion. Bubba Jamison stomped into the dining room, his angry face unshaven, his plaid shirt untucked, his tanned feet bare beneath rumpled khaki slacks. He didn't resemble the suave guy I was accustomed to seeing about town.

This rough-looking man had a dangerous edge.

Morgan Gilroy's pale face zoomed into my thoughts. He'd

named his murderer. The killer could be Bubba Jamison. The excitement I'd felt about landing this career-making job departed in an instant, leaving in its place a breathless uncertainty. I forced myself to take a breath of rose-scented air.

Was this Bubba a stone-cold killer? If so, standing here in his house, planning to spend days alone digging in his isolated yard was not a good idea. Even worse, my presence here was decidedly dangerous if Bubba Jamison knew of my suspicions. Much worse if he'd been the watcher over at the Smiths' house earlier this morning.

Breath stalled in my lungs as I froze, a gazelle at the watering hole of lions.

"I expect they're right where you left them." Muriel gave a negligent wave of her hand. Bracelets jangled from the motion.

Bubba marched up to his wife, sending a blast of alcohol-laden breath my way. "Don't get smart with me. Where are my shoes?"

His anger lashed out at me on the psychic plane. My fight or flight instinct triggered again at the seemingly disproportionate emotion over a pair of missing shoes. I could bolt out the French doors, race around the house, and speed away in my trusty pickup.

Only, his high-performance vehicles could surely catch me before I hit civilization again. Where would that leave Muriel? Did he intend to do her harm?

"Find your own darn shoes." To Muriel's credit, she didn't flinch or back down in the face of his strong emotion. "I'm not your maid."

He stomped off, the slap of his bare feet loud on the slate floor.

I inhaled my relief. "I should go."

"Don't. Please stay." She leaned toward me and spoke in a whisper. "Bubba's been acting strange lately."

No kidding. It wasn't lunchtime yet, and he was sloshed. Not a good sign for their marriage. Even if this was atypical behavior, the man was rattled. Something had pushed him out of his comfort zone.

Was it murder?

# CHAPTER 32

Fear trickled down my spine like beads of sweat. The Jamisons' house was luxurious and plush, but if it was the home of a murderer, this place was a deadly Venus's-flytrap. One snap of its powerful jaws and I would be dinner.

I didn't want to be a victim.

I wanted to live a long life, to see my parents age gracefully, to see my beautiful daughter flower into womanhood. I needed to get out of here.

I fumbled for my business satchel. "I've caught you at a bad time. Let me sketch out my ideas, and we'll talk contracts another time."

Muriel's dark eyes flashed in alarm. "Not on your life. I want my garden installed as soon as possible."

How quickly could I sprint out of here? My life was sacred to me, a precious gift I could ill afford to waste. Was I in danger? Why couldn't I tell?

I summoned a desperately professional smile, the one that was both authoritarian and reassuring, and hoped God didn't strike me dead for lying about my schedule. "I would like to accommodate you, but my previously scheduled jobs have priority."

Thoughts spinning wildly, I pulled out my calendar and considered the mostly empty pages. How long would it take me to figure out who killed Morgan Gilroy? One week? Two? I didn't want to be stuck out here alone until Morgan's killer was

184

behind bars. "My first opening for a job this size is two weeks from now."

Muriel wrinkled her thin nose. "That won't do. My parents are visiting in two weeks. I want them to see my new fountain."

My smile tightened. "Even if the exact fountain you want is locally available, installing it and landscaping the area with mature plants wouldn't give you the same immediate effect as the library. It takes time for a constructed space to look natural and to attract butterflies."

"Buy the damn butterflies. I want the garden done in two weeks. I'll pay extra for a rush job. In fact, I'll give you a five-thousand-dollar retainer right now."

I could do a lot with five grand. Visions of paid tax bills, full larders, and new, "normal" clothes for Larissa swirled through my thoughts.

I didn't know for sure that Bubba Jamison was the murderer. And if I took the Jamison job, I could keep an eye on his comings and goings. I'd stay one step ahead of the sheriff.

The lure of easy money beat the safe approach hands down. "I'll make it work."

"Wonderful." Muriel produced a checkbook. Both the leather checkbook cover and the checks were embossed with a giant M. "I knew this was going to work out. We already had such a great initial connection. We were destined to work together."

I groaned inside. Whatever she meant, it couldn't be good. "I don't follow you."

Her pen slanted over a check. "Our interest in the beyond."

"Excuse me?"

"The beyond." At my confused look, she clarified. "The whole dreamwalker thing. I want to also talk with you about visiting with Aunt Eugenia. I have a message to get to her."

I sucked in a slow rose-flavored breath. Muriel was a little whacked out, but if her checks were good and she left me alone to do my job, she could be as flaky as she wanted. She handed me the check and signed my standard contract without glancing at the fine print.

"Do you want to go through the contract first before we change subjects?" I asked.

"I trust you. With us having the same interests, you won't screw me."

I studied the check, making sure she'd signed it, making sure that the zeros where were they were supposed to be. It felt darned good to see those zeroes on a check made out to me, darned good to know I wouldn't have to worry about this month's bills.

"Let me show you around the house before you leave," Muriel said.

I made polite noises at the swanky furniture, the ornate drapes, the original art, and vaulted ceilings, but I didn't know what to say about the last room she showed me. Oversized animal heads protruded from every wall. There were bears here, bobcats, big-racked deer, two wild boars, a buffalo, and some animals I didn't recognize. A zebra-looking animal pelt lay on the floor between two leather-covered chairs.

"Wow." I hoped this animal display was fake, that they had decided on an outdoor theme for this very masculine room.

"It takes your breath away, doesn't it? Bubba hunts big game across the country and overseas. He used to go with my daddy, but then he found a group from down here that hunts more primitively. Bubba chased down that wild boar on foot with a hunting knife."

I blinked at the animal head she'd pointed to. Boars were fierce. Running one down with a knife was aggressive. Very much like something a killer would do.

My fingers and toes tingled. I gagged on the lump in my throat. I had to get out of there right now. "I'm late for another appointment. Thanks for the tour."

I hurried out of her house. A few miles away, I pulled into the busy parking lot of a country convenience store to settle my nerves.

Bubba Jamison had a dangerous, mean edge. He'd been a doctor before he retired here. He was experienced at hand-to-hand combat with knives. He had a drinking problem. And he'd been one of Morgan's business partners.

Could it be that simple? Were those facts enough to establish motive for Bubba Jamison as a killer? My hands tightened on the steering wheel. My vision blurred as I marshaled my thoughts.

I should call the sheriff. I should let him know that he'd turned a vengeful murderer loose on our town. I should tell him to bring all of his deputies and arrest Bubba Jamison.

There was a sharp rap on my rolled-up truck window.

I startled and glanced up to see scrawny Bubba Paxton leering in my window, a demonic look on his austere features. I gulped.

Oh, no.

Another Bubba.

# CHAPTER 33

Heart racing, I eased the window down to greet the crackhead evangelist. He was dressed like me in jeans, a T-shirt, and work boots. "Hey, Bubba."

"I thought that was you," he said in a soothing voice. "I need a favor."

Crap.

After last night, I owed him a favor. I did not want to be in his debt, but I had no idea what he wanted from me. The fevered look in his dark eyes worried me as much as my recent brush with Bubba Jamison.

My skin crawled as I calculated the risk of talking to a Bubba. Cars putzed around in the busy parking lot. People bustled in and out of the convenience store. I was relatively safe here. If I screamed, someone would help me.

From my depths, I summoned a measure of external calm. "Yes?"

Light and shadow played over his gaunt face. "A friend of mine got into some trouble with the law—"

"Imagine that." I refused to be gentled by his modulated voice.

He scowled at me, his voice roughening. "It wasn't his fault. That bust was totally bogus. The drugs were planted on him. Anyway, my buddy's serving time, and he needs someone to look after his pets."

Business. I could deal with a business conversation. I quoted him my daily pet-sitting rates. No way was I cutting my fee for his druggie friend. I didn't want to cultivate a low-end clientele. I had my reputation to consider.

Bubba's head jerked back. "Nah, he can't pay. His assets got confiscated. He's got nothing but the shirt on his back, so I'm helping him out. I'll keep the snakes . . ." His voice trailed off.

Maybe it was the stricken look on my face that stopped him. Or maybe it was the burst of adrenaline that puffed up my chest and had me shaking a finger at him. "Darn right you will. I only do dogs and cats. Nothing slithery."

He nodded in a considering manner. "I'll keep the feeder mice, too. It's the yippy dog that's the problem. The thing hides from me and pees on my clothes. He hates me. I can't get anyone else to take him. Please do me the favor of keeping him for a few months."

My head reeled. Snakes and feeder mice, oh my. I didn't want anything to do with that part of the animal kingdom. Give me a snarling dog or a hissing cat any day.

If I had to choose, I'd take the peeing dog over the other critters hands down, but why should I be saddled with a druggie's dog? There would be vet bills and food costs. Much as I loved animals, I couldn't take on another financial burden.

I opened my mouth to say no, and I fully expected to say no, but something else came out. "Show me your setup for the dog. Maybe I can suggest something that will make his stay more tolerable."

Relief edged through his eyes. He smiled for the first time since he'd approached me. "Great. I mean, it's not as great as you taking him, but if you could keep him from peeing everywhere it would be a big help." He glanced over at his tricolored rust bucket of a car. "You want to ride with me to save your gas? I'll bring you right back."

Panic shot through me. I was not getting stuck in someone's

vehicle again. That's how I'd gotten caught up in Morgan Gilroy's death in the first place. I'd much rather be in control of my own destiny.

I didn't know if Bubba Paxton was in the clear for Morgan's murder, but he'd helped me bring Daddy back from that dreamwalk. If he'd wanted to kill me, all he'd have had to do was push me off the crystal bridge last night. I would have been as lost as Daddy.

This Bubba had made a few wrong turns, but he was making amends to society. Those didn't sound like the actions of a killer.

I hoped like crazy that my assessment was correct. I was banking my life on it.

In any event, I wasn't riding with him. "No, thanks. I'll follow you. Let me get a soda first from inside."

He nodded and retreated to his vehicle. In minutes, I was following Bubba Paxton to Pax Out, a church I'd vowed never to step foot in. The sugary drink boosted my energy, so that I felt nearly human by the time we pulled into the grassy parking lot.

Pax Out had gone up seemingly overnight. Like most other prefabricated metal buildings in our area, the church was tethered to a concrete floor. Mounds of earth graced the side yard; half a dozen port-a-lets stood like soldiers bordering the parking area. From the looks of the excavation trenches, it appeared they were installing the septic system.

A putrid smell wafted in my truck. I wrinkled my nose.

Raw sewage.

Ugh.

No wonder the little doggie hated it here. With his sensitive nose, this stench would be intolerable. Poor thing.

We parked beside the little wooden cottage on the back edge of the two-acre property. The weathered structure needed a coat of paint and a new tin roof.

In spite of my efforts to be objective, doubts crept in. I couldn't stop thinking what was inside that house. Snakes. Mice. And a misbehaving dog. I berated myself for thinking this was a good idea. I knew better than this. My muscles tensed.

The sagging stairs groaned as we walked up to the door. I reviewed my plan of action: poke my head in the door, suggest he take better care of the dog, and haul ass.

As the door opened, I heard a dreaded sound of my childhood nightmares, the warning rattle of a dangerous snake. I'd been only five, but I'd come upon a rattlesnake in the woods near our home. Fear froze my limbs and saved my life. Later, my father said I'd been very brave, but I knew different. I'd been inches from death. After that, I never walked in the woods without a grown-up or a big stick.

That same paralyzing fear caught me. I couldn't move a muscle. Inside were four huge illuminated glass cages of snakes and an oversized aquarium of white mice squeaking. From the corner of the room came the insistent high-pitched yip of a small dog.

The handgun tucked under the seat of my truck was of no comfort. It was too far away to save me. What had I done? Why had I let this murder suspect talk me into coming here?

"Shut up," Bubba Paxton roared. He turned to me. "See what I mean? The dog is useless. He hides and barks and pees. Come on in. I'll show you his food bowl."

Nope. I wasn't going in there. Not when the place was loaded with killer snakes. I inhaled shakily, imbibing a nauseating brew of human sewage, dog urine, and a thick musk coming from the snakes. I took a step back.

"Watch that board," Bubba warned through the sharp yipping of the dog. He grabbed my forearm as the rotten board gave, hauling me to safety on the threshold. I was awed at his strength. He wasn't any bigger than I was, but there was no way

I could have lifted someone with one arm like he did.

My heart pounded in my throat. I didn't want to be here, and I especially didn't want to go into Bubba's crumbling house. "I can't," I managed to say.

"What? I can't hear you over the stupid dog. Hold up a minute." With that, Bubba stomped inside, past the rattling snakes and squeaking mice. "Come here, you little ingrate."

The dog's high-pitched yap grew louder and more insistent. The odor of fresh urine wafted toward me. I knew how terrified the little guy felt, trapped in there with those deadly serpents. I'd pee myself, too, if I had those things for roommates.

Heck, I'd have to check my undies when I got home as it was.

Bubba got down on hands and knees and chased the dog around, cornering him behind the shabby easy chair. If I was watching this on television, I might think it was funny, but this snake-infested house was no laughing matter.

The dog's protests changed to pitiful crying, melting my heart. "Don't hurt him," I said.

Bubba stood, a quivering Chihuahua secured in his large hands. "Not a chance that I'd hurt him. But he bit me twice, which I don't understand. I don't get small dogs. Give me a hunting dog any day."

As he walked toward me, I tried to block the sound of the rattling snakes. "Do you hunt?"

He snorted as if I'd asked a stupid question. "Yeah."

"How does that fit with your new persona as a peaceful preacher?"

He shrugged as if there was no ethical conflict. "Hey, I gotta put food on my table. Plus when the mice run out, I'll need to supply these beauties with small game."

The doggie in his hands howled. I couldn't leave this terrified baby here with these snakes. I just couldn't. "What's his name?"

"Elvis. My buddy Charlie has quite a sense of humor, eh?"

I reached over and scratched the furry place between his ears, cooing at the little pooch. "May I hold him?"

"No problem."

He transferred the dog to me. I felt the animal's heart racing through his thin skin. The poor thing probably thought he was snake food. "Shh," I soothed, gentling his tremors with my voice and my touch. I glanced up at Bubba. "He can't stay here. He's too afraid."

Bubba nodded. "Will you take him? I know it's asking a lot, but I hate to see this little guy so scared."

Elvis pulled himself together enough to lick my face. My heart melted. How much trouble could one little doggie be? "Who's his vet? How long are we talking about?"

"I have that information. So you'll do it? You'll keep him for Charlie?"

I mentally kicked myself to the highway and back for being a softie. But I had no real choice. This environment was unacceptable for this dog. "How long?"

"Just a coupla weeks, two months tops. He should get out in May. I've got his food and he's up to date on all his shots."

I sighed out a deep breath. "Okay. For a few weeks. I'll do it."

"Thanks. You won't regret it."

A few moments later, I had Elvis stashed in my truck, his gear on my floor mat. He bounded up to the top of the bench seat and barked all the way back to town.

My ears rang. Oh, man, this was going to be a long few weeks.

I got my revenge when I wrestled the dog into the kitchen sink and washed out four pounds of dirt from his coat. He ultimately submitted to my ministrations and I thought I'd seen the last of his overexcitement.

But as soon as my back was turned, he took off after my

other client's pet, the Maine Coon cat, who'd been watching the proceedings from the doorway. Sulay fluffed out her fur, stood her ground, and swiped the smaller dog with a razor-sharp paw. Elvis yipped, halted, and dashed under the kitchen table. Muffin, the Shih Poo I'd inherited from a wayward client, watched from a chair.

The house filled with blessed silence.

Finally.

With balance restored, I set about doing the rest of my chores. I took care of my other pet clients, cashed Muriel's check, and sat on my patio to sketch out a wildflower garden for the Jamisons. The early afternoon sunshine warmed my shoulders, loosened my thoughts. I was no closer to learning who killed Morgan Gilroy, unable to solve June Gilroy's loss at sea, and unwilling to face my father after his near disaster at the jail.

Birds chirped noisily around me, and I drowsed in that peaceful half-asleep, half-awake world. I didn't have the resources of the sheriff's office to solve a crime, and I for darned sure didn't want to upset Louise Gilroy by asking questions about her shaky marriage and missing child.

If my daughter went missing, I'd come apart at the seams. Larissa was my top priority, and as long as I kept that in the forefront of my thoughts, I'd be fine.

A dark cloud passed over the sun and the birds quieted. An unsettling feeling came over me again, that slide of cool air over the ruffled hairs on my arm. I shivered, certain that someone was out there in the not-so-distant woods line, that someone was watching me.

But who?

And why?

With trembling hands, I gathered my stuff in what I hoped wasn't too rushed a fashion. Heart racing, I strolled inside and locked the door. I pulled a knife from my knife block and inched closer to the gun safe.

My home was secure, but I wasn't.

When would this faceless enemy strike?

# CHAPTER 34

On Saturday, mourners packed into the upright pews of tiny St. Luke's Episcopal Church. White and black rubbed elbows with the rich and poor in the humid, darkly paneled church. Thick clouds of perfume clotted the air, hitching in my throat as I leaned against the back paneled wall and dreamed of drawing a full breath again.

In his white robes, portly Father Silas proclaimed Morgan had gone to a better place. He'd gone all right, but the trip hadn't been his idea. Some Bubba had assisted him, quite possibly a Bubba in this church. I tuned out the fervent prayers and nearly inaudible amens as I searched for the Bubbas.

My brother-in-law occupied a prime front-row spot in the Gilroy pew. Morgan's ex-wife, Patty Gilroy, rested her blond head on Bubba Powell's broad shoulder, her seventeen-year-old daughter bridging the gap between Patty and Morgan's brother. Connie Lee's finger absently twirled in her shoulder-length dark hair. The entire pew appeared to be listening to the minister, but I had my doubts about Bubba's attention span.

He'd skated from one dicey situation to another his entire life, always hoping for a big score to make his father proud, but his efforts were in vain. The Colonel expected his sons to be soldiers, only Bubba never fit the mold. He'd been a goofy guy who'd lost the girl he loved. Now he was back in his childhood sweetheart's good graces. Would Patty keep him grounded and focused?

I'd never seen my brother-in-law in this charcoal-gray suit before. Bubba's left arm extended along the top of the pew. That flashy gold watch looked new, as did the gleaming cuff links. None of the items were standard department store fare. Did he come into some money recently? Why didn't I know about it?

I loved Bubba Powell like a brother, but in many ways he was a stranger. He'd talked to Roland and me about his get-rich-quick schemes, but we'd never talked about his hopes and dreams. He'd had a boom-or-bust mentality as long as I'd known him.

Maybe the upgraded clothing was a new aspect of his wheeler-dealer image. Or maybe Ritchie Gilroy had lent him a high-end suit so that he wouldn't disgrace the family. Stranger things had happened.

Louise Gilroy's pillbox hat and minimalist black dress looked New York chic and ultra feminine. With her pale coloring, she resembled a fragile china doll on display, except for her trembling lower lip, which I noted when she turned her head. Were the minister's words of solace a comfort or salt in her wound? Would she finally be moved to arrange a memorial service for her missing daughter?

Three rows back, Mama sat beside Bubba and Eunice Wright. Mama's lime-green jumper had seen better days; so had Eunice's shiny chartreuse suit. Bubba Wright sat perfectly still between the color-splashed women, his head bowed in prayer. This Bubba had won the battle against Morgan by hanging on to his waterfront property, but at what cost?

Had Bubba Wright paid for his victory with his soul?

Across the carpeted aisle and four rows back, scrawny Bubba Paxton was wedged between two plus-sized women, reminding me of a junior-sized burger slapped onto a giant sesame-seed bun. Was he looking at the packed house and wishing he had the same attendance at Pax Out?

As I watched, he turned and a smile flitted across his thin lips. I glanced up in time to catch Connie Lee beam one back at him. The friendly gesture alarmed me. Were Bubba Paxton and Connie Lee a couple? She was a minor and he knew better. He must have felt my gaze. He turned and stared back at me. I did not get the same welcoming smile he'd flashed Connie Lee. If anything, his dark gaze narrowed in a calculating manner.

Another flash of movement caught my attention in the back row where Bubba Jamison slouched in the aisle seat. To get such a prized spot in an Episcopal church, the Jamisons must have arrived an hour early. Muriel fidgeted beside him, poking at her hair, plucking invisible lint from her navy-blue sheath, searching for items in her designer purse. I didn't understand Muriel's distress, and I didn't get why her husband didn't try to quiet her down.

Dulcet tones poured from the pipe organ and the assembly clambered to its feet. Charlotte stood on tiptoe, leaned in, and whispered, "Where's Larissa?"

I leaned close to her ear. "Daddy's watching her." Sheriff Wayne Thompson stood between me and the door, his thickly muscled arms barred across his chest, exerting untold pressure on the shoulder seams of his suit coat. He scanned the crowd as well. Did he know which Bubba had killed Morgan?

Finally, the minister and the Gilroy family filed out, concluding the service. Mourners rose, gathered their things, and conversed in hushed tones. Charlotte and I joined the queue heading through the church to the catered reception at the parish house.

Charlotte spoke softly out of the side of her mouth. "There's a murderer here."

I shot her a worried glance. "You know something?"

She shrugged. "Every armchair detective watches the funeral

to collar the murderer. Wayne was looking. So were you."

"Charlotte!" I shot her a heated warning glance. "We're in a church. At a funeral. Show some respect."

"Don't play the respect card on me." She squared her rounded shoulders. Light glinted off her glasses. "If I'm going to stay on top of my game, I need an angle to cover the funeral."

"Leave well enough alone, Charlotte. You don't want to draw the killer's attention."

"Bah. A killer wouldn't come after me. I'm the press. I am their conduit to the world. I have built-in immunity."

We trudged into the covered walkway between the church and parish hall. Fresh air replaced the perfumed stew in my head. Relieved, I drew in a deep breath. "You keep thinking that way and Bernard Rivers will be writing your obituary."

"Killjoy." Charlotte pinched her nose. The din of conversation around us rose with each step we took. She leaned in close again. "I have to capitalize on my momentum, or I'll wind up on the back row again. What if we're looking at this the wrong way? What if all the suspects are guilty?"

I scoffed. "Get real. Organizing a crime of that complexity would take a mastermind. Who could pull that off? None of the sheriff's persons of interest are brain-trust material."

"I disagree. A brain trust isn't necessary," Charlotte said. We signed the guest book by the door and strolled toward the elegant crystal punch bowls. She leaned in to me again. "Motivation is the key. If we only knew who wanted Morgan dead the most, we'd have our mastermind."

"Interesting theory."

Across the jam-packed room, Connie Lee embraced Bubba Paxton. Due to that furtive smile they'd exchanged in church, I watched them like a hawk, half-expecting to see an extra caress, an intimate glance, something that would tip me off as to the true nature of their relationship. Disappointment surged as I saw nothing out of the ordinary. They seemed genuinely happy to see each other.

On the other hand, Bubba Powell and Patty Gilroy were not happy about the prolonged embrace. Their rigid body language and scowling faces told a much different story. Bubba Powell didn't want Bubba Paxton anywhere near Connie Lee.

Why?

I needed to know.

Bubba Paxton pivoted on his heel and left the building. His sudden exodus piqued my curiosity.

"See that?" Charlotte jerked her thumb toward Bubba's back. "It proves my point. This place is loaded with undercurrents and intrigue."

At least four people, including inveterate gossip Mrs. Grumble, overhead Charlotte's unfortunate remark. I grabbed Charlotte's arm. "Bathroom. Now."

She tried to jerk free. "Oh, for Pete's sake, Baxley. Chill out."

My grip tightened. I hauled her out of the fray, so angry I couldn't speak. I backed into the bathroom. Stella Arnot had decided ten years ago that this room needed a feminine touch, and she'd wallpapered the small space with giant roses, making it seem even smaller. Everyone hated it, but no one wanted to pull the wallpaper down and start over.

"What?" Charlotte said. "What is wrong with you?"

The middle stall was occupied. I placed a finger to my lips and caught Charlotte's eye.

Her eyes lit with comprehension. She moved toward the mirror and renewed her mauve lipstick.

The commode flushed and a teary-eyed Muriel walked out. With a curt nod our way, she washed her hands and exited.

The door closed behind her. "Did you see that?" Excitement animated Charlotte's features. She jabbed me with her elbow. "Muriel was pale and crying. No one else, not even Louise Gilroy, cried during or after the service. This means something."

She had me there.

Delight warred with common sense. I could take care of myself if this got ugly, but Charlotte was a marshmallow. She could easily get snared in the killer's web. If she got hurt, it was on my head. I'd dragged her into this mess.

I rubbed where she'd jabbed my stomach. "Time out. This isn't a game. The stakes are real. Morgan's killer is no lightweight. He killed once to remove a threat. If he perceives you to be a threat, you could be his next victim."

For a second she wavered and I hoped she'd take heed of my warning. I should've known better. Charlotte was at least half bloodhound; she wasn't about to be put off the scent.

She got in my face. "Don't be like this. Don't shut down my ideas. I'm on to something with the Bubbas, aren't I?"

I remembered hearing Morgan whisper "Bubba done it." Charlotte had seen the collection of Bubbas at the jail. Plus, she was my best friend. I hated keeping secrets from her. I crossed to lock the bathroom door and hoped I was doing the right thing.

I reached around her and locked the door. "You are on the right track as far as I can tell, and it scares the snot out of me." I swallowed thickly. "You've got to let the sheriff do his job."

"I want this." Her voice trembled with emotion. "You had a life out there in the world. All I've ever known is Sinclair County. I want to experience other cultures, but I've been stuck here my entire life."

She wouldn't listen to reason. The chance to achieve her dream reporter job was blinding her to the danger. I had to do something. "Do you own a gun?"

"No. Do I need one?"

I parroted one of Roland's pet phrases. "Every household should have at least one gun. I'll lend you a handgun."

She turned from me, resting both hands on the sink. "I hate guns. I'm a lousy shot."

"You're my best friend. Come by and get my pistol this afternoon. Keep it in your nightstand."

She blinked rapidly and then lifted her gaze to meet mine in the mirror. "You think I need a gun?"

"Yes. Have you noticed anything suspicious? Like someone following you?"

Fear coursed through her eyes. "No." She was quiet for a moment. "This is serious, isn't it?"

"Deadly serious."

An insistent pounding on the bathroom door startled me. Charlotte scurried behind me. I opened the door.

"What's going on in here?" Mama's hand stayed coiled in a tight fist. In her lime-green dress, she looked like a slender glass of lime sherbet.

"Baxley is refreshing my funeral etiquette." Charlotte edged past my mother. "Now that I've mastered the course, I'm due for my reward, which I plan to take in crab dip."

Mama stepped into the void, hands planted on her hips. "Why won't you speak to your father?"

# CHAPTER 35

A little voice whispered in my ear to flee. Another voice whispered that it was too late. I clung to the door handle wishing for salvation. I knew the Lord kept his eye on the sparrow, but I wasn't sure he watched Sunday school bathrooms. That was probably an invasion of privacy.

My gut tightened. I did not want to have this conversation. I'd rather be fondling white mice in Bubba Paxton's snake shack than trying to keep a lid on Mama in a public place. "I will talk to him."

"Humph." Mama squinted at me, an aging gunslinger inappropriately garbed in a bright dress. Her long braid shook as she spoke. "Here it is Saturday, and you haven't spoken a word to him since Wednesday. Tab thinks you're mad at him."

Sadie and Caroline Parker edged up close behind my mother. An outsider might think there was a line for the bathroom. But everyone in town knew the Parker sisters kept the phone wires humming with the latest gossip. I thanked my lucky stars that they weren't hardwired into the Internet or the entire world would already think I was mad at my father.

Keeping one eye on the gossip duo, I tried to defuse Mama's anger. "I'm coming by the house after the funeral, Mama. I have to pick up Larissa."

"You don't fool me. You're gonna blow in and out of there like a summer thunderstorm. Your father needs more than that. You saw how vulnerable he was the other night. This is serious."

It was serious. Which was exactly why I didn't want to have this conversation in public. Hell, I didn't even want to have it in private. But this setting was worse, much worse. I didn't want my secrets bandied around the church bathroom or anywhere else in town. "I will talk to him, Mama."

"Promise?"

My shoulders sagged. "Promise."

Mama fixed me with a stern look. "I'm tolerant of many things, but your father's feelings aren't to be trifled with. You do the right thing, or this could get downright unpleasant."

A sinkhole opened in my gut. Mama and Daddy acted like free spirits most of the time, but they had plenty of unwritten rules they expected me to follow. Guilt rode me hard.

She was right. I had been avoiding my father. I didn't want to talk about his near miss in the psychic realm, and I certainly didn't want to discuss his findings. Once we talked, I would have to think about things I avoided, things that I'd swept under the rug to survive.

I could get mad at Mama for loving Daddy more than me, but what was the point? Her husband was hurting and in her mind, I had the power to make it right. A power which I didn't care to invoke at the moment.

I edged past her, nodded at the pastel-clad gossip sisters, and made a beeline for the dessert table. Chocolate was the solace I craved. Who needed lunch when there was chocolate to be had? I was halfway through my third brownie and on the road to recovery when Bo Seavey, the coroner-turned-bartender, tapped me on the shoulder.

"Baxley, long time, no see." Even in his dark suit, Bo appeared to be all elbows and knees.

"You saw me on Monday, you old goat."

"And we were going to get a drink together at the Fiddler Hole."

"I don't do drinks with strange men."

"Dr. Sugar is no stranger. You've known me your entire life."

I gestured with my brownie before taking another bite. "Exactly my point. Anyone who was the county coroner for decades is a strange person."

"Now, now, no need to cast slurs on my professional resume. You don't see me saying that you're rolling in dog poop or drowning in poison ivy."

The rash on my leg was almost gone, but his mention of poison ivy brought back the need to scratch the itchy skin full force. I swallowed wrong and coughed up a piece of brownie. He clouted me on the back, knocking me off balance. For a man of slight build, his punch had some heat in it.

"Easy there, Dr. Sugar," I said. "I have no intention of having a date with the autopsy table."

"You'll recover, sweet thing. If you change your mind about that drink, let me know."

I waded through the perfumed crowd and sucked down another glass of very tart fruit punch. My eyes watered but I didn't dare cough for fear of attracting Dr. Sugar again. I covered my mouth with my hand and cleared my throat a few times.

Automatically, I scanned the room for Bubbas. Bubba Jamison had his hand on teary-eyed Muriel's shoulder. Funerals must not be her thing. Bubba Powell stood beside Patty and both of them watched Connie Lee like hawks. Bubba Wright and Eunice were seated at the table with other shrimpers, chowing down on the luncheon. I didn't know how often they got meals from the Yummie Shop, but they were putting a dent in these fancy groceries.

Charlotte made her way around the room, talking to people about Morgan. I hoped someone had a good word to say about the man. Otherwise, Charlotte would end up with a negative piece about a selfish man.

A woman I recognized from the bank greeted me. At her side was a woman I couldn't place. My look of confusion prompted an introduction.

"You remember Aunt Bubba, don't you, Baxley?" the bank woman said.

I managed a polite smile, but ice formed in my heart. The ground seemed to shift. Would I plunge into the vats of hell? "Sure. It's nice to see you again, ma'am."

A few minutes later, I made my excuses and headed straight for the sheriff. His knowing smile broadened as I approached. I'm sure he hoped I'd meet him in the storage closet for a quickie. He could keep dreaming. That wasn't going to happen.

"We've got a problem," I said. "There are more Bubbas."

# Chapter 36

A muscle ticked in Sheriff Wayne Thompson's clean-shaven cheek. He motioned me into an empty Sunday school room off the social hall, closing the door behind us. "Don't go asking for trouble," he said.

Neither his sharp tone nor his puffed up chest impressed me. "I'm not a deputy you can boss around. I'm Jane Q. Citizen offering you a tip to help solve your case."

He stepped closer, moving into my personal space, his cheap cologne as offensive as the perfumed church had been. His proximity rattled my nerves. What did he expect? Someone had to do his job.

His nostrils flared a bit. "You said, and I quote, 'we've got a problem.' That's not a public service announcement. That's Baxley sticking her nose where it doesn't belong. Stay out of this."

"Bubba Powell is my brother-in-law."

"Bubba Powell isn't your responsibility."

"Like hell he isn't. Roland watched out for him and so will I."

"You're no elite Special Forces operative. You consult for me on my terms, and I say give this a rest for now. No point in stirring up a hornets' nest."

I forced in a deep breath, searching for calm in this maelstrom of emotion. "I can take care of myself. Roland taught me self-defense."

Sensual awareness flashed through his heated gaze. "Want to go one-on-one with me? Think you could take me?"

I got right in his face. "Get over yourself, Wayne. I'm not interested in dating you. I want to close this case. There has to be something more I can do."

The air thickened in the small space. "With the dreamwalking pipeline shut down by that Rose woman, there's not much else you can do. Whoever killed Morgan could strike again, and I don't want to put you in jeopardy."

I waved off his caution. "You've already looked at Bubba Paxton, Powell, Jamison, and Wright. Now there's Aunt Bubba and God knows how many more Bubbas we've overlooked."

"Aunt Bubba? You mean Viola Hornshaw?" He scoffed and stepped back. "She couldn't drive a knife into a man's heart like the killer did. Aunt Bubba is not an official suspect, whereas the four men you named are persons of interest."

"Bubba Powell didn't do it."

He leaned down into my face. "Powell is screwing the ex-wife. He's got motive."

I ignored his macho display. "Bubba never stopped loving Patty. Her father forced them apart. They're finally living out their love."

He straightened and shook his head dismissively. "If Patty and Bubba wanted in each other's pants back then, parental disapproval wouldn't keep them apart."

My jaw dropped. Were we talking about the same people? "I don't believe you."

He fingered a strand of my white forelock. I'd worn my crazy hair loose today instead of hemmed in by its customary ponytail. "Sweetheart, you were the only virgin in our graduating class. Every other female in school put out on a regular basis. Your virginity was a hot topic back then. We all wanted to do you, even your precious Roland."

My weight shifted to the balls of my feet. My fists clenched at my side. "Roland wasn't like that."

Wayne snorted. "He sure had you snowed. He was exactly like that. Now he's gone and you're here alone. With me. What do you say we make up for lost time?"

I could take him down. He deserved it, but assaulting a law enforcement officer would complicate my life. I skirted around him, edging closer to the door and freedom. "Not a chance. Find another Bubba. Mine didn't do it."

"Get laid and quit causing problems for me."

I exited the classroom, grateful for the normality of heavily perfumed air and the thick buzz of conversation. Wayne Thompson had a lot of nerve, saying those nasty things about Roland.

Food.

I needed food.

Should I go dessert, fruity drink, or main course? Shrimp fisherman Bubba Wright passed by with a plate heaped with steamed shrimp. That looked good. Bertie Robins passed by with a piece of Mrs. Day's Cocola cake. Hmm. That looked good, too. Real good.

Dessert it was.

My path to the heavenly bliss took me past Bubba Wright again. I heard him laughing about his early-warning system. The others laughed, too. Willy Plano asked Bubba about playing the race card.

"I'll play every card I got if it lets me keep what's mine," Bubba Wright said.

His gaze caught mine, and I was stunned by the fierce heat in it. For the first time, I saw steely determination in him. Violence, too. There was no doubt in my mind that Bubba Wright could take extreme measures to protect his dock and Shrimp 'n' Stuff business.

I hurried away, selected the largest piece of pre-sliced cake, and dug into the mouthwatering treat. There weren't too many slices of this cake left. I'd better hang close in case I wanted another piece.

As I stuffed the last delectable bite in my mouth, Connie Lee approached the dessert table. I wiped the cake crumbs from my mouth and followed her gaze to the various platters of treats. "They're all good."

"I'll bet they are," Connie Lee said. "No sweets for me though. I have to watch what I eat and drink."

Mental head slap. I'd forgotten about her diabetes. She'd just lost her father, and she couldn't drown her sorrows in chocolate. She was pale and stick thin. That black dress must be a size two. My maternal instinct surged. "How are you feeling?"

"Tired. I'm tired all the time. It's no fun going to dialysis three days a week. I need a new kidney, but I'm way down the waiting list."

"My brother-in-law told me he went over and got tested."

Her lips twitched. "Bubba insisted. We'll find out on Monday if he's a match. I hope he is, but chances are slim to none."

"Bubba wants to help you."

"Bubba wants Mama to marry him. Getting married is all they talk about. Well, that and the money for my medical needs. Almost every phone call we get is from creditors wanting money. Mama won't marry him until I'm healthy again."

I wondered about her earlier enthusiastic hug of Bubba the evangelist. "Are you close friends with Bubba Paxton?"

She nodded, her features softening. "Pax understands me. I love talking to him. He helps me with my issues."

Her gushing praise of Bubba Paxton amazed me. Obviously Connie Lee thought of the former druggie as a friendly shoulder. Or was it something more? "He's your boyfriend?"

Her nose wrinkled. "Ew. No. He's, like, way too old. He's my counselor. He taught me the positive power of prayer."

"I see." I couldn't take Bubba Paxton seriously as a spiritual counselor. Once a crackhead, always a crackhead, as Roland used to say.

There was an abrupt splintering sound from the center of the room, as if a punch bowl had shattered. At the noise, Connie Lee ran to her mother. I stood on tiptoe to see what had happened. The minister's wife wept over a broken platter, which I immediately recognized as her late mother's pickle tray.

"I don't give a flying goddamn if you are ready to go!" Bubba Jamison bellowed into the too-quiet room. He grabbed a handful of potato chips from an ornate serving bowl and tossed the chips in the air like confetti. "I'm not ready to leave. I'm staying here to party and thanking God that this lying, cheating son of a bitch is dead."

# CHAPTER 37

"Bubba, lower your voice." Muriel's imperial voice dripped culture, money, and class. "You're making a scene."

"Damn straight. I am making the scene." Bubba Jamison climbed up on the food table, his gleaming oxfords mere inches from the deviled-egg platter. He raised both arms in a victory salute and gyrated his hips. "Everybody, listen up. I am the last man standing. I win. I got the money. I got the girl. I got it all, baby."

To my right, Sally Redman sputtered in octogenarian outrage. She whipped her walker across the room and whacked Bubba behind the knees with a bag of sandwich rolls. "Get yourself down from there at once, young man. This is neither the time nor the place for such a vulgar display."

"I can buy and sell everyone in this room," Bubba said. "I am the King of Sinclair County."

"Get down from there right now or I'll tell Daddy." Muriel's shrill threat torpedoed through the silent crowd.

"To hell with the lieutenant governor. I can buy and sell him, too." Bubba strutted across the table, narrowly missing Mrs. Fisher's crystal bowl of cole slaw. A jigging foot knocked the silver olive tray. Black and green olives scampered across the floor like marbles on holiday. "I'm top dog now."

Muriel sent me a desperate "do something" glance. I didn't know why Bubba was acting out, but I didn't want to get tangled up with a crazy person. Guilt sluiced through me. I had already banked Muriel's check, and I wasn't giving the money back. Hence Muriel was my client, and I was on her payroll.

Where was the sheriff? Why didn't he do something? Or the church elders? I scanned the room, willing someone else to step forward and take charge of the situation, but nobody moved. It was as if I stood in a frozen tableau, a step in time ahead of everyone else.

I swore under my breath.

I had to do something.

But what?

Muriel had already tried reason and threats. Miss Sally had hit him with a bag of rolls. Neither woman had gotten his attention. A surprise tactic would jar him into a different mindset and hopefully make him compliant.

Hustling plants and animals for a living had made me strong. I hefted the nearest bowl of fruit punch and slung the contents at him. The ice ring of strawberry slices hit him in the solar plexus, sticky red juice dripped from his beak of a nose.

"Get off that table right now, Bubba Jamison!" I yelled.

The sound of my voice released the crowd from their earlier thrall. The room sprang to life. Rosa Canchetta chortled, picked up a deviled egg, and chucked it at Bubba. Her neighbor, Ward Hillsby, grabbed another and hurled it at the man on the table.

Two kids reached into the potato chips, crunched up big handfuls, and threw them in Bubba's direction.

Charlotte's camera flashed. Others whipped out their cell phones to take pictures.

The punch bowl weighed a ton, so I put it down. Bubba sputtered and tried to dodge the food thrown at him. One foot went in the baked beans and down he came. The table buckled, with the steamed shrimp, pulled pork, barbeque sauce, rolls, and fruit salad dumping over on the man.

Bubba moaned.

The crowd howled with laughter.

Silent tears flowed down Muriel's face.

I winced. My intervention had made the situation worse.

The sheriff stepped forward and escorted Bubba out. "Come on, King of the County. Let's hose you down outside." Wayne glanced in my direction. "Do not leave. I want a word with you, Baxley."

Mrs. Fisher pulled her surprisingly intact crystal bowl out of the mess. Three church ladies stepped forward for their dishes as well. "I'm sorry." I gestured at the mess. "I'm so sorry. I was trying to help."

Rosa Canchetta patted my back, her face wreathed in smiles. "Don't fret, dearie. This is the best funeral I've been to in years."

I gulped. Trudy Brown scowled at the red blotches on her lace tablecloth. "I'll pay to have that replaced," I said.

"A little bleach should do the trick," Trudy said. "If not, I'll let you know."

Muriel remained frozen in place while everyone scurried around her. I knew just how mortified she felt. I wanted to be anywhere but here. I took her arm. "Come on. Let's go wash up in the ladies' room."

She complied.

"I'm so sorry," I said. "I thought I could shock some sense into him with the punch. I will return your deposit on Monday."

Muriel glanced up from drenching a paper towel in the sink. "Why would you do that?"

"I think it would be awkward for us to work together after this, don't you?"

"I want my fountain and butterfly garden. Bubba isn't going to ruin that. Besides, I won't release you from the contract I signed." Muriel mopped her pale face with the wet towel. With wonder, I noted that none of her mascara ran. She still looked gorgeous.

I blotted my steaming face with another wet towel. I brushed potato chip specks out of my two-tone hair and off my dark pantsuit. I hadn't lost my gardening job, but I'd come darned close.

Thank goodness Larissa hadn't been here to witness my impulsive behavior. Though Bubba Jamison had acted inappropriately, my behavior hadn't been much better. No telling what caption Charlotte would put under Bubba Jamison's picture. "Sinclair County king egged," or "Food fight at homicide victim's funeral," or "Don't mess with big, bad Baxley."

I groaned and washed my warm face again. How would I ever live this down?

I looked over at Muriel. She still held the towel over her mouth. Her eyes were closed, and her shoulders shook.

My throat constricted. If the sheriff didn't arrest me for inciting a riot, the manners police surely would. Worse, my actions had adversely impacted my client. "Oh, Muriel. I'm so sorry. I can't apologize enough."

She lowered her towel and gasped out a huge laugh.

I covered my mouth in surprise, then, as she kept laughing, I joined in. We slid down the wall and sat on the cool tiles covering the bathroom floor. I tried not to think about the huge wallpaper roses towering over us.

"Bubba looked so shocked when you threw the punch at him," Muriel gasped out between bouts of laughter.

"He did."

"He's such a zero. I don't know why I married him."

I kept my mouth shut. The client was always right.

Muriel's laughter trailed off. "I was going to divorce him, you know. Morgan had almost convinced me to marry him."

I blinked. "You and Morgan were together?"

She scrubbed her face with her delicate hands. Her bracelets jangled. "Yeah. I was stupid enough to believe his smooth lines. Then I realized he only wanted me for Daddy's political connections. I broke it off with him a week before he died. I thought Bubba didn't know anything about the affair, but he did. You know what?"

"What?"

"Morgan told him out of spite."

My pulse quickened. "That's not good."

"Bubba confronted me about it, and I admitted to the affair. I never thought he'd take it so hard. He had three affairs in Atlanta before we moved here."

I bit my tongue again. There was nothing good I could say. Bubba Jamison was an adulterer. Muriel wasn't much better. I couldn't imagine ever cheating on Roland. If he'd been unfaithful to me, I'd have known it. There was no way I'd stay with a man who outright violated our sworn vows.

"This is so messed up," she said.

I silently agreed with her. "What are you going to do?"

She shrugged. "What I always do. Call Daddy for damage control. Bubba's a zero, but he's my zero."

The parish hall had emptied when we returned. Except for the broken banquet table by the door, you'd never know there'd been an epic social disaster. I trailed Muriel to her Mercedes. She waved good-bye with her cell phone in hand.

I had no doubt that her father would make things right for her. Bubba Jamison was lucky to have Muriel to cover his indiscretions. How mad had he been about her affair with Morgan? Had he been killing mad?

The sheriff tapped me on the shoulder. "A word."

He looked put out with me. Goody. We were even. "I'm all ears."

He waggled a finger at me. When he spoke, his teeth flashed before my eyes. "That was a stupid stunt you pulled in there."

"Gee," I spouted off. "If the sheriff had stepped forward to get the crazy man off the food table, the outcome might have been different."

"The sheriff was busy. He was collecting evidence."

"So was I. Muriel had just ended a flaming affair with Morgan Gilroy." Heat suffused my face. Why on earth had I blurted that out?

He digested the news. "That puts a new spin on the out-of-control actions of the King of Sinclair County. It gives him two motives to kill Morgan."

With my spontaneous utterance, I'd given him the upper hand. I needed to rebalance the energy in this equation. "What did you find out?"

"This is my investigation."

"Come on, tell me. What did you find out?"

He shook his head.

"At least tell me which Bubba did it," I persisted.

"I'll give you this much. Nothing I learned today cleared any Bubbas. Every one of them could have killed Morgan."

"Now you're sounding like Charlotte. She thinks his murder was a conspiracy plot."

"Stop asking questions. Go home. Set aside your loyalty to Roland's loser of a brother, and you'll realize I'm trying to help you."

"I'm leaving, but only because I'm ready to go home. I hope there aren't any more funerals in this county for a very long time."

He put his hand under my elbow and walked me to where I'd parked in the shade, near the crumbling brick wall bounding St. Luke's Cemetery. Oddly, I felt comforted by the action. I wasn't softening toward him. I wasn't stupid enough to do that, but I no longer felt bereft. This was another reason I'd come home. To feel this sense of extended community.

We stopped at the driver's door to my truck. Glass fragments sparkled in the afternoon sunlight. A fist-sized hole gaped in my window. A broken brick lay on the passenger-side floor mat.

An arctic wind howled through my soul. The rose tattoo on my hand heated. I arched an eyebrow at the Sheriff. "You were wrong. Looks like I do have a stake in this battle. I take malicious damage to my property very personally."

# CHAPTER 38

"This is getting to be a habit." A wan smile touched Mama's worried eyes.

I held onto my flower-power tea mug for dear life. Tendrils of steam curled into my nostrils, soothing my frayed nerves. "I don't understand why someone broke my truck window. What did I ever do to anyone? I'll bet you anything the cost of a window is the same as my insurance deductible. I'm out a couple hundred dollars and for what?"

"I'm glad Tab took Larissa fishing. I'd hate for her to see you rattled like this."

Mama's comment rubbed me wrong. "You don't want her to know that I have emotions? I have plenty of those. They are mushrooming by the hour, growing on the crap that keeps multiplying in the dark."

"What's this all about?" she asked. The weather channel TV station blared in the background. Wind chimes tinkled outside. A breeze fluffed the tie-dyed curtains away from the open window.

"Someone is trying to scare me."

Mama's eyes widened in alarm. "Oh?"

I paused to take another sip of tea. "Someone thinks I will cave because of these behind-the-scene tactics."

"Maybe you should talk to Wayne about your concerns."

I shook my head. "I'm not entirely certain the sheriff isn't responsible. He wasn't surprised by the hole in my truck window."

"Maybe he didn't want you to know he was upset."

"Every time I see him he's upset at me. He's been very open about his disapproval of my actions. Only not this time. I told him to quit dragging his feet on the investigation. I bet he thinks I'll solve this case before he does. Maybe he's scared I'll run for sheriff next election."

Mama sipped her tea. She'd selected the cup with a peace symbol on one side, a yellow happy face symbol on the other. "Wayne is a good sheriff."

"He's not getting to the bottom of this murder investigation fast enough for me."

"These things take time."

I couldn't sit here and drink tea when I wanted to track down the Bubba who had caused all this anguish. I rose and paced the tiny kitchen. "There's a killer running rampant in Sinclair County. What if he comes after us? Are you willing to bet Larissa's life on Wayne's laid-back investigative approach?"

"Morgan's killer hasn't murdered anyone else in almost a week. You're over-dramatizing the situation. Larissa is a beautiful child with her whole life ahead of her. Morgan made many enemies. If you ask me, he got what he deserved."

"His bad karma caught up with him?"

"Absolutely. You can't escape your destiny." Mama pursed her lips. "Which reminds me. You need to have that talk with your father. You promised me you'd do that for him."

I was a mother in my own right, but here in this house, I was Mama's daughter. "I will. I keep my promises."

As if on cue, the screen door creaked opened and Daddy and Larissa strolled in. My father favored his right leg. "Y'all okay?" I gave them both a hug.

"We hiked all the way to the dock, Mom," Larissa crowed.

The dock was two miles from here. No wonder Daddy was limping. Four miles was a long way to walk for an out-of-shape sixty-year-old. "Catch anything?" I asked.

"The tide was wrong," Daddy said. "Not enough water in the creek to shake a stick at."

We chitchatted for a few minutes about mostly nothing, then Mama caught Larissa's eye. "You ready to help me with my basket-weaving project? I've got all the fixings set up in the oak grove out back."

Larissa crowed her excitement. "Sure."

They left, and it was just Daddy and me in the kitchen. "Sit down, Daddy. You must be exhausted."

"You ready to talk?" He eased into the wooden chair across from me, his clenched hands resting on the faded green tabletop.

I nodded, wishing the lump from my throat. My crappy day was about to get worse. "Talk away."

He nodded, his face solemn. "I went looking for Morgan the other night at the jail. My guides told me he was there, but I couldn't find him. I wish he'd shown himself so that we could solve his murder, and you'd stop worrying yourself thin about Larissa's well-being."

My gaze focused on the white oven door in the gold stove. "I can't stop worrying. Larissa is all I've got."

"You've got us, too. Don't ever forget that."

"I appreciate that, but you won't be around much longer if you keep pulling hare-brained stunts like going over the bridge. I made a deal with a demon to get you back, and now that demon has sealed Morgan's lips. I dreamwalked this morning at the jail and found Morgan, only he can't talk. A dark spirit has him trapped."

"What kind of deal?"

"I have to pass information along to a woman in Tampa. I didn't want to agree to anything, but time was running out.

Helping the demon was the only card I had to play."

"That's dangerous."

"I realize that."

"We can't give them a voice in our world. That's against the rules."

"No one gave me a rule book. Like I said, I was out of options. You'd been gone too long."

"I couldn't hear you calling me. There were so many other voices and it was so dark."

"Why did you go over the bridge?"

"I'd given up on finding Morgan and hoped to find Roland. He isn't dead."

I stared past Daddy's lined face to the sagging curtains and repeated the official party line. "The Army says he's dead."

"The Army messed up. Roland doesn't walk among the dead. What are we going to do about it?"

"What can we do? I know in my heart that Roland loves his family. He'd do anything in his power to come home to us. Therefore, it's not up to him. That's the only thing that makes any sense."

"We can look for him among the living."

Fear rippled through me. I threw up both hands to ward off the suggestion. "No. Absolutely not. Neither one of us is doing peyote buttons or any other hallucinogenic substance to enter the spirit world of the living. If Roland is alive, he'll turn up. I know it. I believe that with all my heart."

Daddy studied me for a long moment. "Is that the way you want to leave it?"

"Yes. Do not under any circumstances endanger your life again. Do you hear me? If you die, Mama will be inconsolable, and she'll come live with me."

"I'll do as you ask. But I'd rather do something to help you."

"I have bad dreams," I blurted out. I drank the tepid tea, felt it plunge down my throat and clank in my empty stomach. My fingers tightened on the old, cracked mug.

He looked thoughtful. "Are the bad dreams related to Roland's disappearance?"

I rose, ignoring the trembling in my rubbery knees. "Someone is out there, killing people in our community. Someone busted the window of my truck today. I can't let down my guard for a second. I won't let them harm Larissa."

My words settled heavily on his bent shoulders. He slumped forward, his hands cupping his chin. "Yes, of course. Larissa must be protected."

"Why does Bubba Paxton know private stuff about me?"

"He's spent a lot of time here. He must have absorbed the information. Something is off with his aura. Did you feel it?"

My head cocked to the side. I'd never thought to use Daddy's insights to identify the killer. Was he sitting on an untapped fountain of information with his aural readings? "Off? How?"

"Every now and then I get a pulse of something unhealthy from him."

My expectations plummeted. "Not unusual for a crackhead."

"He doesn't do drugs anymore."

Roland's pet phrase popped in my head. Once a crackhead, always a crackhead. But I didn't say it. Seems like I was swallowing a lot of my words today. "The sheriff considers Bubba Paxton a person of interest in Morgan's death."

"I heard that. Not sure I agree, but the boy has made some whopping mistakes, that's for darn sure."

"Paxton told me his job was on the line."

"Churches are businesses at their core. Expenses and income are their yin and yang." Daddy leaned back in his creaking chair, a speculative look in his eye. "Larissa told me about the little dog you're keeping for Pax. She seems quite fond of Elvis the Chihuahua."

I chewed my lip. Holding everything in wasn't my style. Had Daddy sensed changes in my aura because I was not being true to myself? The thought added to my anxiety.

My fingers absently traced the painted flower on my mug. "I hope she doesn't get too attached. The owner will want the dog back once he gets out of jail."

"Wait and see. Things have a way of working out," Daddy said.

His words stayed with me throughout the afternoon and into the night. I'd checked the locks and deadbolts on the doors, double-checked the new window locks. My hand slid to the pistol under Roland's pillow, making sure it was within reach. Sulay the cat guarded the foot of my bed. Elvis and Muffin had pulled guard duty in Larissa's bed.

My fortress was as safe as I could make it.

I rolled back to my side of the bed, listening to the familiar sighs and creaks in the darkened house. This place had belonged to my grandmother, and she'd kept it up until her health failed. I hoped to pass this family treasure along to Larissa.

Daddy's prophetic words surfaced again. *Things have a way of working out.*

Things had worked out poorly for Morgan Gilroy. For June Gilroy as well. One had been murdered, one drowned.

Was the broken window in my truck a warning for me to mind my own business? Maybe it was something as simple as a kid acting out. But that theory didn't ring true.

Whoever killed Morgan knew that I was asking questions. They knew I wanted justice to be served.

If so, the sheriff was right.

One of the four original Bubbas killed Morgan. I ticked them off on my fingers.

Was it Bubba Jamison, the self-styled King of Sinclair County? He had a strong motive, since his wife and Morgan had an affair. In his big-game room, he had hunting trophies aplenty. Stabbing a person wouldn't be too different from hunting large game.

What about Bubba Wright? He'd fought off Morgan's buyout of his waterfront property, but at what cost? What was this early-warning system he'd been talking about? Did he really have an alibi for Morgan's death, or had his entire church family lied for him?

Bubba Paxton was no saint. He'd been to prison for dealing crack and now counseled innocent girls like Connie Lee, Morgan's daughter. Plus, Morgan had threatened to take his church away. Was that a killing offense?

I didn't want Bubba Powell to be the killer. My screw-up brother-in-law deserved a break. But he had a major blind spot when it came to Patty Gilroy, Morgan's ex-wife, to the point that he was willing to donate one of his kidneys to Patty's daughter. If Morgan had threatened Patty, Bubba Powell would have moved heaven and earth to keep her safe.

Darn. The more I learned about the four Bubbas, the guiltier each of them looked.

Was the sheriff having the same problem trying to eliminate suspects?

I gripped the white cotton coverlet and pulled it up to my chin. I wasn't afraid of the dark, but I didn't like it very much. I closed my eyes tight against the things I could barely see and concentrated on what I knew.

Morgan Gilroy hadn't been a nice man. He'd taken what he wanted from everyone, freely indulging his desires at everyone else's expense. His bad karma had caught up with him.

What about June? She was a kid, same as Larissa. She didn't have bad karma. She wasn't swindling every person in the county. She didn't deserve to die.

Sleep fuzzed my mind.

There was something about June I should be remembering.

Some connection I hadn't put together that hovered just out of reach.

If only I could remember.

# CHAPTER 39

"Don't point that gun at me." I sidestepped so Charlotte didn't blast a deadly hole in my chest. Being gunned down by my best friend in my own backyard would be the ultimate irony.

"I don't like one-handed anyway." Charlotte gripped the pistol with both hands. She crouched down, arms fully extended, sticking her butt out. "Do I look like a really hot chick with a lethal weapon?"

"Absolutely."

"You know, I didn't want to borrow your gun, but now I'm liking the idea." She twirled and took aim at my prized froggie planter of geraniums. "Prepare to meet your maker, dirtball."

I gently pushed the nose of the gun towards the lawn. "Get serious, Charlotte. Don't make me take the bullets away from you. I want you to be protected."

She scrunched her freckled nose, her glasses riding a wave of skin. "Maybe you should loan me a hunting knife instead, since that's what the killer used last time."

"You don't have the agility or strength to use a knife against someone who's used to hunting or fighting. The gun stacks the odds in your favor."

Charlotte laid the sleek weapon on the hood of her gray Jetta. "I don't have a permit to carry a weapon. Should I put it under my seat? Will the gun go off if I slam on the brakes too hard?"

"Under your car seat is okay when you're out and about. Or you could put it in the side of your door or the glove box. Take it inside at night. I keep Roland's gun under his pillow."

Her head bobbed, and she danced backwards to stay aligned. The sun caught the dial of her large-faced watch. "Geez, you are a whack job."

Her reluctance to grasp the facts irritated me. "I'm prepared. We still have a murderer running loose in Sinclair County. Speaking of which, did you note who the sheriff spoke to yesterday?"

"During the reception?"

I nodded. "He acted like he'd found the Rosetta Stone, but he wouldn't tell me anything."

"He watched the Bubbas. He was near your brother-in-law when Powell's phone rang."

"Oh?" My frustration mounted. Charlotte was holding something back. I was certain of it. But would it help or hurt my brother-in-law?

"I didn't hear anything, but Bubba Powell ended the call abruptly, grabbed Patty and Connie Lee, and left. They didn't see Bubba Jamison make a huge fool of himself or you inciting everyone to riot."

My wafer-thin hold on my patience snapped. "I did not."

"You were so bold. I swear, you seemed ten feet tall. I should've snapped a picture of your David and Goliath moment."

Dread slithered across my spine. Was my respectability dangling by a fat punch bowl? "But you didn't, right?"

"Nah. I'll probably get fired for not snapping that one, but I did get a great shot of Jamison afterwards. Too bad I can't use it."

"Why?"

Charlotte grinned. "Kip confiscated my camera and my memory card. He deleted the image files on all our newspaper hard drives. He got a phone call yesterday less than an hour after the fray from the lieutenant governor, no less."

Muriel hadn't wasted any time. How many other messes like this had she cleaned up for her husband? With such a magic wand, many mistakes could be erased.

Was murder one of them?

I shivered in the late-afternoon sunshine and surveyed the moss-draped oaks rimming my yard. I would do well to stay on Muriel's good side.

Charlotte's round face filled with expectation. I rallied for her sake. "What? No freedom of the press protest?"

"Nada. Zip. Zilch. Kip folded like the worm he is. Well, he folded after they offered him fifty-yard-line seats at the Georgia–Florida football game." Charlotte patted the deep pocket in her vested maroon shorts set. "Lucky for both of us, he didn't remember my flash drive. I've got the picture saved there."

"I'm sure there were plenty of incriminating pictures out there. Half the crowd had their cell phones out snapping photos."

"Even so, it won't make the paper."

Insects buzzed around us. I slapped at a fly and missed. "What about the sheriff? Did you notice anything else about him at the reception?"

Charlotte gave me a sidelong glance. "What's with you and the sheriff? Is love in the air?"

Heat steamed up my T-shirt collar. "Ew. Definitely not. He implied that he'd discovered many clues at the reception. I got nothing. Well, only a little something I overheard from Bubba Wright. Anyway, Wayne wouldn't tell me a blasted thing. His secretiveness fired up my competitive instincts."

Charlotte winced. "God help us all."

Her remark fired me up even more. Wayne's ineptitude was no joking matter. "He's not doing his job. A killer is on the loose. We are all in danger."

Charlotte pretended to play a violin. I tapped her shoulder. "Stop that. I'm serious. So is the killer. And someone busted the window on my truck. If you've got something else, I want to hear it."

We both leaned against her car while Charlotte seemed to consider my request. "Maybe we could team up," she said. "Compare notes, that sort of stuff."

"That's what we're doing."

"You're grilling me, but you haven't told me anything I don't know. If we're equal partners, you need to spill."

I didn't want Charlotte to get hurt, but it made sense to tell someone what I knew. It might as well be Charlotte. "Bubba Wright joked with his friends at the funeral about his early-warning system. What was he talking about?"

"Hmm." Charlotte's fingers tapped on the warm car hood. "Early-warning system. Sounds like an alarm. Is it a burglar alarm system?"

"Those things are pricey. I can't see him putting a burglar alarm in at Shrimp 'n' Stuff. It has to be something else. Seems to me like he got advance notice of something."

"Yeah. That sounds right. Advance notice. But of what?"

"That's where I keep getting stuck. Do you think it's something at the bank? Or about one of his boats? What's on the horizon? Think, Charlotte. You're the reporter. You live the events on the local calendar."

Charlotte huffed out a breath. "I know when the historical society is meeting next, which properties are being sold for nonpayment of taxes, which churches advertise in the paper. When you come down to it, I don't know much of nothing."

"Wait a minute. Taxes. Wasn't there something about the tax base changing in the paper not long ago?"

"You're right. There was." Charlotte clapped her hands with gusto. "The city and county managers appointed a task force to find ways to fund the infrastructure we need to attract more industrial growth. Those findings haven't been released yet." Her voice rose on a hopeful note. "I think we're on to something."

"Was Morgan Gilroy on that task force?"

"Crap. I don't remember if the task force members were listed in the article." She squeezed her eyes shut. "But Bernard knows. He wrote that story. Please don't make me ask Bernard anything. He finally is showing me some respect. I don't want to change the balance of power again."

"Maybe it won't come to that. If the task force decided something, who else would know?"

"The tax assessor's office. They review the recommendations before they go up to the city and county government levels."

"Interesting that nothing has leaked from that task force, isn't it? Usually word spreads like wildfire."

Charlotte nodded her agreement. "Very curious indeed."

Excitement skittered through my veins. This felt so right. Everything seemed to be falling into place. "On the one hand, we have an impending negative tax decision. On the other, we have a man who won't sell out to the condo people. Chances seem good that they would levy higher taxes to force him to sell, all in the name of progress."

"Yeah. I'm buying that. But I'm also remembering that piece I wrote about the homestead exemption. If Bubba Wright filed for that, he is immune from higher taxes."

I vaguely remembered a rule from when I'd filed for my homestead exemption. "Isn't that only if you live on the property?"

"It is, but I'll bet you anything, Bubba figured out a way around that."

"We're on to something, Char. I can almost taste it. Who does Bubba Wright know in the tax office?"

"Besides the tax commissioner, three women work over there. Amber, Nettie Sue, and Jaconda."

My heart skipped a beat. "Jaconda? Wasn't she the tall, thin woman sitting beside Eunice Wright at the funeral?"

"Yes. Oh. My. God. We are too good. Now what?"

"Now we know what Bubba's early-warning system is. He dodged the tax bullet. But what would he do in retaliation?"

"Nobody messes with Bubba Wright down at the docks. His word is law."

"And being in the fishing industry, he'd be very familiar with knives. Plus he'd be strong enough to physically overcome another man."

Birds twittered in the nearby trees. A squirrel scampered across my lawn. It seemed a rather ordinary setting to be talking about a man's murder.

"I don't know," Charlotte said. "Bubba Wright had twenty years on Morgan. You'd think Morgan would see an attack like that coming and get out of the way."

"You're right." Defeat huffed out of me. "I was so sure we were on to something. Bubba Wright could've done it only if he sneaked the knife in, if Morgan didn't expect it."

"That may be how the killer did it. Morgan kept in pretty good shape, so the attack had to be a surprise."

"Yeah. The element of surprise is critical. Morgan probably had guns and knives stashed all over his house. Bubba Jamison has a slew of weapons. I saw them the other day when I was bidding on a gardening job out there. Bubba Powell has his share of guns and knives, and I bet Bubba Paxton does, too."

Charlotte scowled. "Every man in this county has at least one gun and one hunting knife. Most have sets for each vehicle, boat, and house."

She was right. Guns and knives were as plentiful as the Spanish moss hanging from the trees. "What if we're looking at this the wrong way? What if the knife was Morgan's? What if it was on his desk and someone came to see him? That someone was very upset. In the heat of the moment, the person grabbed the knife and stabbed Morgan."

Charlotte glowed with approval. "I bet that's exactly how it happened."

"If only we knew why. Then we'd know who." I caught her eye. "You can't breathe a word of this to anyone. Not until the killer is locked behind bars. Whoever killed Morgan will target us if he knows we're closing in on him."

"My lips are sealed." She picked up the pistol and shoved it under her seat. "I can't get killed now, not when my journalism career is finally taking off."

"Mom!" Larissa yelled to me from the house. "Uncle Bubba is on the phone."

I caught Charlotte's eye. "I need to take that call."

"You be careful, too."

Careful seemed grossly inadequate, but it was all I had. "That's my plan."

# CHAPTER 40

"Baxley, you got a minute?" Bubba Powell's voice boomed through the phone.

I'd believed one hundred percent in my brother-in-law's innocence when Morgan was first murdered; now I wasn't sure. The rough edge to his voice caused my fingers to spasm on the cell phone. I glanced around my cozy living room to make sure no killers lurked in the corners.

The coast was clear.

I sighed with relief and focused on Bubba's question. I hoped I had more than a minute. I hoped I had a lifetime to live. A minute wasn't nearly enough. I prayed my brother-in-law wasn't the killer. I forced life into my voice. "Sure. What's up?"

"I'm in trouble. I need your help. Can I come over?"

Butterflies slam danced in my stomach. I flopped down on the sofa in my den. How many times had Bubba begged for help? And yet, given the circumstances of the recent homicide, I had to put my safety first. Was my Bubba a killer? I didn't know.

Worse, I didn't want him in my house.

That realization sickened me. But I couldn't put Larissa at risk. I couldn't leave her alone either. "Not a good idea," I hedged. "I might be coming down with something."

"Christ. That's no good. I can't risk an illness. Did you hear the news? I'm a tissue match for Connie Lee. We're having the transplant surgery on Tuesday."

Surgery. Meaning Bubba would lose a kidney and Connie

Lee would have a second chance at living her life. An ending and a new beginning. Words tumbled out of my mouth. "Wow. I'm stunned. A match? What were the odds of that? A zillion to one? That's great news for Connie Lee. But are you sure you want to give up your kidney?"

"I'm positive. There's no doubt in my mind."

There was an extra nuance in his voice that caught my attention. A measure of pride, perhaps? I traced the plaid pattern of the sofa armrest with my thumbnail. "How can you be so sure?"

Silence swirled in the line. My pulse drummed in my ear.

"She's mine," Bubba said.

I wasn't sure I'd heard him correctly. "Excuse me?"

"She's my biological daughter. Patty and I had one last fling before her wedding. Connie Lee is my kid."

I glanced around to make sure Larissa wasn't in earshot. No kid in sight, just the big cat hunkered down in the nearby wing-back chair, eyes at half-mast. I sagged into the sofa, hugging a cushion to my stomach. "Are you sure? How long have you known?"

"The hospital tests proved it. I found out today."

"Wow. Does Connie Lee know? Or Patty?"

"Patty knows. We haven't told Connie Lee yet."

I couldn't quite catch my breath. If Bubba was Connie Lee's dad, then she was my niece. "I didn't expect this. Did you?"

"I'd hoped for it, but Morgan had made such a big deal about Connie Lee having the Gilroy high cheekbones and his mother's personality that I didn't push the issue. Now I wish I had. All those years we spent apart. Wasted."

"They weren't wasted. You had two wonderful kids. A wife."

"But I wanted Patty. She told me that Morgan threatened her. If she left him before Connie Lee turned twelve, he'd make sure Connie Lee never got a dime of his money."

"How odd. Do you think he knew the truth of her parentage?"

"I wouldn't put it past the bastard. His threats kept Patty and me apart for years, until she finally had enough of him and moved out. By then, Morgan had already set up a trust fund for Connie Lee."

"All this time, Patty never suspected the two of you were Connie Lee's parents?"

"What can I say? Patty likes sex, and she wanted Morgan's money. As time went by, she learned money didn't buy happiness and she wanted out. But it was too late. Connie Lee was sick, and Patty couldn't afford the medical expenses on her own."

This puzzle of financial dependence intrigued me. "How did she gather the courage to leave him?"

"She got a good lawyer in Atlanta, one Morgan couldn't intimidate. Or so she thought. Muriel Jamison recommended him. The guy promised her everything, but as the divorce dragged on, he did less and less for her."

Oh dear. Poor Patty. Muriel had been Morgan's playmate. She'd probably fed him all the divorce details, further screwing Patty.

"That's why I need your help. I borrowed money to help Patty with Connie Lee's bills, since Morgan wouldn't pay for the dialysis. Connie Lee would be dead without those dialysis treatments. I had to do it."

This was the Bubba I knew. The one who tilted at windmills. The one who believed every scam artist that came along. "Who lent you money? You have the worst credit rating in three states."

He gulped into the phone. "They are very bad people. Loan sharks out of Jacksonville. I've got to pay them fifty grand by nightfall tomorrow or I'll be sleeping in the graveyard next to my brother's empty coffin."

I shuddered.

The shadows lengthened in the room, adding an ominous tint to this conversation. I flicked on a lamp, welcoming the soft glow of light.

I was a decent person, a mature adult. I took care of my financial responsibilities. How had Bubba missed that basic life lesson? "I don't have that kind of money. I've been strapped ever since Roland died. Sell your car. Sell your place."

"I can't scrape together enough cash in time. Please. I need your help."

"My hands are tied. The Army hasn't released Roland's death benefits. I mortgaged this house to start my landscaping business. My truck is ten years old with a busted window. What do you think I can do for you?"

"You have a good credit rating." His voice grew more persuasive. "You can borrow the money. I know you can. Please. Do this for me. For your niece, Connie Lee. I'll repay you. I promise."

My gut recoiled. "That's not fair. Roland and I bailed you out of debt four times, and you've never repaid us a dime. We loaned you the money we'd saved for Larissa's college education. I'd like to help you, but I can't. I just can't."

"Don't do this. Please. I need your help."

"You have another option."

"No. I don't." Desperation tinged his voice.

I held firm. If I didn't, I'd be bailing Bubba out for the rest of our lives. Hell. Truth be told, Roland and I should have cut him off a long time ago. "Call the Colonel and Elizabeth. Tell them the truth."

"Dad hates me. He won't loan me a dime."

"He might do it for his granddaughter."

Bubba swore up one side of the phone line and down the other. "Don't leave me high and dry. I'm a desperate man."

"Cuss all you like. It won't change anything. I'll nurse you back to health after the surgery, but that's the limit of my generosity."

He said a few more choice words and ended the call.

I drew my knees up to my chest. Bubba was Connie Lee's biological father. Bubba owed a loan shark fifty grand. Lack of money seemed to be Bubba's recurrent theme song. And his life kept intersecting with Morgan's. Now Morgan's alleged daughter was actually Bubba's kid, my niece.

Wheels turned in my head.

Connie Lee had had numerous medical tests during her life. What if Morgan knew of her true parentage all along? What if Bubba belatedly realized Morgan had kept his daughter from him on purpose?

There was no doubt in my mind that Bubba could have killed Morgan over such a thing. I could see him storming into Morgan's house, arguing, picking up a knife from the desk, and stabbing Morgan, over and over again.

Oh. God.

Morgan's death might very well have been a crime of passion. Bubba Powell's passion.

Larissa strolled through the living room, Muffin and Elvis trotting at her heels. "Mom, you all right?"

"Yeah. Sure."

I might never be all right again.

# CHAPTER 41

Monday dawned clear and warm, a great day for being outdoors with plants and animals. I was looking forward to a peaceable day. I had plenty to do, and I preferred to stay busy. With any luck, my full calendar would prevent me from spending the whole day worrying about Morgan's murderer.

Inside my kitchen, the animals' turf war appeared to have been settled. As I poked around the stove making breakfast, the Maine Coon cat claimed the high stool by the telephone, tail flicking lazily. Down below at floor level, Muffin and Elvis kept one eye on me and their food bowls, the other on Sulay the cat and pack leader.

After I put Larissa on the school bus, I started my daily rounds. The Smiths' boxers, Peaches and Babyface, bounced excitedly through their brisk walk. Remy at the auto repair shop estimated the cost of my new window. I phoned the amount in to my insurance company. Just as I thought. The bulk of the expense would come out of my pocket.

My mobile phone shrilled. "Pets and Plants. How may I help you?" I asked.

"How did you get this number?" the muffled voice asked.

I glanced at the display window. No phone number. Instead it read "restricted." "Pardon me?"

"You called me the other day. Left a message."

My heart raced. Could helping Rose, the tattooed woman, be this simple? "Raymondia? Is that you?"

239

"How did you know my sister?"

"It's complicated."

"You've got one minute to explain or I'm hanging up."

"I talk to dead people," I blurted out. "Your sister gave me the message. Said it was about the bank robbery money."

"What? You psychic or something?"

"Something. Look, I don't want to get tangled up in your life. Rose is holding a friend of mine until I can prove I talked to you."

"Proof?"

"Yeah. Tell me something that only the two of you would know."

"Is Rose okay?"

"She's scary as hell. I don't know what okay is for her."

"That's Rose." The speaker paused. "Thing is, even if I believe your crazy story, her message makes no sense."

"That's your problem. I don't make this stuff up. Please help me out. I need to rescue my friend."

"Oh, all right. What will it hurt? Tell her I sat on her glasses in second grade."

The call ended. I pocketed the phone and felt better than I had in days. Finally, I had something to tell Rose, but Rose had to wait her turn. I had to attend to my living clients first.

The statuary place out on the highway had the fountain in stock I wanted for the Jamison job. I arranged for it to be delivered to Muriel's north county home on Wednesday. After that, I indulged myself in the fun of wandering the lush lanes at Sunny Days Nursery, wishing I could take every plant home. Instead, I loaded up the back of my truck with enough goodies for Muriel's butterfly garden and drove home. Then I busied myself with yard work, pulling crabgrass, Virginia creeper, and dollar weed from my flower beds.

Through all my activity, Morgan and the Bubbas hovered at

the edge of my mind. Morgan had been dead a week, but his killer remained a mystery. Figuring out who killed him was hard. It seemed Morgan had been at cross-purposes with all the Bubbas.

Bubba Wright had rejected Morgan's outright bid for his land. But when Morgan tried an end run by getting Bubba's taxes raised, Bubba'd had forewarning, thanks to his niece at the tax assessor's office. Losing his land would have deprived Bubba of more than his physical property. He'd have lost his heritage, his livelihood, his boat, and the joy of fishing.

In Sinclair County, no one came between a man and his fishing. That alone was enough to inspire murderous rage from the most sainted. Morgan's ploy to gain Bubba's land, land that had been in his family for generations, was a brazen move.

Bubba Wright had his back to the wall, all right. Thanks to me, his entire church family had vouched for his alleged whereabouts at the time of the murder. Even so, Bubba Wright had a strong motive to kill Morgan and, quite possibly, the opportunity.

Bright sunlight warmed my shoulders, easing the chill of murder from my bones. A bead of sweat trickled down the channel of my spine. A living thing, that bead of sweat, a reminder that I was solid flesh and blood and influenced by my physical environment.

Like the Virginia creeper, which had threaded itself through my pampas grass. I studied the many-tiered weed garland with some amazement. Had it grown a foot an hour? I'd weeded out here last week, or maybe the week before. No matter. This weed was toast now. I yanked hard on a lower strand, wishing I could root out a murderer just as easily.

Bubba Jamison could easily be the killer. He had motive coming out the wazoo. He'd been cuckolded by his wife and his hunting buddy. From what I'd observed of his erratic behavior,

Jamison operated under a hair trigger. With his finely honed hunting skills, he could have easily killed Morgan.

Muriel was his alibi for the murder, but I saw firsthand how she erased his unseemly behaviors. She'd stare me straight in the eye and point-blank lie when it came to protecting her husband. Had she lied about his opportunity to kill Morgan?

I scooped up the clump of weeds and hauled it over to my wheelbarrow. How discouraging that I couldn't rule out Bubba Wright or Bubba Jamison. Maddening, actually. The focus on murder suspects should be narrowing, but it wasn't.

Though Bubba Paxton had turned his life around, he wasn't in the clear. He'd found God while serving time for dealing crack. He'd sweet-talked Morgan and pals into building him a church. He'd even counseled Morgan's daughter. But when attendance at Pax Out fell off, the investors wanted to pull the plug on Bubba.

He had a criminal record, and a history of doing stupid stunts. Keeping four rattlesnakes in his tiny house was proof that he hadn't grown new brain cells. He wanted to keep his job as preacher at Pax Out, the church that bore his name. I could see him flying off the handle if Morgan called him over to tell him he was fired.

How far would a man go to protect his lifelong dream?

The shade beckoned. I moved over to my ivy bed. Dollar weed had made steep inroads here. I hated dollar weed. Those underground runners tunneled through the ground at warp speed. I got my trowel out and made sure I got every inch of that stuff, the pungent aroma of turned soil centering me, helping me feel connected to the earth.

Bubba Powell had a strong motive to kill Morgan. Connie Lee was his daughter, not Morgan's, as everyone in town had assumed. Morgan had kept Bubba apart from Patty, the love of his life, for years.

Bubba must have hated Morgan with a passion. He'd wanted to give Connie Lee his kidney to ease her suffering, a selfless act he would have gladly done years ago if he'd known she was his flesh and blood. He could have been enraged by Morgan's high-handedness and killed him to avenge Connie Lee's suffering. I'd seen the Powell brothers in hunting mode often enough to know that Bubba was adept with weapons and killing game.

The thought ate at me in a terrible, gnawing way. No question about it, my Bubba had been pushed to his limit. I'd started this with the goal of clearing my brother-in-law's name. Now I didn't know if that was possible.

I tore out a big clump of crabgrass, rocking back on my heels. Dirt flew everywhere, spraying on my face, in my striped hair. I brushed it off.

How could anybody live with murder hanging over their head?

It wasn't any consolation knowing Morgan was an unpleasant man. Sure, he'd gotten what he deserved, but still, he was dead. You didn't come back from that.

There was one redeeming aspect to this mess. With so much evidence pointing toward the Bubbas, it was highly unlikely we had a crazed serial killer in our midst. Chances were high that Morgan's death was the direct result of a personal grudge.

Which meant Larissa wasn't at risk. I sighed the tension from my shoulders.

I gathered up a mound of dollar weeds and tossed it in my wheelbarrow. Crickets chirped. Birds sang. It was a good day because Larissa was safe.

That busted window was grounds for caution though. Someone had sent me a cautionary message. Only the message wasn't clear. Was I supposed to stay away from the Bubbas? Or was I supposed to quit trying to solve Morgan's murder?

Too bad Roland wasn't here. He excelled at analysis.

I needed someone to talk to about all of this. My heart cried out for my husband, wherever he might be. Daddy was right about Roland's disposition. Even though the Army had declared Roland dead, he wasn't. I didn't have any direct proof, but deep inside I knew the truth.

Roland was alive.

I didn't understand what kept him away. No matter how I looked at the facts, nothing made any sense. He'd loved being in Special Ops. He loved Larissa and me. I lived with the hope that he'd make his way home.

Someday.

I pulled my phone out of my pocket to check the time and saw the message icon on the screen. I'd missed a call. I accessed the message. "Baxley? Louise Gilroy here. Come get Precious. I can't take care of her anymore. Call me."

Poor Louise. She sounded so tired. So defeated. Morgan's funeral must have exacted a terrible toll on her. Had she hit bottom? Did she realize June wasn't coming home?

My heart went out to her. She didn't need more stressors in her life right now. I returned her call. "Louise, don't do anything hasty. I'll be right over."

# Chapter 42

Though it was mid-afternoon and a pleasant eighty degrees outdoors, the volatile climate inside the Gilroy house hit me full force. Louise's anger and unhappiness whirled like twin tornadoes. Underneath the turbulence throbbed a disturbing malaise. Shivering, I pulsed more energy around me, to hold the negativity at bay. I rubbed my bare arms and perched on the edge of the leather chair. "I came as fast as I could. What happened?"

"I can't control Precious." From the adjacent sofa, Louise nodded toward her Labrador retriever. Precious had settled down by the door after greeting me. "The dog runs off every time she goes outside. Then Ritchie stomps around here, saying Precious isn't worth a damn because she won't come when he calls her. He wants the vet to put her down or else I have to drive her over to the dog pound. I'm at my wit's end. Please, say you'll take her."

Precious didn't deserve abandonment or euthanasia. I'd kept her for Louise several months ago and the dog wasn't mean or disobedient. But animals were sensitive to imbalance. Undoubtedly, Precious needed a break from the emotional chaos in this household.

Much as I wanted to rescue Precious, I believed she was good therapy for Louise. "I appreciate your thinking of me. I do. But please wait a few days before you make a decision. How long has Precious been running off?"

Louise pinched the bridge of her thin nose. With her pale coloring, ice blond hair, and black sheath, she reminded me of a fairy-tale character who'd spent her life conversing with mirrors. "Two weeks. She cries to go out, and then she runs away. Ritchie has zero tolerance for her bad behavior."

I seized on that thought. "Sounds like Precious needs an obedience refresher. If she was better trained, you'd keep her right? She's a member of your family, after all."

As soon as the words left my mouth, I wanted to take them back. I mentally kicked myself to the marsh and back. Poor Louise. She'd lost her daughter, her brother-in-law, and was on the verge of losing her pet.

Louise paled, further increasing my guilt. I swallowed around the lump in my throat, rubbed the goose bumps on my arm. "I apologize for that insensitive remark. I'm your friend, Louise. I'd hate for you to make a rash decision now that you'll regret later. Precious has a sweet disposition. She'll be a good companion again once this behavior problem is addressed."

Louise gripped her trembling hands together in her lap. "I can't give her the discipline or exercise she needs. I'm ruining June's dog. That's why Ritchie says she has to be put down."

I made myself breathe. Precious was too nice a dog to be destroyed. Louise loved this dog, but grief had clouded her mind. "There has to be a better solution. Does your vet offer obedience classes?"

"It's too late. This can't wait one more day. Ritchie said he'd shoot the dog if she runs off today. I can't bear to have that on my conscience."

Precious looked at me with mournful eyes. I couldn't see this gentle dog being destroyed over a minor behavior issue. She needed consistent attention, something Louise couldn't give right now. I thought about taking her home with me, but we were already busting at the seams.

"I could come over and work with her, if you think that would help," I offered. "If that doesn't work, I can help you place her with another family."

Louise sniffed back her tears. Precious padded over and placed her triangular head in Louise's lap. My friend froze for a moment, and then she cautiously stroked the dog's head. "That sounds reasonable. I don't know what has gotten into her lately."

"I've got a new landscaping job starting on Wednesday, so I need to come early in the day to work with Precious. Is that okay?"

"I've got an even better idea. Use your key and take care of Precious as if we weren't here. Walk her morning and evening and work extra with her on obedience. I'll pay you, of course."

This was a good deal for me, but I felt lousy about taking her money. "I don't want to take advantage of your grief."

"Don't be silly. It will be a relief not to worry about the dog."

"What about Ritchie? Will this suit him?"

"Ritchie's been pushing me to do more since June—" She paused momentarily, straightening her posture. "I made the decision to do this instead of killing the dog. He'll have to adjust."

Her smile stopped short of her sad eyes. I feared for Louise's well-being. In the months her daughter had been missing, Louise had aged ten years.

"I'll get started right away." I stood and clapped my hand against my jeans. "Come on, Precious. We're going out for a walk."

I breathed a sigh of relief once I stepped back into the warm outdoor air. Precious tugged at the leash until I asserted control. I didn't need a degree in pet psychology to know she wanted to romp in the woods. I kept her on Honeycreek Lane, hiking to the head of the road and back. My eyes darted over to Morgan's shadowed driveway as we passed the entryway, but I wanted nothing to do with Sparrow's Point.

Back in Louise's yard, I practiced basic obedience commands with Precious. She came, sat, and heeled on command. Exercise had helped. With a surge of satisfaction, I returned the tongue-lolling dog to her owner. "I'll be back tomorrow morning, Louise."

She waved at me from the sofa, an empty highball glass on the coffee table. "There's a retainer on the counter, dear. Thank you."

Inside my truck, I glanced at the amount on the check. Two hundred dollars. Almost exactly what I needed to cover my busted window. Funny how life worked out.

While waiting at the bus stop that afternoon, my cell phone rang. I flipped it open, enjoying the drowsy sunshine on my shoulders. "Pets and Plants. How may I help you?"

"Stay away," a thin but otherwise nondescript voice warned.

I gripped the phone tight in disbelief. "What?"

"Stay away," the voice repeated, sounding distant and muffled.

I didn't recognize the caller's voice. I checked the caller ID. Restricted. My breath hitched in my throat. "Who is this?"

"Keep your nose clean, or else."

I glanced around the road. Not a single car in sight. Only me and a couple hundred pine trees in the neighboring forestry tracts. At my feet, Elvis contented himself by licking his private parts. Muffin snored next to Elvis.

Nothing made me madder than someone telling me what to do. I wouldn't stand for it. This was the twenty-first century. I had rights. I wasn't anyone's victim. "I don't know who this is, but I don't appreciate being threatened or harassed."

"You've been warned."

The phone went dead.

Waves of disbelief rolled through me. Adrenaline surged

through my veins, kicking my senses into hyperawareness. The distant school bus approached in a flash of lights and low-throated diesel rumble.

The little dogs at my heels yipped at the sound. I picked them up to quiet them, wishing my unease would calm so easily. I had to be smart about this phone call.

With a Zen-like clarity, I recalled the skills Roland had taught me about threat analysis, skills I'd laughingly learned because I didn't need them. Roland had been adamant and his forethought filled me with assurance.

I had two options.

Be bullied or take action.

Even if I cowered under the threat of harm, that was no guarantee of safety. I couldn't gamble with the future and well-being of my family.

My only real option was to take action.

But action against what?

# CHAPTER 43

I tossed my phone at the sheriff. "Trace the number. Find out who called."

Sheriff Wayne Thompson unstacked his heels from his desk, easily one-handing the phone as he rose. Overhead, a fluorescent light flickered. A faint tang of Pine-Sol hung in the air. "What's got you so stirred up, hon?"

"I'm not your *hon*." I worked to relieve the tension in my jaw. "I'm a tax-paying, law-abiding citizen who received a threatening phone call. Arrest the bad guy who harassed me."

The sheriff's friendly expression sobered. "What happened?"

A tide of emotion threatened. I fought it back. I would not cry here. I blinked rapidly. "I got a call a few minutes ago. I didn't recognize the voice or the phone number. The person told me to stay away. He said I'd been warned."

"The caller was male?"

"I'm not sure. The voice sounded weak and distant. Like a sick person in China."

Wayne's intensity abated. He chuckled and nodded his head. "Good one. You had me going for a moment."

Was he going to pat me on the head and send me away? My stomach lurched. "I'm serious as a heart attack. Someone called and threatened me. I want him arrested."

"Why would a sick Chinese man care about where you go?"

"It was a figure of speech, Wayne. Give me credit for having half a brain." I pounded my clenched fist on his cluttered desk, toppling a stack of papers. "I want you to look into this right now. Call one of your technology-friendly deputies in here and identify the caller."

He whistled appreciatively. "Roland was a lucky man. You're one fiery woman."

How dare he reduce this to sex? I swore aloud. "Do your job."

"Relax, hon. I don't need a deputy. I've learned a few things over the years."

I paced the office while he called his football buddy at the phone company and obtained the number. Anger boiled like a bitter brew in my gut. I wanted this threat neutralized at once. I could handle just about anything head-on, but I couldn't fight a nameless, faceless enemy.

"It's one of those disposable cell phones. Can't be traced." His gaze narrowed. "What's going on? First your truck window and now this. Who have you pissed off?"

"That's just it." My hands twirled like color guard flags. "I walk pets and create gardens. Sure, I've consulted for you on this case, but my dreamwalks haven't helped solve Morgan's murder. I don't understand why I'm being targeted, and I'm scared. Don't you get it?"

My voice rose with each word I spoke. This was not my fault. Tears spilled down my cheeks. I couldn't hold them in any longer. There was only so much stress a woman could handle in one day.

Heat flamed my cheeks, but I didn't turn tail and run. I expected Wayne to take care of this for me, right now. He was the sheriff, the highest ranking law enforcement officer I knew.

"Sit down. I'll be right back." He stepped out and returned with two Cokes. He took the chair next to me and waited. "What's going on?"

My attempt to compose myself hadn't worked. Information

whirled dizzily in my head. I ran my thumb over the condensation on the aluminum can as I tried to sort out what to say. Despite our past, he acted like I was another run-of-the-mill brainless female. My actions today hadn't encouraged him to think otherwise. I had to pull it together.

I drew in a shallow breath of courage. "That's just it. I don't know."

"Is this about the case?"

He didn't have to say which case. Morgan's homicide was the only elephant in the room. "What else could it be? I've never had a broken truck window before, and I've certainly never been threatened before."

He took a long pull from his soda. "Who have you been talking to?"

"I've talked to them all. Two Bubbas are clients. Bubba Paxton helped me with Daddy the other night and begged me to board a dog for his druggie friend. I couldn't say no. And you already know I went to see Bubba Wright when this whole thing started. If I'd known where this would lead, I'd go back in time and stay at your house with Dottie while you answered Morgan's distress call."

"There's no going back."

His crisp tone helped center me. "Roland used to say that, too. I can't handle this by myself. I'm a single parent. If anything happens to me, Larissa won't have a mother or a father."

He regarded me steadily. "You're not going to cry again, are you?"

I choked out a harsh laugh. "No. I'm done with that. I need answers."

"Answers are dangerous." He leaned back in his chair.

"So are angry women. Tell me what you know."

His lips tightened. "I'm not that moved by a few tears. The expedient solution is to remove you from the line of fire. Take your kid and head out of town for a few weeks."

I tapped my chest. "Single mother here, remember? I don't take vacations. Can't afford them."

"Visit a friend then."

"My friends are too far away. It would cost me an arm and a leg in gas money to drive across the country."

"What about the Colonel and Elizabeth?"

My breath stalled. "What about them?"

"Go stay with them in Jacksonville for awhile."

"Not on your life." My free hand spasmed on the wooden chair armrest. "One look at the tattoo and the hair, and they will have me declared an unfit parent so they can get custody of Larissa. I will not willingly walk into that viper pit."

He leaned forward, pushing the woodsy fragrance of his aftershave my way. "That's pride talking. Be objective. Someone sent you two warnings. This same someone may be a killer. Heed the message. Stay away from the case."

I ignored his invasion of my space and stuck to my guns. "That's just it. I don't know who to stay away from. I have to work. If I don't work, I can't pay my bills."

"Move into my place with Dottie and the boys. No killer in his right mind would try to get in there."

"No thanks. I'd rather eat mud pies." A vision of June's watery death surfaced in my thoughts. I shuddered.

Wayne noticed the movement. "What? You know something else?"

"I was thinking back to June's disappearance."

He looked away. "That kid's face still haunts me."

"Me, too. Daniel Huxley told me he found gator wallows in the high marsh. June could have had boat trouble, tried to walk home through the marsh, and stumbled into a gator."

"That thought crossed my mind. Don't mention it to the Gilroys. They don't need that image in their heads."

My grip tightened on the half-empty soda can. "Poor Louise. She believes June will walk through the door any day now. June isn't coming home."

Phones rang. Someone made copies on the machine outside his office. Shoes squeaked down the tiled corridor. Normal sounds of daily life. I drew comfort from the ordinary setting.

"Thank you for listening," I said. "I've been going out of my mind with worry."

"You always were wound a little tight. But you've got good reason to worry. I haven't collared Morgan's killer yet."

"About that," I started.

His palm shot out. "Don't give me another lecture about how innocent Bubba Powell is. He's guilty as sin, and we both know it. Morgan had scarlet fever as a kid and was sterile his entire life. Connie Lee isn't Morgan's daughter."

"I know she's Bubba's kid." But I hadn't known Morgan was sterile. My blood iced as another thought occurred to me. When did Bubba Powell learn the truth?

"That makes him a suspect. Morgan was murdered in cold blood. That's against the law."

"Morgan ruined people's lives. He went after all the Bubbas." Darn. I wasn't going to let that slip. I wanted to pump Wayne for info, not spill my guts.

"What do you know?"

"Morgan wasn't a nice man. Now my family's safety is being threatened. Do your job. Nail the killer."

The sheriff studied me. "When were you going to tell me about the call from Florida?"

I nearly dropped my Coke. "How do you know about that?"

"You had me run the numbers on your phone."

"Oh. Well. Not much to report. The voice was muffled. I couldn't even say it was definitely a woman. The caller wanted to confirm the message I had. They gave me a message for Rose."

"I don't like this."

"Me neither. Daddy warned me about being an information conduit for the other side. I do not want to open any portals. Rose could wreak serious damage here."

"But if you have a bargaining chip, Rose would let Morgan talk to you."

I shuddered. "I'm not facing Rose again until Mama has both my necklaces recharged. A packet of crystals won't be enough to protect me. I need my top artillery to face down a demon."

"Do it. As soon as you can. I've got a bad feeling about this case."

# CHAPTER 44

That evening Larissa and I carried a vase of bright pink azalea blossoms I'd snipped from the yard over to Bubba Powell at the hospital. He appeared to be the picture of health, tan skin glowing against the white sheets and pale blue gown.

I wasn't sure what to say to Bubba. On the one hand I wanted to applaud him for being noble. On the other, I wanted to protect him from undergoing voluntary surgery and organ donation.

"You sure about this?" I asked once we'd exhausted the safer subjects of weather and Larissa's school projects.

"Dead sure," he said.

My gut tightened at his unfortunate word choice. Did Bubba kill Morgan? I gazed deep into his eyes, searching for the truth. His emerald green eyes reminded me of my husband and my daughter, people I trusted. In the past, Bubba's affable grin would've seemed harmless, but I looked past his disarming mug tonight. In his eyes I saw a steely determination.

Bubba Powell had been pushed to his limits. Of that I was certain.

"How's the food, Uncle Bubba?" Larissa hopped up on the hospital bed with him, swinging her jean-clad legs to and fro.

Larissa didn't know Connie Lee was Bubba's daughter. I couldn't tell her without having a frank discussion about sex, something I wasn't ready to do. Right now Larissa believed sex and babies went with marriage. And I'd like for her to believe

256

that for at least ten more years.

Like that was going to happen.

She probably already knew about the birds and bees but didn't want to embarrass me by mentioning the subject. I was comfortable with that.

Bubba shrugged. "Don't know. I won't get any food until after my surgery tomorrow. Listen to my stomach, and you'll hear it growling."

Larissa put her head close to his tummy and came up smiling. "Yep. You're hungry all right. Want a candy bar?"

"No food for me tonight. Tomorrow's the most important day of my life."

"You're doing a nice thing," Larissa said. "Helping Connie Lee out like this. But what if you need that kidney later?"

Bubba managed a wan smile. "One day you'll understand."

He caught my gaze. "If anything messes up tomorrow, Baxley, I'm counting on you to watch over my family."

Though the surgery was routine, it was still dangerous. "I'm proud of you for stepping up, Bubba. Roland would be proud of you, too."

"I've made some bad decisions through the years. If I die on the operating table, at least I will have done one good thing in my life."

My throat tried to close. I forced words out. "You're not going to die."

"No, you're not gonna die." Larissa slid the faded pink plastic bracelet off her wrist and handed it to him. "Wear my lucky bracelet. It will keep you safe."

A sigh slipped from my lips. Larissa hadn't taken that bracelet off since her friend disappeared. She'd worn it nonstop because June had given it to her. I leaned in to hug Larissa.

At first I thought Bubba would refuse to take it, but he surprised me by wearing it. He held up his arm and grinned.

This time the smile reached all the way to his eyes. "What do you think? Is it me?"

I gave his shoulder a fond pat. "You're going to be the coolest looking kidney donor in the operating room."


That night I checked and rechecked the locks. I glanced in Larissa's room three times. Both dogs and the cat were in there with her. Finally I went to bed. Sleep, when it appeared, was fitful.

Funhouse faces loomed and disappeared in my dreams. Snatches of conversation came at me, as if I were on a cosmic bus plugged into a universal party line.

My grandmother scolded blue jays in her yard. Maternal pride surged as June and Larissa giggled over cookies and milk at my kitchen table. Daddy tended his herb garden under the oak trees. A young Wayne Thompson flirted with me. My mother-in-law looked down her nose at me in my beautiful wedding dress. Roland carried me over the threshold of our honeymoon suite and kissed my clothes off.

The images came faster. Morgan lying in a pool of blood, his dying words screaming through my head. "Bubba done it!"

*Which one?* I hollered back at him. He writhed under his dark spirit gag.

Bubba Wright smiled secretively, his gold tooth winking at me as he said, "I beat Morgan at his own game."

Bubba Paxton appeared next, his wiry body constricted by anaconda-sized rattlers. "Save me, Baxley. Morgan is squeezing the life out of me."

Bubba Jamison strutted on my mental stage in full entertainment regalia. Light gleamed off the rhinestones on his white pantsuit. "I'm the King. All my mistakes are erased. My permanent record is clear."

A tuxedo-clad Bubba Powell twirled onto my mental stage,

dancing with Patty in an opulent ballroom setting. "She's my heart, Baxley," he said. "I'd do anything to make her happy."

The stage darkened until a pair of eyes glowed in the inky twilight. I moved and the eyes tracked my movement. Rose. She was watching me.

My heart raced. If I didn't run, I would be this predator's next meal.

I darted through the darkness. My heart pounded. I had to get away. I had to reach safety. But which direction was safe? I couldn't see anything.

I stumbled, plunging into a bottomless void. My hair trailed behind me like kite streamers. Wind rushed past my face, bringing tears to my eyes.

"Help!" I cried. "Someone, help me."

But no one came.

That wasn't right.

I should have someone.

I cried out for my someone. "Roland, where are you? I need you."

My gut chilled and superheated.

A heavy weight bore down on my chest. I struggled to draw a full breath.

The low-pitched growl of a motor reached my ears. Oh, God. Whatever this was, it was bad. I clawed my way back to consciousness.

My eyes opened wide. Thin rays of sunlight beamed through the sheers framing the window. My chest rumbled, and I glanced down into the Maine Coon cat's furry face. I pushed the purring cat aside. "Off, Sulay."

Dreams were powerful conduits between the visible and invisible, only I had no idea how to interpret this one. Warily, I got Larissa off to school, worked with Precious at the Gilroys', and walked the Smiths' boxers, but the unsettling images stayed with me, returning in waves throughout the morning. As I waited at the repair shop to get my truck window fixed, my cell phone rang. Daniel Huxley. I took the call.

"Hey," Daniel said. "You were talking about boats and the marsh the other day. I've got a Coastal Watchdog inspection run this afternoon along the coastline mid-county. Thought you might want to tag along."

A boat ride sounded like fun. But how could I have fun, knowing someone was after me and my brother-in-law was on the operating table? "This might not be the best day for me. I need to stay close to the phone. Plus, I've got a ton of work to do."

"Bring your cell phone. The work will keep. I can't postpone the boat ride because we're supposed to get rain tomorrow. The tide is perfect today. Say you'll come."

"I want to, I really do. I can't remember the last time I went out in a boat."

"I scan north and south of the marina. Tell you what I'll do. I'll scan the northerly route with you, then I'll bring you back to the dock before I do the other section. That way you wouldn't be on the water too long."

He sounded so accommodating. I wavered between fun and work, between responsibility and goofing off. "Sounds tempting."

"I thought you'd want to see where June's boat was found."

"I do." Heat rushed to my face at the words I'd said to Roland during our wedding ceremony. It felt wrong to say them to another man. "I mean, I'll go with you. What time?"

"Half an hour."

"I'll be there."

It was only after I hung up that I remembered Daniel hoped

for more than a friendship with me. I'd need to get that squared away before I stepped foot in his boat.

This was not a date.

# Chapter 45

Daniel Huxley's brown eyes gleamed with masculine approval as I walked toward his speed boat. I felt as if I'd worn a string bikini instead of my knee-length green shorts, ivory polo, ponytail, and a red ball cap. His fingers closed around my wrist, steadying me as I left the relative safety of the dock.

I grabbed the boat's center console to check my momentum, breaking the physical contact with him right away. He radiated strength beneath his "Save-the-Planet" T-shirt, palm tree–print swim trunks, and brown Docksiders. "Thank you for inviting me on your boat ride," I said.

His sun-bleached eyebrows waggled suggestively. "It's my pleasure to have a beautiful woman on board the *Sea Cat*."

Heat suffused my face. "About that, Daniel. I hope I haven't given you the wrong impression. I'm not looking for anything more than friendship."

His gaze sharpened for a moment. If I hadn't been watching closely, I'd have missed the cool speculation in his eyes. When his features relaxed, my senses went on alert. He was hiding something.

"Friendship is a good starting point," he said.

In light of the recent trouble I'd faced, his changeable emotions worried me. I'd accepted his invitation to learn more about June's last minutes on earth. Until this minute, I'd thought of Daniel as innocuous, but now I doubted my perception. Daniel was an unknown, or worse, a killer.

Sunshine played across the shimmering water. Gulls winged by, circling and landing on the tall dock pilings. Salt air, tarred wood, and gasoline created an uncertain ambiance. What had seemed like a golden learning opportunity now seemed fraught with danger.

I needed to get off of this boat.

I glanced over at the marina. "I don't know what I was thinking. I shouldn't be here. I have way too much work to do."

Daniel's hand rested lightly on my shoulder. "I understand your caution. It took me a long time to be social after my wife died from cancer."

"I'm sorry for your loss." Warmth radiated from his touch, calming my fear. I took a deep breath and relaxed. I didn't doubt his sincerity now that he'd opened up to me. He'd been hiding his grief. "I try not to obsess about my husband, but I miss him. I still expect him to come walking through my front door."

He busied himself checking the console gauges and untying ropes. "My cousin Louise is that way about her daughter. It's tough to lose a kid the way she lost June."

I nodded, thankful he'd broached the subject of the missing child. "Not knowing is hard. Do you think June is still alive?"

"No. It's been too long. June wouldn't walk away from her life. Her parents indulged her every whim. If they'd insisted she always have someone in the boat with her, perhaps her accident wouldn't have happened."

Or perhaps two kids would've been lost at sea. Panic struck my heart with lightning bolt intensity. Larissa could've been in that boat with June. If Mama hadn't insisted Larissa stay with her and Dad that day, my kid might've been in harm's way.

"Is that why you asked me to come with you today?" I asked.

The engine vibration shook the bottom of the boat as the powerful props turned. The sharp smell of fuel lingered in the air. I held on to the console as we eased away from the floating dock.

He idled the boat down the creek. "Partly. I enjoy your company, but your questions about June the other day got me to thinking about her disappearance. I wanted to see the marsh again under similar conditions, and we're in another full-moon phase. Today's flood tide should be equal in height to the one on the afternoon she disappeared."

I nodded, jamming my hat securely on my head. After we passed the last mooring, he eased the throttle forward. The wind cut right through my clothes. I moved behind the canopied console, standing next to Daniel.

"You cold?" He jerked his thumb toward a rear bench compartment. "I've got a windbreaker in there."

"It's warmer back here out of the wind. I'll be fine."

We traversed the labyrinth network of tidal creeks, startling herons and egrets. Rafts of marsh rack floated by. Bleach bottles bobbed above crab traps. My troubles eased and I felt free for the first time in days. I could get used to boating regularly. "You've got a great job."

"This is the best part. Identifying and prosecuting people who aren't adhering to conservation laws is controversial. I catch heat for doing my job."

"Does it happen a lot?"

"I've been arrested a few times." At my startled look, he clarified, "For trespassing on a developer's land. Nothing truly criminal."

"You're right. Riding around in the boat is definitely the best part of your job."

"Today I'm checking out the Ryals Brothers' development. They've banned me from their land, so I check on their construction from the river. I also check to make sure other property owners are being good stewards of the marsh."

We cruised by the building site, slowing to photograph the broken sediment-barrier fence. Tide encroached through the opening, covering the flat, clear-cut land.

After Daniel made notes, we were on our way. We slowed to pass the Gilroy docks. Morgan's came up first. A small skiff was the only vessel at his dock.

Ritchie and Louise's dock was just to the south. There were no boats tied up at their dock. Daniel pointed to an aluminum boat upended near the high-tide mark. "There's June's boat."

My heart stuttered. "I didn't know they'd kept the boat."

"That's it all right. Louise wouldn't hear of getting rid of June's boat. Ritchie wanted me to take it to the dump, but Louise put her foot down. The boat stays until June comes home."

An idea leapt into my mind as I stared at the beached boat. If I touched the boat, there might be residual vibrations that I could identify. Lucky for me, I already had a built-in excuse to be on the Gilroy property. This evening when I walked Precious, we'd come down to the marsh, and I'd check out the boat.

No telling how many people had touched that boat before and after it had been recovered. Even so, few of those people would have been in the grip of a powerful emotion like the killer had been. If, of course, June had been killed and not accidentally drowned.

Daniel sped up again once we cleared the docks. We traveled due east, through wider creeks until we reached the edge of the sound. Across the water, two barrier islands created a wide throat between the sound and the Atlantic Ocean. The boat slowed and turned into the high marsh.

He cut the motor and raised it, using a paddle to pole us across the marsh grass tips. He lined us up between the tallest oak on the island and a cluster of mainland palms. "This is where June's boat was found. By the time I got here, the tide had gone out. Bubba Wright and I bogged through the marsh to reach the boat."

I glanced east to the island and west to the mainland. Swimming across the strong currents in the sound would take an Olympic-caliber swimmer. Ten-year-old June wasn't that strong of a swimmer. Acres and acres of marsh and water separated us from the mainland. Walking back to the mainland would be an extreme challenge for an adult. I doubted whether a child could manage the feat.

"Why didn't she stay with the boat?" I startled at the unexpected sound of my voice. I hadn't meant to say that out loud.

"I've asked myself that over and over." Daniel rubbed the side of his face. "June knew the basics of boat safety because I taught her. I can't think of any reason she would've come out this far without checking the boat plugs. And even if she forgot them at first, she would've put them in once the boat started taking on water. She was a smart kid."

"Something else must have been wrong."

"That's what I concluded too, but the Gilroy brothers didn't want to hear that." He shook his head. "They could be such Bubbas sometimes."

His remark floored me. I huffed out my surprise. "Bubbas?"

"Yeah. Brothers. Bubbas, brothers, same thing. Bubba is what they called each other in private when they wanted to get a rise out of each other. The Gilroy Bubbas. They had a whole Bubba ritual." He shook his head dismissively. "You'd think they didn't have a brain between them when they were in Bubba mode."

I drew in a shallow, considering breath.

*The Bubbas.*

The brothers' name for each other was a missing puzzle piece, a corner piece in this murder mystery jigsaw puzzle, which brought two trains of non-related thought together. My brain whirred. Morgan's murder had been a crime of passion. He'd also been the person June was supposed to be spending her last afternoon with.

What if he'd lied about her not showing up? What if something had happened to June while she was at his house?

I didn't have any answers, but the questions felt right.

Dead right.

The two Gilroy deaths weren't coincidence. They were related. One Bubba remained. Ritchie Gilroy. He'd been above suspicion the entire time.

He'd been on the scene right after the police arrived. He'd been at Morgan's funeral, and the threatening phone call I received came after I visited his house. He certainly had opportunity. He knew how to handle a knife, so there was his "means." And if Morgan was responsible for June's disappearance, Ritchie had a strong motive to murder him.

Had we been looking in the wrong direction for Morgan's killer all this time?

A cool ocean breeze ruffled the short hairs on my neck. Now, more than ever, I needed to touch that boat.

Once I was back in my truck, I called Mama. No answer. If I wanted my necklaces, I needed to go by there and pick them up. They waited for me on the kitchen table, along with a note saying my parents had gone to visit a sick friend.

I put Roland's necklace on, stashed Mom's new necklace in my pocket, and made a plan.

# CHAPTER 46

"What's up, Mom?" Larissa's book bag thudded on the floorboard. She bounded into the truck, her golden hair shimmering like a curtain around her. Pride filled me as I watched her. Even though I wasn't a material success, I'd brought this person into the world.

"I need you to stay with Charlotte this afternoon." I pulled out behind the school bus onto the highway, headed to town. I'd phoned Charlotte for help since my parents were in the wind. My friend was delighted but asked me to bring Larissa to the newspaper office while she typed up her last story of the week.

Alarm splashed across my daughter's face. Her creamy skin paled, accentuating the freckles on her nose and cheeks. "Is Uncle Bubba okay? Is it Connie Lee?"

I was as wired as a squirrel under attack by a tag team of mockingbirds. Alarmed that Larissa's intuition had picked up my distress, I shielded my turbulent emotions. "Your uncle is fine. So is Connie Lee. Something else has come up. I need you to keep Charlotte company."

Her lower lip stuck up. "I wanna come with you."

"I need to do this alone."

"I could help you."

"One day you'll understand."

Her voice shook with emotion. "I understand right now. You think I'm a dumb kid who can't look out for herself. But I can táke care of myself."

I kept my eyes on the road, taking a deep, cautionary breath before I spoke. "You're remarkably grown up for ten, but I'm erring on the side of caution. Today I want you with someone I trust implicitly."

"Aww, Mom." With that, Larissa lapsed into troubled silence.

I was glad of the respite, though her verbal compliance didn't fool me. Sure enough, her energy inched across the void between us, sniffing around my mental shield. I held firm. Larissa did not need to know my plans.

At the paper, Charlotte bustled out of her tiny office and cooed over Larissa. "We're going to have so much fun. I've got way-cool arts and crafts sites bookmarked on the Internet."

"Whatever." Larissa's shoulders slumped, and she shot me a pouty look. I sympathized, but I couldn't be her best friend. I was her mother. That took precedence.

"Thanks, Char." I edged toward the door. "I appreciate the favor."

"I expect a home-cooked meal out of this," Charlotte joked.

"Done." Relief sighed out of me as I left. Larissa was in good hands. I could do this without worrying about her or having to hurry home.

My truck roared down the highway. I turned on Honeycreek Lane and parked in Ritchie and Louise's driveway. A glance in their garage window confirmed both cars were gone.

Good. I exhaled thankfully. I didn't want the Gilroys to see me down by the boat. Questions churned through my head as I pulled the spare key from under the planter. Even if I discerned the truth, how could I prove it?

Without proof, the sheriff wouldn't believe me.

Inside the house, Precious sounded off. Her insistent barking centered me. I had a job to do. About time I acted like a police consultant instead of a fretting mom. The boat was a lead in the case, and I was checking it out. If I got a reading on a particular person, the sheriff could question him. It could point to solid evidence.

Precious greeted me like a long-lost friend, licking my hands, jumping up, sniffing my shoes, her nails clicking on the ceramic tiled floor. Poor thing. Living in this house without June must be like living in a mausoleum.

I snapped the leash on the Lab's red collar and headed down to the waterfront. No need to meander around the yard when no one was here to notice my direction.

Precious sniffed around the aluminum boat with interest. I circled the small craft, looking first for anything visual that might trigger a memory, but the exterior appeared unremarkable. The drain plug was securely installed in the stern.

I stopped by the rear transom. Precious tugged on the leash, urging me forward, but this was where I needed to be. I took a few deep breaths and braced for the momentary sense of disorientation.

My hands trembled. I reached for the boat, the sun-warmed aluminum feeling oddly cool to my touch. After another deep breath, I dropped my guard.

Sensations roared in like a nor'easter. I reeled under the assault, dropping to my knees, fighting to hold the connection. Anger, fear, and sadness thundered from fingertip to brain. Stone-cold fury rocketed through next, taking my breath away. On its heels, a vision unfolded. An image of a lumpy canvas duffel bag lying on the bottom of the boat flashed into my head.

*June.* She was in the bag. She was too still. Waves splashed over the bow and saltwater sprayed in my face. Thickly muscled arms lifted the bag and heaved it overboard. The bag clunked against the side of the boat and sank below the dark green water.

The boat traversed the throat of the barrier islands and

motored into the marshy creeks. I heard another splash. The
boat floated into the marsh. I heard the slap, slap of swimming
arms. Nausea swirled through me, and I fell away from the
boat. My fingers were stiff with cold. I rubbed feeling back into
my hands, welcoming the warmth of the late-afternoon sun on
my face.

June had been buried at sea.

She hadn't been alive at the time. She had drowned before
she'd been tossed overboard. If Morgan had been involved, he'd
lied about her being at his house. He'd lied about her swimming in his pool. Larissa's vision had been of June in clear
water. Pool water.

I needed to see Morgan's pool again, to try to sense the actual
event.

Driven by that thought, I stumbled to my feet, only to realize
I was alone. Long shadows crossed the lawn. Distant marsh
hens called. But the dog was nowhere in sight. "Precious!"

Irritation crackled through my heightened senses. That
darned dog. She'd probably gone to the woods. To that muddy
bank where she'd been digging the other day. I sprinted through
the woods, calling her name as I ran.

Sure enough, I found Precious in the ravine. Her powerful
paws carved through the soft earth. She stuck her nose in a
spot, snuffled, and moved farther down the bank.

My heart pounded. Was the dog looking for something in
particular? Because my thoughts were on murder and death, I
considered that Precious might have zeroed in on something
related to the homicide. If that were true, I should test my
sensory perception down here.

With my senses running wide open, I fanned my fingers along
the bank, searching for a disruption in the energy field. I
strained to concentrate.

Nothing.

I felt nothing emanating from the bank.

I backed away, stepping in the thin trickle of water. I wobbled, nearly righted myself, then fell into the mire. An acrid stench engulfed me. Gross.

I staggered to the opposite side, planting my hand on the sloping bank. The resulting jolt nearly knocked my shoes off. My rose tattoo heated. Something was here all right, but it was on this side of the ravine.

Grabbing a pointed stick, I dug. Precious came over, sniffed, wagged her tail, and dug with me. Moments later, the dog pulled an object from the bank.

There was so much mud clinging to it, I couldn't make it out. Using my sharp stick, I cut at the mud, revealing the rubber sole of a sneaker. A few more scrapes and I saw bright curlicues and swirls. My daughter's artwork.

This hand-painted shoe was an exact match to one in Larissa's closet. June and Larissa had painted these shoes during spring break and then mixed up the set of sneakers. Larissa's shoes were in her closet.

This muddy shoe had belonged to June Gilroy.

# CHAPTER 47

Precious clung to the shoe and whined pitifully. A low keening sound rumbled in my throat. Grief and shock whirled through my system, weakening my knees. Instinctively, I ramped my shields back up and summoned the courage to face this chilling reality.

"I miss her, too." I rubbed the dog's mud-dotted ears and tried to make sense of this physical evidence. June's body had been disposed of at sea, but her shoe was here. Could she have died in the creek?

There was only an inch or two of water here in the drainage ditch. During a rain, the volume increased, but during a drought, like we'd had when she disappeared, the ditch dried up. It didn't seem possible a healthy ten-year-old who knew how to swim would have drowned here.

I believed June drowned in Morgan's pool. So why was her shoe here? The psychic signature emanating from the shoe matched what I'd detected in the boat. Which implied to me that whoever had dumped June at sea had also hidden her shoe here in the bank.

Which furthered my resolve to visit Morgan's swimming pool at Sparrow's Point.

I scrambled out of the ditch and strode toward Sparrow's Point, Precious at my heels. Sticks crunched under my sneakers as I hurried through the dappled sunlight. Even if Morgan had been responsible for June's death, I had no proof. Which led me back to Ritchie. How would Ritchie learn of Morgan's deception?

Morgan wouldn't have bragged about killing his niece. From what I'd seen, he had enjoyed June's company.

Could he have acted inappropriately with her?

A shudder ripped through me. Child molestation sickened me. Wouldn't a sensitive like me have known if that was going on?

Wouldn't June have been sad or distant or reserved instead of her usual happy-go-lucky self? Wouldn't my maternal radar have noticed something big like that?

Wait. I was grasping at straws. Maybe I hadn't missed anything.

Maybe June's death had been an accident.

But then, why hadn't Morgan stepped forward? Why put his brother and Louise through the torture of not knowing what happened to their child? That didn't make any sense.

I stepped clear of the shaded woods line onto the thick cushion of Morgan's lawn and surveyed the property. Thick clumps of orphaned Spanish moss dotted the grass, giving the yard a neglected feeling. No vehicles were in the driveway.

I exhaled in relief. Though Ritchie and Louise weren't at home, I'd worried they could be over here preparing Morgan's estate for sale. It was just me and the dog and the pool.

Precious padded resolutely at my side, the shoe clamped firmly between her powerful jaws. Mud crusted along her snout, legs, and barrel chest. After being in the ditch, I looked and smelled a mess, too, with mud smears on my clothes, skin, and hands.

The pool water sparkled in the sunlight, a veritable psychic Oz. My energy barriers ramped up another notch and my pace slowed. If this was the site of June's death, I would sense her last moments, but so what? Even if I dreamed the event, I wouldn't have tangible proof to give the sheriff.

One thing at a time.

At the brick-edged concrete, I toed my muddy sneakers off to keep from tracking a mess on the pool deck. The hard surface felt cool on my bare feet. A shiver of dread rippled down my spine.

My palms dampened, and my mouth went dry. Nerves, I told myself. I could do this. I'd faced down angry demons.

"Stay here, Precious."

The dog sat, June's shoe in her jaws.

Gingerly, I approached the calm water, half afraid that I would sense something, half afraid I wouldn't. I crouched down on the sunny pool coping, opening my senses to the fullest extent.

The psychic blast knocked me on my butt.

Images careened in my head, a remnant of June's last day alive. She had frolicked in the pool. "Throw me the ball, Uncle Morgan," she'd cried. Morgan had thrown a foam ball from the pool deck to her. Sometimes she caught it, most times she missed.

"Call the jump," she'd shouted.

"Dive," he'd said. He'd had her spin and cannonball and more. Then his phone rang. He picked it up and debated with his caller. He walked toward the house, disagreeing with whoever was on the phone.

June continued to jump and dive. After a few minutes, she tried another spin, only she slipped on the diving board and hit her head as she fell into the water.

My vision darkened to a narrow shaft of light. Water rippled.

Time passed.

Morgan retuned to the pool, running and shouting for help.

No one came.

He dove in and brought June up, but it was too late.

Much too late.

June was dead.

He cradled her in his arms, weeping.

The vision faded and I was blasted by the bright sunshine of reality. I drew in deep breaths to steady my racing heart. June had been here. Morgan had lied about that. He'd told so many lies, it's a miracle he'd kept them straight. Maybe that's what tripped him up in the end.

Behind me, the sliding glass door of the house opened.

My gut filled with dread as I turned.

Ritchie Gilroy stepped out of the shadowed doorway.

# CHAPTER 48

Ritchie's face contorted in a mask of fury. "Why couldn't you leave well enough alone?"

My body temperature plummeted from volcanic to ice-cold. I scrambled to my feet, wishing I knew how to send a reliable telepathic message. I tried it anyway, beaming my thoughts in broadband style to the universe, hoping a nearby sensitive would hear my distress call.

*I'm in trouble. Send the police to Sparrow's Point.*

I hoped someone out there received the message. But just in case they didn't, I prepared to defend myself from this deadly Bubba. The first task was to make myself appear to be a non-threat. "Ritchie," I stammered, "what are you doing here?"

"I'm the executor for Morgan's estate. What are you doing here?"

"Precious got away from me. This is where we ended up. I didn't think anyone would mind if I sat by the pool for a moment. I'll just get the dog and be on my way."

"Not so fast." He studied the mud on my hands and T-shirt. "That dog been digging in the drainage ditch again?"

I edged toward Precious, hoping against hope Ritchie didn't see the muddy shoe between the dog's paws. "I'll bathe her before I allow her back in your house. I'm sorry to have disturbed you."

Ritchie strode over to Precious, his face reddened with every step. "She found the other one, didn't she?"

"I don't know what you're talking about." The distant woods line wouldn't offer much in the way of a sanctuary if Ritchie came after me. He regularly competed in marathons, which meant I couldn't outrun him. Plus, I'd removed my sneakers before I walked out on the pool deck. There would be no running anywhere in bare feet. I adjusted my course to take me to my muddy shoes.

Sweat moistened my palms, beaded my brow. Trying to appear nonchalant took a toll on me. I wanted to sprint out of here at the speed of light. Instead, I jammed my toes in my muddy shoes and used my finger to roll the heel part up the back of my foot.

So far, so good.

"Don't lie to me." He pointed to the shoe Precious guarded. "That's June's shoe. Where did you get it?"

No way was I telling him that I traced the psychic signature on the shoe. His interest in the object was a bad thing. It further cemented the certainty in my mind that he was tied to Morgan's death. "Precious dug it out of the mud bank."

He covered his eyes with a hand for a moment. "I told Louise to get rid of that dog."

My pulse hammered in my ears. If I made a mad dash, I could beat him to the mansion. I could lock the door. What was I thinking? Ritchie had a key to the house. The lock would slow him down for a few seconds. Then what?

No, I was far better off out here in the open. I kept my weight on the balls of my feet, ready to fight if he approached. His large size gave him the edge in hand-to-hand combat. The only thing I had going for me was the element of surprise. If he came after me, I'd have one chance to take him out. I'd better not waste it.

I strengthened my telepathic distress signal.

Richie suspected I knew what had happened to June. How

was that possible?

He grabbed for the shoe. Precious growled at him, hunkering down over the prize. I darted around both of them, catching the leash in my hand and tugging the dog my way. "I'll take her home and get her cleaned up now."

"Not so fast. Precious, sit," Ritchie commanded in a stern voice.

The dog complied, howling as Ritchie ripped the shoe from her muddy mouth. When Ritchie approached me, I backpedaled. Now that I was off the pool deck, the woods were much closer.

But if I fled, he still had the dog. Precious could track me with her eyes closed. The only option I had was to stand my ground. I hated having no options.

Ritchie pressed the shoe to his chest. "My sweet June. I can't believe she's gone."

"I'm sorry about your daughter, Ritchie." I kept my eyes on his hands, hands that most likely killed his brother in cold blood.

He stared at the glass-slick water in the pool. "Morgan was supposed to be watching her. I trusted him to keep her safe, but he didn't. I believed him about June not showing up here on that day. I believed my brother and doubted my daughter. All that time, I didn't believe in June because Morgan wouldn't lie to me. But he did, and you figured it out, didn't you?"

I gulped as his unfocused gaze dialed in on me. Every hair on my body snapped to attention at the unwholesome energy radiating from Ritchie. "June would have come home if she could. She wasn't the type to run away or kill herself," I said.

"But you know about Morgan and June? About how she died?"

"Ritchie, don't beat yourself up. Accidents happen."

His bitter laugh echoed across the empty yard. "This was no accident. It was neglect. My rotten brother didn't keep a close eye on June while she was in the pool. When he found her dead body, his first thought wasn't me or my wife, it was saving his precious hide." Ritchie's hands coiled into tight fists. "His business deal meant more to him than our peace of mind."

I watched him, waiting to see where he would strike. Yet, even knowing it was coming, he blindsided me. In one fluid motion, he latched on to my arm. His seething emotions ignited the rose tattoo. Frantic, I pulled against the restraint.

His grip tightened. "Tell me what you know."

# CHAPTER 49

Ritchie's hand scalded my arm as if the demon once again had hold of me. Revulsion swept through me, scattering my wits. Blood pounded in my ears, deafening me.

It was too late. Too late for June. Too late for Morgan. And now too late for Baxley. He was gonna kill me.

To heck with my mental distress beacon. Unless I did something, I would die. I locked down my thoughts and tried to erect a mental barrier. Nothing happened at first. I gasped aloud as threads of Ritchie's malignant energy choked me. A shudder ripped through me, and I grabbed that energy pulse and focused on building an energy barrier.

Raw energy crackled in the air. The mist of my mental shield grew thicker and I allowed myself a shallow breath. White light flooded my head, restoring order to my panicked thoughts, allowing me to focus on my physical well-being. Shielded but jazzed on the white lightning of adrenaline, my regular senses heightened.

The crimson mask of fury on Richie's face contrasted sharply with the blue sky. The sharp scent of chlorine from the pool blasted through my nostrils. Palm fronds rustled in the slight breeze. From distant Honeycreek Lane came the whir of tires on pavement.

Roland used to say there were two kinds of people in the world: doers and quitters. At the time of his lecture on the subject, I'd decided to quit a volunteer effort, but his disappointment changed my mind. I drew on that wellspring of confidence.

"I'm not a quitter." I reeled at the unexpected strength in my voice.

Ritchie shook my arm, lifting me half off the ground, rattling my teeth together. "You should've quit a long time ago. You should've stayed the hell away from the Gilroys." He shook me again. "How did you figure it out? Morgan talk to you from the grave? Is that how you know?"

Anger made me bold. "You killed your own brother."

His eyes gleamed with dark malice. "Morgan was a selfish pig. All he cared about was the next deal coming down the pike. He put making money before family. It cost him his life."

Ritchie's face contorted in fury. I couldn't breathe. One wrong word on my part and he would kill me. No one had heard my extrasensory plea for help. No one knew I was here at Sparrow's Point. Not family, not the cops.

My fate hinged on my wits and the self-defense moves Roland had taught me. I hadn't practiced those kicks and throws in a while, but I hoped it was like riding a bike. If I wanted to see Larissa tonight, I prayed that was the case. I let my shoulders slump and hung my head.

"Tell me how you figured it out," Ritchie snarled, his other hand cupping my throat. Fingers dug into the cords of my neck.

Fear rode me hard. I tugged at his wrist. He was so big. So powerful. So enraged. My hope dimmed. Tears spilled out of my eyes. "Morgan told me. He was still alive when the sheriff and I arrived."

"Liar." Ritchie yanked down on my left arm and sneered in my face. "If good old Wayne had heard a deathbed confession, I'd a-been in jail last Monday night. Tell the truth."

If he'd move in front of me, I could kick him toward the pool, but from the side, my angle was bad. His fingers dug in a little more. My words spilled out in a high-pitched shriek. "I am telling you the truth. Morgan said Bubba killed him. That's why Wayne interviewed Bubbas."

Ritchie's eyes widened, then narrowed again. "Damn, I should have killed that bastard outright. But I wanted him to suffer for what he did. For killing my June. She was a true Gilroy. Morgan's daughter wasn't even his flesh and blood."

He shook me again. "Who else knows?"

I managed to gasp in a bit of air. "What?"

"Who else did you tell?"

"No one. I'm telling the truth," I sobbed. Closing my eyes against the tears and pain, against the tangible signs of my physical weakness.

"Look at me. Who did you tell?"

"No one." I gazed into the crazed eyes of a gilt-headed killer. Had I gambled my life waiting on the perfect moment to fight back? His thumb and index finger pressed against my windpipe. I tugged at his choke hold. "Please, Ritchie. Let me go."

Valuable seconds ticked off my life-clock. My intuition screamed to act now. I tensed as he released my left wrist, stepping forward into perfect kicking position.

A branch broke off to my left. Ritchie froze. He glanced over his shoulder, the whites of his eyes showing.

"Hold it right there, dirt bag." Charlotte's crisp voice rang with authority.

I gulped in a sigh of relief. I'd been rescued. There was my best friend in her Charlie's Angels pose, crab-walking closer, gun extended like she planned on leveling a whole team of commandos. For a plus-sized woman, she was amazingly sure-footed.

My relief was short-lived. Charlotte's tongue and pen were lethal weapons, but she didn't know how to shoot my pistol. She'd never squashed a bug, much less shot a man.

Ritchie swore. "Where did you come from?" He whirled around, thrusting me between him and the gun. One hand tightened on my throat, the other cinched around my waist. Baxley Powell, the human bullet shield.

"The cops are on their way, Ritchie," Charlotte said. "Let Baxley go."

He backed up, disarming my plan to lash backward with my foot to his knee. He dragged me close to the pool. The stench of his fear clogged my nostrils. I prayed Charlotte had the gun on safety as I put my plan into action. I sagged like a defeated rag doll. My dangling arms found each other, my fingers interlocking in a two-handed fist.

My hands powered up and over my head, striking Ritchie's right eye. My foot slashed out at his kneecap. I twisted away as he struck my face in a glancing blow.

"You'll pay for that." His hands went to his eye. I powered my mega-fist into his groin. He crumpled to the pool deck.

Charlotte ran up, holding the pistol like a dirty diaper. "That was so fab. You're an Amazon. Where'd you learn to fight like that?"

My hands throbbed. Cold sweat trickled down my back. Nausea swirled in my throat. I didn't have time to explain, not with Ritchie writhing at my feet. "Gimme the gun, Char."

She handed it to me, steering clear of the groaning man on the concrete. "You didn't need firepower. I had no idea you were so talented."

"Get up," I said to Ritchie. "Sit in that chair by the pool where I can keep an eye on you until the sheriff arrives." I glanced over to Charlotte. "You called the cops, right?"

She nodded toward the woods. "Larissa called them. They'll be here any minute."

"Larissa's here?" I croaked, rubbing my aching throat.

"She's in the car." Charlotte's round face blanched. "She's

pretty shaken up."

"I don't want her near this." I called the dog. When Precious came, I unhitched her leash and handed it to Charlotte. "Tie Ritchie's hands behind the chair."

"With pleasure. Good thing I spent all those summers at Girl Scout camp. I can tie him up with six kinds of knots."

"Make sure they're tight."

Moments later, Ritchie was secured, and Charlotte was on her way back to wait with Larissa in her trusty Jetta. I allowed myself a full breath, but I relaxed. Pain throbbed through Ritchie Gilroy's eyes, pain and a crazed look. I couldn't believe he'd hidden his madness for so long.

"You think you've got me?" Ritchie said. "You've got nothing. There's not a single piece of physical evidence that ties me to Morgan's murder. That woo-woo stuff won't hold up in court. I'm a free man."

I leaned close to his snarling face. "You killed your brother. You physically assaulted me. You won't be free for a long time."

"My lawyer can make short work of your transparent claims. I'll have you arrested for trespassing. You assaulted me."

"Uh, Baxley," Charlotte said. "Larissa's here."

# CHAPTER 50

"Stay back, Larissa," I warned. Adrenaline rushed through me like a fire hose run amok.

My daughter ignored me. She stopped at the edge of the pool, kneeled down, and dipped her hand into the still water. For a long moment, she said nothing. Then she stood, tears rolling down her pale cheeks, and stumbled back toward the woods. Precious followed her, June's shoe clamped firmly in her jaw.

It didn't take a psychic genius to know that my daughter had just had another vision of her friend's death. I wanted to go to her, but I couldn't. I needed hard evidence to seal Ritchie Gilroy's fate. Morgan's negligence had cost June her life, but Ritchie had crossed a line when he'd murdered his brother.

No way I wanted a killer walking our streets, living in our community as a free man.

I shot Charlotte a questioning gaze.

"I'll go with Larissa," Charlotte said.

My friend hurried after my daughter, catching Larissa when grief bowed her double. Her gulping sobs wrenched my heart. Her friend died of accidental causes, but Morgan's cover-up led to his murder. Negative energy crackled around me like sheet lightning, raising the hair on my arms.

Unconsciously, my hand went to my green pendant. As I touched the smooth moldavite, my thoughts steadied. My driving sense of purpose returned.

"How did you figure it out, Ritchie?" I asked. "Did Morgan let something slip in casual conversation?"

Ritchie Gilroy spewed off cusswords like volcanic cinders, hot and deadly. "You blinded me."

"Better learn to deal with the pain. Prison is a rough place."

"I'm a Gilroy. Money will make this go away."

He sounded as arrogant as his brother. I wouldn't trick him into admitting anything. I had to outwit him. "Your house looks out over the water. Did you see Morgan tow June's boat out?"

He snorted. "You think I would have waited nine months to kill him if I'd seen that? I'd have confronted him right away."

Pulse hammering in my ears, I tried to process the information I had. I settled on the lead that brought me here. "It was the shoe, wasn't it?"

"I want my lawyer."

"It *was* the shoe. Precious found the other shoe first, didn't she? She found it and brought it home, and she wouldn't give it up."

He glared at me with his good eye. "One glance at that shoe and I knew Morgan lied. June wouldn't take those shoes off for nothing. She practically slept in them. So for them to end up muddy and discarded, something bad had happened to her. I ran over here and that monster laughed in my face. He said the damage was done, and he'd cleaned up the garbage. Case closed."

My insides curdled. Morgan's words had been cruel, ruthless, and mean-spirited. They'd fueled a man distraught by grief into performing a heinous act.

I stroked the stone around my neck, until my sympathy dissipated. Seeing the shoe had triggered Ritchie's rage, but was that too circumstantial for a conviction?

I needed more. And the only way to get more was to try to read Ritchie's thoughts. There must be something else he was hiding. Something that would cement his guilt.

The energy coming off him was an ugly, seething mass. I recoiled at the thought of entering that maelstrom. But it was the only way. If Ritchie wasn't convicted for murder, he'd come after Larissa and me. That was unacceptable.

Once the sheriff got here, I would not have another chance alone with Ritchie. The time to do this was right here, right now.

Releasing my pendant, I edged forward, both arms extended in front of me. I didn't have to immerse myself in Ritchie's energy field. All I needed to do was touch the edge to get a reading.

"What're you doing?" Ritchie reared back as if my good energy were virally contagious.

I inched forward. "You're hiding something. I need to see it."

He scooted his chair backward, edging closer to the pool. "Stay away from me."

The urge to touch my pendant was overwhelming. The green stone seemed to be calling to me to hold it, to keep the bad energy at bay. That contrary message diluted my current intent and kept my shields from dropping. Did Roland's gift interact with my psychic abilities? If so, I needed to take it off. I needed every bit of intuitiveness I possessed to do this.

Hmm. I halted, removed the green necklace, and dropped the other one out of my pocket. Instantly, I plunged into chaos.

# CHAPTER 51

Evil threads surged around my head, snaking through every orifice. I fell to my knees. With each thread pulsed a gruesome vignette of events related to the Gilroy deaths.

June's accidental death unfolded before me. Morgan's grief-stricken expression when he found her. His dumping her body from the boat played out again in my head, only this time I got a fix on the waterway markers. He returned home, drinking scotch from the bottle on the pool deck, and spotted her shoes. He buried them in the soft bank of the ravine.

Ritchie came upon Morgan in his office. They argued fiercely. Morgan said he'd taken out the garbage. Ritchie grabbed the knife and stabbed his brother. They argued more. Ritchie's voice rang in my ear. "You killed the only true Gilroy. I'll make sure Connie Lee doesn't receive a dime from your estate. You screwed me for the last time."

"I screwed your wife, Bubba," Morgan gloated.

Ritchie stabbed Morgan again. And again.

He bent Morgan's finger until it broke. "Die, you self-centered prick."

The visions repeated. Ritchie grunted with each knife thrust. Morgan moaned. The metallic smell of blood engulfed me. Blood dripped down my fingers.

Suddenly, I plunged into June's last moments. She couldn't move. The water rocked her body, pulsing her hair in front of her face. She held her breath until she couldn't. Water flowed in, filling her lungs. She struggled briefly. I struggled briefly.

I floated.

The pungent scent of chlorine permeated my thoughts.

Cool air washed over me, and still I floated in a void, neither living nor dead. In between worlds.

Spirits gathered on one side. Were they hoping I would join them?

I wasn't ready to die. I had a daughter to rear.

From far away I heard voices. Female voices. Charlotte and Larissa. I focused on their voices, and the void brightened. I felt a huge pressure on my chest.

I fought against it. If I opened my mouth to breathe, I'd drown. But the pressure insisted.

The voices. I heard them again. A man's voice this time.

I coughed. Water ran out of my mouth. The world spun as I wrenched open my eyes.

Warmth seeped up my right arm. I looked toward that comforting presence. Larissa kneeled beside me, worry clouding her eyes. Her hands were wrapped tightly around my fist.

"I'm here, Mom."

I wasn't sure if she'd said that aloud or whispered it in my head. My fingers brushed across the smooth stone on the pool deck. My moldavite pendant.

My thoughts cleared.

"She's back," Charlotte said.

I gazed over at my friend. She was soaking wet, her lacy pink bra beaming through the thin white blouse. Her smile warmed me the rest of the way. "What happened?" My voice broke as I spoke.

"You had a seizure or something. Larissa said you would die if you weren't moved. I tackled you into the pool. Then I nearly lost you there as well."

I sat up. The pendant was near my hand. I grabbed it.

"Not so fast, hard head," Sheriff Wayne Thompson said. "Let Bo Seavey check you out first."

I searched his face. "The ex-coroner? Am I dead?"

"Nah," he said. "We were down at the Fiddler Hole having a drink when the call came in. He came along for the ride."

Bo gestured with his black bag. "Never a dull moment out at Sparrow's Point, eh, Baxley?"

"I'm due for some dull times." I glanced around. "Where's Ritchie?"

"In the back of the squad car. Virg and Ronnie secured him while the rest of us brought you around."

Bo whipped out a stethoscope. "Whoa," I said. "That thing been on any dead people?"

"Relax, hon. Dr. Sugar is on the case."

With a steady heartbeat and working lungs, I passed his exam with flying colors. I sat up on the warm concrete, clutching a soft blanket around my shoulders. I coughed again. "I'm fine."

"Charlotte's been feeding me a crazy story." The sheriff squatted beside me, dousing me with his woodsy aftershave. Concern ringed his dark eyes. "You found June's shoe, realized the missing girl was dead, and hiked to Morgan's place. Is that right?"

"Almost. The dog got free while I was tending her. She dug up June's shoe in the woods. We walked over here, ran into Ritchie, and he went nuts. He killed Morgan."

Disappointment flooded Wayne's eyes. His lips tightened. "Impossible. He's one of the few men in this town who aren't named Bubba."

"Ah, but he was. He and Morgan called themselves the Bubbas. Daniel Huxley told me about it. He said they had a whole gag going about the Gilroy Bubbas. Ritchie is a Bubba. Worse, he's a cold-blooded murderer."

Wayne stilled. "What proof do you have?"

I ignored the turbulence around Wayne. I had no reason to

be afraid of him. "The shoes. June took them off before she drowned. Morgan overlooked them during the cleanup and later buried them in the ravine. When the dog dug up the first shoe, Ritchie confronted Morgan about his daughter's death. Morgan taunted Ritchie, who then showed no mercy. He said he's gonna drain Connie Lee's trust, keeping the money for himself. I believe he's already raided one account. One that has a ram as its logo."

"I know that fund," Bo Seavey said. "I have stock with them."

Precious walked up, shoe in mouth. "That's evidence," Wayne said.

"Good luck getting that one from her. You might have better luck with the one locked in Ritchie's gun cabinet."

"How do you know about that?" Wayne cocked his head to the side.

A marsh hen cackled in the distance. "A little birdie told me."

# CHAPTER 52

"Ya done good." Daddy beamed from ear to ear.

"Easy, Dad." I glanced around my parents' crowded kitchen, keenly aware of my father's booming voice. His euphoria filled the house.

Mama patted my shoulder. "Cat's out of the bag now, little one. Everyone knows you're one of those *smart* Nesbitts."

Steam from my teacup wafted up in my face. The heat felt good. I wasn't sure when I'd be warm all over again. The chill in my bones seemed permanent. "Not smart enough to avoid a confrontation with a killer."

She clucked dismissively. "You're smart as a whip and don't you forget it. Without arming Charlotte and sending that mental distress signal, Ritchie would have killed you in a mudcat minute."

Larissa padded into the kitchen and slipped into my lap. I hugged her. "Thank you for hearing my distress call."

"You were doing fine when we got there, Mom," Larissa said. "Charlotte is still raving about how you took Ritchie out with your self-defense moves. You'll be headline news in the paper."

As soon as we were released from Morgan's, Charlotte had dumped us at Mom's and raced back to file her story.

"If Charlotte knows what's good for her, she'll focus her story on something else." I stroked Larissa's hair, marveling at how perfect she was. "All I've ever wanted to be is your mom, and I nearly messed that up."

She gazed up at me, her green eyes full of adoration. "You're the best mom I ever had."

Her earnest expression tickled my funny bone. "I'm the only mom you've ever had."

The sheriff sauntered into the kitchen like he owned the place and sat down in the empty chair beside me. "Start from the beginning."

I leaned close and lowered my voice so no one else would hear. "Bubba done it. That was the beginning. Those three incriminating words from Morgan's mouth."

He dismissed my attempt at humor with a wave of his hand. "I know that part. How'd you end up in so much trouble today?"

"When I couldn't make any headway with Morgan's murder, I focused on June's disappearance, but I didn't have much luck there at first. When the dog dug up June's shoe, I caught a break. You did find the other shoe at Ritchie's house, didn't you?"

"We got him all right. And there was blood on the soles of his Docksiders. I'm willing to stake my career on the blood being Morgan's. Plus, according to his computer records, he'd hacked into Connie Lee's inheritance. He dumped the stolen money in a local account under his name. It was a matter of time until Patty and Bubba Powell learned the funds were missing. Once that happened, their lives would have been in jeopardy. Locking Ritchie up is the only way to stop the body count from escalating."

"You sure you've got enough evidence?" Larissa tensed. "I don't want him coming after my mom and me."

The sheriff nodded. "Ritchie Gilroy is looking at a hefty sentence. He won't see natural daylight for a very long time. I never suspected him because we had so many other Bubbas. And those four Bubbas had plenty of reason to kill Morgan."

"Makes you wonder, doesn't it?" I drew in a full breath. "On a given day, how many routine actions look guilty when viewed in another light? It's never a good idea to lift up the rocks of people's lives. No telling what might crawl out."

"You think of anything else you forgot to tell me at the scene?"

"Nope. I can't remember anything else."

He studied me intently before he rose. "Call me."

Not happening.

# CHAPTER 53

The next evening, I got Larissa and the animals settled and realized the longer I put off confronting Rose, the more I dreaded it. Nothing for it but to go see her. The tattoo on my hand had been bothering me, too. Maybe now Rose would remove her mark.

I closed the bedroom door and placed all the loose crystals around me on the bed. I wore Roland's moldavite pendant and looped the moldavite and amethyst one Mama had made for me around my tattooed hand.

Taking a deep breath for courage, I accessed the dream portal and crossed over. I figured I'd find Rose with Morgan, so I focused on his image. A transparent version of his library appeared before me, and he sat behind his large desk. The black covering still obscured his mouth and nose, but he appeared not to be paying any attention to it.

"Morgan?" I asked.

He looked up and tugged at the spirit glommed onto his face.

"Easy. I don't need you to tell me who killed you. I figured it out on my own. I came up here to tell you Ritchie is locked up and will be for many years."

The darkness fell from his face. "Thank you. And Connie Lee? Is she okay?"

"She's getting there. Ritchie nearly stole her entire inheritance before we caught him, but her finances are secure now."

"I didn't deserve her," he said.

"You cared for her. That's what a parent does."

"Ritchie hates me because of what happened with June."

"I saw what happened. June's death was an accident."

"I shouldn't have covered it up. Ritchie was right. I was only thinking of my bottom line at the time. But I messed up so much more. June's gone, I'm gone, Ritchie's in jail, Louise is lost in booze, and Connie Lee nearly lost everything."

"We all make choices. We have to accept the consequences."

"What I wouldn't give for a do-over. Do you think June will ever forgive me?"

"You could find her and ask her. She's up here somewhere."

"This is a big place. I drifted for a bit, then Rose plunked me down in my office. It felt so good to be in familiar surroundings that I haven't left my chair."

"Can't you let go and move on?"

"I have too much to do. Maybe one day I'll move on. About Connie Lee—"

"What about her?"

"I'm not stupid. She's your niece."

"I wasn't sure you knew."

"I did. But I didn't want anyone else to know she wasn't mine. I loved her like she was my own."

"She'll be fine. Don't worry about her."

"Her kidneys—"

"She had a transplant. She's doing much better."

Color flooded back in his face until Morgan looked almost human. "That's a relief."

There was a sizzle, a blast of sulfur, and Rose appeared. "You're back."

Her eyes glowed red. I avoided looking at them. "I am. I found Morgan's killer without his help. I also did what you asked. Your sister said she sat on your glasses in second grade."

"You've been busy." Rose studied me intently and seemed to reach a decision. She crooked a finger at me. "Come into my office."

With that, Morgan and his library faded from view and a flat expanse of gray plain appeared. "How'd you cross back over the bridge?" I asked.

"You don't know everything, Baxley Powell."

"Agreed. But as my county's dreamwalker, I need to come here for my clients. Is there going to be a problem between us?"

"Depends."

"Oh?"

"Depends on what you want. We're watching you, in this world and yours."

"We? Who is watching me? Are you talking about the person in my woods? That watcher?"

"Can't say."

"What about my husband, Roland Powell? What can you tell me about him?"

"Nothing."

"Why not?"

"There's a certain rhythm to life and death, a certain balance that has to be maintained. When someone like you travels between worlds, the fabric of existence is at risk. Things are meant to be revealed in their own time."

"Wait. Are you talking religion or philosophy or something else entirely?"

"Balance is all important."

Rats. She wasn't going to give me anything else. "I did what you asked, passed on that message. But my father says I shouldn't carry messages back to earth."

"Tab understood the rules. That's why we were anxious when you took over. You were an unknown."

"Did I pass muster?"

"The jury is still out on that."

"What about this tattoo on my hand? Will you remove it?"

"You will carry my mark. It will not come off."

Tattoo removal was a painful process. Maybe it wouldn't be so bad having a tattoo.

I didn't understand Rose at all. I thought she'd gotten trapped on the other side of the bridge. "What are you?"

"Interesting question. You ready for the answer?"

My mouth dried. I nodded. Her red eyes blazed dark blue. Three sets of glistening white wings unfurled, then closed and vanished.

Rose hissed and belched sulfur as she faded. Her voice resonated in my ear. "I'm undercover."

# CHAPTER 54

Not much had changed in the Fiddler Hole in a decade. The bar counter had a few more dents and scratches, the utilitarian bar stools had more bare wood exposed on the rungs. Faded photos of the tiny crustaceans for which the bar was named dotted the walls. Nothing said good times to coastal natives like mud flats, fiddler crabs, and fiddler holes. Due to state law, patrons could no longer smoke in Georgia bars, but I still wanted to turn on the overhead light to dispel the gloomy atmosphere in here.

"I can't believe I let you talk me into this." I gripped my frosty beer mug with both hands. "Your wife is going to be pissed."

Sheriff Wayne Thompson grinned and pushed over a paper bag of cash, which I tucked in my jacket pocket. "Got news for you, hon. Dottie stays pissed at one thing or another."

Dottie had two good reasons to be pissed. She was stuck in bed for the rest of her life, plus her husband didn't believe in fidelity. I couldn't be too sad for her. Dottie built her own hell when she married Wayne.

If not for unfinished business and collecting my off-the-books pay, I wouldn't be here. But I needed to know answers that only Wayne knew. Hence the call and the meet.

We'd beat the rush for happy hour. I didn't know if this would take five minutes or five hours, but I was prepared to sit here all afternoon to draw answers out of the sheriff. With Mama meeting Larissa's bus and keeping her overnight, I didn't have to watch the time.

I steered the conversation away from his unhappy wife. "I wanted to talk to you about Ritchie Gilroy. How goes the case?"

"He's our guy all right." He leaned in conspiratorially. "Remind me not to get you mad. You sure cleaned his clock."

"I did what I had to do." His woodsy fragrance surrounded me, only it no longer repelled me. Through the course of this investigation, Wayne had earned my respect. I fingered the condensation on my beer mug. "You have enough evidence?"

He took a long pull from his beer and licked the foam from his lips. "Our prosecutor says we have a strong circumstantial case, but he's pissed we didn't nab Ritchie at the murder scene with the knife in hand."

"Not much chance of that. He was long gone before we arrived. And then he touched the knife before you processed it. Make sure the murder charge sticks. I don't want any unpleasant Gilroy surprises."

"I can't guarantee anything about the legal system, but the prosecutor feels he can win the case. That's the best I can do."

"What about the other Bubbas? Won't his lawyer use that suspect pool against us?"

Wayne barked out a laugh. "His lawyer can darn well try, but he won't have any better luck than I did. Bubba Wright, thanks to you, has an ironclad alibi. Bubba Powell is the town hero for saving Connie Lee. Bubba Jamison's political connections make him untouchable. No one thinks a spiritual leader like Bubba Paxton could pull off a brutal stabbing. Believe me when I say the other prime suspects are in the clear."

The tightness in my chest eased. This was really over. "You'll testify to that in the courtroom?"

"You know something different?"

I hastened to reassure him. "No. Ritchie murdered his

brother. I'm one hundred percent positive. But accusations can be as damaging as truth, sometimes more so, given the rumor mill in this town. I hope Bubba Powell can get past this and move on with his life."

"Quit fretting. The Bubbas are adults. They can take care of themselves, even your screw-up brother-in-law." He studied me for a long moment. "I'm impressed with how you handled yourself under pressure. Any chance you've reconsidered going to the police academy? You'd be the best deputy I ever had."

"At my age?"

"You pack one hell of a punch. And you have a nose for investigation. The pay is steady and probably higher than your pet and plant sidelines combined."

I tried the idea on. It definitely had merit. I could handle the physical aspects of the job, and routine wage checks would be great. But there were serious downsides, too. I'd have to work for Wayne, and I'd be immersed in a very negative energy career. I didn't need that.

Plants and pets energized me.

Plus, they didn't endanger my family.

"No thanks. Larissa is my top priority. Being a police consultant is a better career choice for me. I work my schedule around hers, and my current career gives me that flexibility."

His warm gaze swept my length. "I have the deepest admiration for your flexibility."

My hackles rose. "Stop that. I am not sleeping with you."

"Can't blame me for trying." He grinned. "You always were hot and mysterious. Now you're hot, mysterious, and a kick-ass babe."

This from the man who'd slept his way right through the alphabet of our senior class. But his clever word choice piqued my curiosity. "Mysterious? How?"

"Just the way you carried yourself, hon. Like you had a secret."

For a psychic kid trying to fit in, of course I'd had a huge secret. "Didn't you think I was one of those weird Nesbitts?"

"That was part of the attraction. A guy could do you and get hunting advice from his dead grandpa at the same time, or so the story went."

My chin dipped. Every time I thought I was communicating with Wayne, he messed it up. Why couldn't he accept our relationship for what it was? Two friends talking about local events.

"Do you have to be so crass?" I slid off my stool. "Everything isn't about sex. You really should go in for some sensitivity training."

He shrugged and rose with me. "Not any point in that. I am who I am."

"You'll never know how hard I tried to fit in."

"You can't hide a star under a wheelbarrow. We all knew you were destined for more than Sinclair County. Roland was sure one lucky dog."

"Destiny, eh? Maybe destiny had a hand in me coming back home. No, wait. It was economics. But now that I'm here, I don't plan to leave."

"Good. We need people like you to return and reinvigorate the county. I could use a little invigoration myself."

"Enough." I lifted my hand to staunch the flow of his flirtatious remarks. "You keep coming on to me like this, and I'll have you arrested for sexual harassment."

He tapped the shiny badge clipped to his belt. "I'm the law, babe. You think one of my guys would lock me up for what comes naturally? Not a chance."

"Natural or not, I've had enough."

303

"You asked me to meet you for a drink. What was I supposed to think?"

"That I wanted to discuss the Gilroy case with you in private."

"You don't want to jump my bones?"

"Not even a little bit."

His face fell. "But there was a time once when you thought about it?"

"In high school, I considered dating you. But it wouldn't have worked. You have the morals of a tomcat."

"Ouch."

"Do you deny it?"

"No. But I'm not the only one who catted around."

I tensed. Air stalled in my lungs. The truth of his words cut into the trust I held sacred. "You saying Roland cheated on me?"

He shrugged.

Tears welled in my eyes. "That's not possible." I pushed past him and fled the murky dive.

All during the drive home I questioned Roland's absences over the years. He was always headed off on assignment somewhere, always in the no-communication zone until hours before he reappeared, spent and exhausted.

No matter how I looked at it, I didn't see him as a cheater. And he'd never, ever, asked his dead grandpa for hunting advice when we made love.

He was missing though.

And alive.

He was out there, somewhere in the world.

I'd find him.

Then I'd have my answers.

Deep shadows lay across my drive when I pulled in, adding shade and coolness to the honeysuckle scented air. I opened the house up and settled in a creaking rocker on the porch. Elvis curled up in my lap. Muffin took the padded chair next to me. Sulay perched on the porch railing, studying me with her steely cat gaze.

I contented myself with truths. Larissa was safe. We had a roof over our heads and enough to eat. I was a crazy Nesbitt, but my differences weren't a closely guarded secret any longer. My parents believed in me, and so did my kid.

I'd come full circle in life. My parents and grandparents had rocked on this porch, same as their ancestors. I'd been a kid here. Hanging Christmas lights on the moss-draped oaks, finding Easter eggs in the border grass, delighting in the wonders of nature. As an adult, I'd finally accepted my intuitive perceptions and dreamwalking.

Even better, I believed in myself.

That was more than most people got.

For now, it was enough.

# ABOUT THE AUTHOR

Formerly an aquatic toxicologist contracted to the U.S. Army and a freelance reporter, Southern author **Maggie Toussaint** loves writing fiction. She's published six romantic suspense novels and six mystery novels, with *Dime If I Know* and *Gone and Done It* her most recent Five Star releases. *Bubba Done It* is the second installment in her new paranormal mystery series. Her debut release, *House of Lies,* won Best Romantic Suspense in the 2007 National Readers' Choice Awards. Her mystery *Dime If I Know* won the Silver Falchion Award for Best Novel: Cozy/Traditional. She's served as a board member and an officer for Southeastern Mystery Writers of America and as an officer for Low Country Sisters in Crime. Visit her at www.maggietoussaint.com, http://www.facebook.com/Maggie ToussaintAuthor, and http://www.twitter.com/MaggieToussaint. Maggie makes her home in coastal Georgia with her husband. When she's not writing books, she enjoys spending time with family and friends.